LYCH WAY

LYCH WAY

✢ THE ✢ UNDERTAKEN ✢ TRILOGY ✢

✣

ARI BERK

✣

SIMON & SCHUSTER BFYR

SIMON & SCHUSTER BFYR

An imprint of Simon & Schuster Children's Publishing Division
1230 Avenue of the Americas, New York, New York 10020
For information about special discounts for bulk purchases, please contact Simon &
Schuster Special Sales at 1-866-506-1949 or business@simonandschuster.com.
The Simon & Schuster Speakers Bureau can bring authors to your live event. For more
information or to book an event, contact the Simon & Schuster Speakers Bureau at
1-866-248-3049 or visit our website at www.simonspeakers.com.
Also available in a SIMON & SCHUSTER BFYR hardcover edition
Book design by Laurent Linn
The text for this book is set in Minister Std.
Manufactured in the United States of America
First SIMON & SCHUSTER BFYR paperback edition February 2015
10 9 8 7 6 5 4 3 2 1
The Library of Congress has cataloged the hardcover edition as follows:
Berk, Ari.
Lych way / Ari Berk.
pages cm.—(The undertaken trilogy ; [3])
 Summary: As his family and friends suffer and fall at the hands of the vengeful
Huntsman from Arvale's sunken mansions, Silas Umber must reach deep into his
complicated bloodline to summon powers and wisdom beyond those required of
a Lichport Undertaker.
ISBN 978-1-4169-9119-9 (hc)
[1. Fantasy. 2. Ghosts—Fiction. 3. Future life—Fiction. 4. Families—Fiction.] I. Title.
PZ7.B452293Lyc 2014
[Fic]—dc23
2013009306
ISBN 978-1-4169-9120-5 (pbk)
ISBN 978-1-4424-3915-3 (eBook)

For my father

CONTENTS

1. Migration 1

2. Beginning at the End 8

3. Cold 14

4. Necessities 25

5. Old Folks' Home 30

6. Night Market 49

7. Rumors 53

8. Vigil 56

9. Fireside 67

10. Wanderlust 71

11. Hosts 79

12. Flow 100

13. River Cruise 109

14. A Wake 119

15. When the Party's Over 130

16. Cold Comfort 138

17. Brunch 143

18. Play 160

19. Fire and Water 170

20. A Word of Welcome 180

21. Lament 182

22. Harmonies 185

23. Burnt Feathers 195

24. Chase 199

25. From Before 208

26. Below 219

27. What Cannot Be 226

28. Remembering Babylon 235

29. Outsider 243

30. Names 257

31. Above Stairs 260

32. Birth Rite 275

33. Turn the Page 284

34. Rotunda 291

35. In Memoriam 296

36. Underworld 299

37. Seconds 307

38. Field 314

39. Veil 319

40. Coda 322

When you have read folktales of this god and that, you have perhaps spoken patronizingly of the old mythmakers and thanked your lucky stars that you lived in a more enlightened age. But those old storytellers were the really enlightened ones, for they saw into the other world and recorded what they saw. Many of the world's favorite gods are said to have lived upon the earth as men. They have so lived. Does that idea startle you? How does a man become a god, and how does a god become a man? Have you ever wondered?

—Elsa Barker, from *Letter From a Living Dead Man*

A bed is laid in a secret corner
For the three agonies—love, birth, death—
That are made beautiful with ceremony.

—George Mackay Brown, from "The Finished House"

CHAPTER 1

MIGRATION

A FALCON TURNED SLOWLY IN THE COLD AIR, its arcs becoming wider and higher with each pass it made over the corpse.

It rose above the cobbled lanes and leaning houses and flew north, past the bare trees whose roots cracked the sidewalks on most of Lichport's crumbling streets. It could see the river in the distance ahead. Then, as though it had changed its mind, the bird banked, and flew back the way it had come. It circled once more far above the body and then stooped, dropping from the sky into a blur until it opened wide its sharp-tipped wings again, briefly holding the air before landing gently on the dead woman's shoulder. The falcon flapped quickly, finding its balance. Dark and light markings flashed from the underside of its wings as it lifted its yellow legs up and down, careful not to pierce the corpse's clothing or flesh with its talons.

The peregrine tilted its head to the side and looked at the woman's dull eye with its bright one, perhaps seeing its own reflection. Leaning closer, the bird moved its smooth beak slowly across the woman's face as though to wake her. It plucked tentatively at the disheveled tresses of hair lying across her face and shoulders. The bird stood atop the body, crouching, vigilant, jerking its head sharply this way and that, attentive to each sound it heard—branches scraping against one another, distant waves falling to shore, anything that moved or stirred the air.

The falcon waited like that for some time before a movement farther down the street caused it to leap into the sky again. Another corpse, desiccated and elderly, shambled toward the woman's body and, lifting it from the ground, carried it away. The peregrine followed above them, unseen and silent, in the direction of Temple Street, where the one corpse carried the other up the stairs and onto the veranda of a large house. On the roof of that house, the falcon perched upon one of the spiral brick chimneys and waited. Inside the house—she knew with the instinct of a mother—was Silas Umber, who in life had been her son.

LEDGER

It is now surely beyond any dispute that
the first death watch, the original Hadean
clock, was built by Daedalus. Hesiod makes
no mention of this episode. True. But
what cared he for the machinations of mere
men? Pausanius, Apollodorus, and Ovid are
all cryptic, and generally reliable, but the
most detailed account is found in the "lost"
portions of Hyginus's Fabulae. No other
versions of this account exist but, in truth,
what classical author would have written
openly on such a matter, particularly in
those long ago times when selfish, vengeful
gods walked closer to the sides of men?
Who would scribe a story that would have
reddened the face of Hades with shame,
only to have such records used against
them when they later arrived in Tartarus's
dark tribunal halls, where more creative
punishments might be meted out over the
long eternities? Then as ever: better to say
little and live long.

Nevertheless, my own careful studies of
the surviving accounts reveal that Daedalus,
on the occasion of his son's death, sought
to confound the work of Hades, the Lord
of the Dead. Mors was then merely the
herald, not yet king, and so it would indeed
be Hades that would take offense at such
an undertaking. Daedalus's cleverness was
considerable. With his son's corpse close
by, he created a kind of clepsydra, or water
clock, and in a small metallic chamber below
where the water pooled, he summoned and
locked up the ghost of his son, so that the
boy would not be lost to him, could not
be taken away into the lands of shadow.
Nor could his son's spirit wander—that
most terrible of fates. Father and son would
remain together. Hades, go hang.

All depictions of the original device are
lost, but its workings we know well enough
from the writings of the those Undertakers,
those inheritors of Daedalus's invention, who
both saw that first Hadean clock, kept it
safe, and who later made their own versions,

each with the technology that time and their own craft afforded them. I suspect, since Daedalus's day, the technique has been more or less consistent. The clock merely kept the time, noted the passing of moments and hours, by the flow and collection of water (and later, by mechanism), a simple reminder of man's fleeting mortality. But, with the spirit entrapped within, when the workings of the clock were halted, when the hole through which the water passed was blocked with wax (or the dial stopped), time halted its course as well, and the dead could be perceived.

How the particular "spiritual" mechanism functions remains a considerable mystery. And surely, long ago, the action must have been performed with some trepidation, for the halting of time would have been an affront to both Hades (who so relies on time's passage to carry death to mortals) and Cronos himself, the miserable Titan who fathered Hades into the world so that the dead might be herded like cattle into pens and thereby remain peasants, even in the afterlife where we might all one day have continued on as kings in our own manors and blissful estates, had things been otherwise.

Still, we may speculate that when the forward motion of time, or its semblance, was halted, the entrapped soul, sensing the moment or lack thereof, would seek to make a way for itself into that Other World that is the inheritance of every soul. Yet, being bound, and though the gate, or Lych Way, be opened, the ghost could make no egress. But the pale light of those shadowlands, passing into our world through the Lych Way as a mist, or rather, a sort of Plutonian ether, might make transparent mortality's curtain, revealing, with time suspended, the presence of the dead yet residing within or about our mortal sphere.

It is perhaps best not to dwell too long upon the miserable irony of Daedalus's creation. For while he sought freedom for Ikarus from that harsh imprisonment Hades would have put upon him below in Tartarus, by setting his son's ghost in the prison of the clock's mechanism, Daedalus himself became Ikarus's unwitting jailor. But in truth, what father does not seek, through love or necessity, or ignorance, to choose for his son that occupation that will keep him gainfully employed and close to home?

—FROM *THE HIDDEN HISTORIES OF THE HADEAN CLOCK*, ALSO CALLED *THE UNDERTAKER'S FRIEND AND BURDEN*, BY JONAS UMBER

CHAPTER 2

BEGINNING AT THE END

HE SHOULD HAVE GONE HOME.

But instead of sitting in the safe quiet of his own study surrounded by his father's things, Silas Umber was stacking books upon Charles Umber's desk in the cold, private library of Temple House. He had promised his mother he wouldn't enter the north wing until she got back. He'd lied. He went in the moment she'd left the house, and he'd been there all night.

The north wing was no longer used. But up until recently it had been the busiest part of the house. It was there his cousin's corpse and spirit had both been hidden and trapped by his uncle. Silas's own life had nearly ended there, and his father's corpse had almost certainly been brought to this part of the house after he'd been murdered. The little library off his uncle's bedroom was also the storage room for numerous volumes of funereal photography as well as Charles Umber's collection of forbidden occult books. Now his uncle was dead. Silas had insisted that none of the books be removed until he'd been able to go through them all. His mother hadn't been too keen for anyone to enter that part of the house, and had locked the doors of the north wing. Silas knew she wouldn't want him to open it again, but that would be an argument for another day. At least he knew that the books and much else were still there undisturbed.

Here was a collection not fit for the public rooms of the house.

Volumes filled with portraits of Lichport's dead, taken, preserved, and prized by his mad uncle. Silas pushed aside the postmortem photographs. He'd seen them. His eyes moved quickly across the titles of the older books: *The School of Night. Compendium Demonii. The Cult and Rites of Canaanite Idolatry. The Book of Abramelin. The Areopagian Grimoire. Demons, Spirits and Spells of Assyrian Sorcery.* Shelf after shelf stacked with books of necromancy. He pulled down two and three volumes at a time, piling them on the inlaid desk. And as his hands passed over these forbidden tomes, the words of his ancestor Cabel Umber crawled in his ears. . . . *You can bring her back. . . . Such arts, dark as they are, are meant to be used by the wise. . . .* As much as Silas hated and feared Cabel Umber, he knew his ancestor was right.

Beyond the desk and the piles of books stood open the large bronze door with its sigil-inscribed surface. Across its threshold lay the Camera Obscura, Charles Umber's room of . . . experiment. That chamber was empty now, its floors and walls scrubbed nearly clean, but traces of the chalk-drawn magic circles remained on the floor. The massive glass ampule that once held the corpse of his cousin, Adam, had been taken away by the Narrows folk, along with all the bottles of honey and other preservatives. But the sickly sweet smell remained, and it distracted him from his reading, making him look up frequently, as though someone, or something, might at any moment come through the door.

He opened another volume. *See,* he told himself, *centuries of people all wanting the same thing, all crying out in spells and chants to bring back the spirits of the beloved dead. What they have done, I can do. And I have more longing and as much aptitude as most. As Undertaker, if I used such spells, surely they would work. Surely the dead would come if I called them.*

He noticed the bindings of some of the oldest tomes were

worn and cracked. Those must have been brought to Lichport long ago, maybe by his own ancestors. Others, it seemed from their inscriptions, had been collected by the Knights of the Eastern Temple, that mysterious brotherhood who built the house's original rotunda and for whom the street, the cemetery, and the house itself had been named. An easy guess, for on the shelves, Silas could see, held between the books, were also pages and documents from the times when the brothers still occupied the property. They looked like mostly ledger pages, lists of objects, long ago stolen out of the East and brought, ultimately, to Lichport. Some of that very collection certainly formed the basis of the assemblage of artifacts gathered by his grandfather and then added to by his uncle: the relics now stored in the attics of Temple House. Silas carefully put those brittle pages aside and turned back to the books. It was in the ancient books of forbidden rites—books his father would have shunned—that Silas was searching for a spell to break a spell.

He read by candlelight. Looking into the wavering flame, he could almost see her face through the frozen water. Beatrice. Her features were blurred but discernable below the ice. Blue-skinned. Wide-eyed. Terrified. Trapped. She was waiting for him, had been reaching out to him in his sleep all the time he was in Arvale. Who else could help her if not him?

Looking up from the books, he noticed that his arm wasn't hurting anymore, and the curse mark had faded. Maybe his return to Lichport from Arvale had worked loose the stitches of the spell? Or maybe Cabel Umber's powers had dissolved as the cousins of the summer house chased him from the gates and back into his prison inside the sunken mansion? Either way, that business was far away now and finished.

The air of the room was freezing.

He knew Bea was cold too.

The thought of her spirit trapped in the dark, icy water quickened his breathing.

Looking down, Silas could see wisps of vapor form on the air in front of his mouth. His fingers were going numb. He moved his hand down to the pocket of his jacket to warm it, but remembering it was filled with dust—the remains of Lars Umber, who'd perished at the Arvale gate—he stopped. He rubbed his hands above the flame of the candle instead.

Before him on the desk was a worm-riddled copy of *The Virgilian Heresies*. He had found, in more than one book, broken versions of some of the spells hissed into his ear by Cabel Umber in the sunken mansion at Arvale. He mistrusted those words and their source, though he could even now feel the power in them. One of the pages bore what looked to be a recent bookmark. As he silently read over the words of the Dark Call—the accursed rite that would forcibly summon a ghost back into its bones—the chamber grew even colder, and the candle dimmed as if the flame crouched in fear. Silas closed the book. More of its pages had been marked, and Silas suspected that his uncle had used such spells to summon certain spirits to his awful purposes, or maybe even to keep poor Adam bound to his corpse.

Silas rubbed his eyes and sighed in frustration. He wasn't sure if he could do it. Such rites required using the bones of the deceased or other "mummiae," or remains. The words were forceful and grim. He'd already found many spells of binding and numerous summoning rites, but the sounds of those words . . . *Command, compel, demand, require, force, order, constrain* . . . He couldn't think of using them on Beatrice. She was not his slave. He loved her. He didn't want to use violent language to drag her spirit from the millpond. He just wanted her back. Back with him, out of his dreams and at his side. He wanted, more than anything, to walk with her again as they had done when exploring together Lichport's streets and monuments. Just to hear her voice again. Wasn't love enough to bring her back? *No,* chided Mrs. Bowe's voice in his mind, *nor has it ever been. Alas! Poor Orpheo! If love were enough to bring them back, the world would be crowded with corpses, forced to endure an eternity of embraces by those weak-hearted folk who could not bear to say good-bye! Let death come and do not look back!*

"No," Silas said aloud to the air.

The candle was sputtering and a chilling draft idled now about the desk where he worked. He didn't know how long he'd been there. All he knew was that he was cold right through. He rose and stretched his back, aching from hunching over the desk. From where it leaned against the wall near the door to the Camera Obscura, a broom fell and loudly struck the floor, startling Silas.

Someone is coming, he thought, recognizing the portent.

My mother is home. . . .

LEDGER

I HEARD OF WHAT HAPPENED TO A
FAMILY IN THE TOWN. ONE NIGHT A
THING THAT LOOKED LIKE A GOOSE
CAME IN. AND WHEN THEY SAID
NOTHING TO IT, IT WENT AWAY UP
THE STAIRS WITH A NOISE LIKE LEAD.
SURELY IF THEY HAD QUESTIONED IT,
THEY'D HAVE FOUND IT TO BE SOME
SOUL IN TROUBLE.

THERE WAS A MAN USED TO GO OUT
FOWLING, AND ONE DAY HIS SISTER
SAID TO HIM, WHATEVER YOU DO
DON'T GO OUT TONIGHT AND DON'T
SHOOT ANY BIRDS YOU SEE FLYING—FOR
TONIGHT THEY ARE ALL POOR SOULS
TRAVELLING.

—PASSAGES FROM *VISIONS AND BELIEFS IN THE WEST
OF IRELAND* BY LADY AUGUSTA GREGORY, 1920.
TRANSCRIBED BY AMOS UMBER

CHAPTER 3

COLD

FROM SOMEWHERE ON THE GROUND FLOOR OF TEMPLE HOUSE, Silas heard noises. Had his mother come home during the night or early morning? He knew she would be furious with him for going into Uncle's upstairs rooms.

Silas got up and walked slowly into the north wing's long gallery. There was gray light in the windows. He'd been up all night and hadn't noticed the morning, or the dusky, clouded noon when it came.

Then he heard the sound of heavy footfall stumbling down the back hallway.

It was not his mother.

He knew every version of her footstep: the quick and angry click of high heels, the slow, drunken slur of house slippers, and all the variations in between. Whoever was walking around downstairs was not Dolores Umber. Someone else was in the house. The loud, slow footsteps made their way through the butler's pantry. Silas moved closer to the wall. He barely breathed.

Downstairs, he heard metal hit the floor. Maybe one of the candelabra falling over. Then nothing. Whoever it was had come to a stop in one of the downstairs reception rooms. The dining room, most likely. Those were absolutely not his mother's footsteps. Someone had broken into the house and was looking for the silver, or worse, hiding, lying in wait for him to come downstairs, or for his mother to come home.

Where was she? Where had she run to so quickly? Dolores had been frantic when she'd left. Where had she needed to go in such a hurry? Was the person in the house connected somehow to her absence? Silas did not like unanswered questions, especially those that came to him in Temple House.

There was more noise from below. Chairs were being dragged across the floor. Was someone stealing the furniture? Silas kept close to the walls to avoid the floor creaking and made his way out into the upper hallway. With even more trepidation, he walked one hesitant footstep at a time through the doorway leading from the long gallery of the north wing and onto the upstairs landing overlooking the foyer.

He walked slowly, carefully placing each foot before following with the other. He tried to keep his back straight, not to crouch, pretending he wasn't scared. But with each step, he moved a little more hesitantly over the carpets. His feet felt heavy, as though some wiser part of him knew that he didn't really want to see what was down there and was trying to hold him back.

At the bottom of the staircase, the statue of the Ammit, the "devourer of souls," stood sentinel over the foyer. The taxidermic representation of the otherworldly Egyptian monster seemed alert too, its brittle ancient lion hairs standing up stiffly on its neck. Silas brushed past the statue, his arm touching it, but he barely noticed. He moved deliberately into the large study that once held so many of the artifacts from his uncle's collection. He walked sideways, looking out the window to see if anyone was outside on the porch. At the fireplace, he picked up an iron poker, casually, as though to examine it, in case he was being watched, then he moved silently down the back hallway and through the butler's pantry. At the closed door to the dining room, he paused, breathing hard. He was sweating. Trying to get a tighter grip, he squeezed the handle of the iron poker so hard his knuckles went white.

He held his breath and pushed open the door.

The corpse of his great-grandfather turned toward him, blocking his view of the dining room.

"Silas. Oh, my child . . . ," said Augustus Howesman. He stepped aside and let Silas see what lay on the dining room table.

All at once, Silas's fingers loosed their grip on the fire iron he held. It clanged twice as its point and then its handle struck the floor. His great-grandfather's mouth was moving but Silas could hardly hear any of the words being spoken. His mind had clamped shut, unable to take in anything more. As he looked upon his mother's body, a ringing like the soul bell rose in his ears. Dolores Umber lay across the polished surface of the table. She wasn't moving, and he knew from her posture and the pallor of her skin that his mother was dead. There, on the same table where his uncle had served them all those trays of preserved food and desiccated meats, was his mother's corpse. He couldn't look at her. He raised his eyes to the ceiling, then closed them. He knew that if he could keep his eyes shut, he'd be okay. He didn't have to accept anything he couldn't see. But the presence of his mother's cold body had changed the quality of the air in the house. It hurt to breathe, and he knew that if he opened his eyes, he would see the walls of Temple House leaning in to crush him. Though the death watch sat untouched in his pocket, in Silas's heart, time had stopped.

Hands held him at the shoulders. He didn't open his eyes. He could feel his great-grandfather now standing in front of him. The ringing in Silas's ears lessened.

"I can't do this. I can't do any of this anymore."

"Silas, I'm sorry. You don't have a choice, son."

"She can't die. Not now . . . I can't . . . I'm not ready . . . not now."

His great-grandfather's face was sorrowful, sympathetic, but his voice grew firm. "Would tomorrow be better? Maybe it would have been better for Dolores to die next year? Or in ten years? When would you have been ready? Silas, if you don't know this already, it's time you did: Death does not care if you are ready. Do you understand me? No one is ever completely ready, especially the living. Silas, come here. Look at your mother. See her now, as she is. It only becomes real when you look. Come on, son."

Silas allowed his great-grandfather to move him toward the table.

His mother's skin looked very smooth, almost as though she'd had no cares in life, had never pursed her lips in anger or drawn her eyebrows together in scrutiny. Only in death had her body finally let go of its worries. She looked younger. He knew his mother had been beautiful in her youth. She'd told him so many times, and he'd seen pictures. But now the fairness had returned to her face and he could see it. Yet, at the same time, death had also added something to her looks, a sharp angle of difference. She was his mom, but something else now too. The foreignness of her familiarity unnerved him. Made him feel like he shouldn't be looking at her as she lay there with her eyes closed, like he was intruding on a private moment.

Memories began to gather about him like onlookers at a visitation. Silas remembered when his mom brought home a cake when he graduated high school. He'd thought it was stupid at the time. He hadn't even gone to his graduation. He'd barely qualified for graduation, he'd missed so many days. They hardly had anything to celebrate. But she had been trying to make the day special. She was trying, and he'd blown her off. Maybe she'd tried more than he noticed. His stomach clenched as the guilt washed through him and flooded everything else from his mind.

He could remember almost nothing before this moment. He had been looking for something upstairs. It didn't matter now. All thoughts of the ghost of the millpond fell away from him. There was only the shape of his mother on the table and whatever needed to be done for her next. Everything else in his mind froze and faded. Even the desires of a moment ago watched him now from across a crevasse. It was like his fever-dreams when he'd get sick as a kid. He was a tiny spot on a vast plain. He'd stretch out his arms on the bed, but couldn't reach anything, couldn't feel the edge of the bed, or the wall. There were no sounds in those dreams, so when he tried to scream, no one could hear or find him.

Again, his great-grandfather was speaking to him. Words of comfort. They sounded like they were coming from another room. The world was muffled, wrapped with cotton.

Silas walked in slow circles around the dining room table while his great-grandfather spoke. He would look down at his mother's face as he went past her head again and again. Even as Augustus Howesman was trying to give him instructions on what needed to be done next for Dolores, Silas was talking to himself out loud.

"I should have come home! I waited too long."

"Silas?"

"I should not have left her alone," Silas said. "I should have gone with her." He suddenly saw something on her arm that seized his jaw and pushed the words back down his throat. Silas squatted and looked closely at Dolores's skin. He gently touched the spot on her arm where the curse glyph, a copy of the one Cabel Umber had placed on him, had been stitched in hair and thread onto his mother's skin. Those careful stitches . . . tiny and so precise. He knew immediately who had made them. The three ladies from the house on Silk Street. They had somehow lifted the curse from him and set it upon his mother. He could still feel the heat of the spell on her skin. This was an old power at work. Had his mother gone to them? Is that where she'd gone last night? His mind was churning, but the simple truth broke through: The curse meant for him was taken by her. She had died for him.

This was his fault. He might as well have killed her himself.

Every part of him ached. Shame and grief covered him like a mourner's shroud.

There was a draft moving across his heart. When he closed his eyes, all he could see was a cold stone inscribed with an equation of loss: his own name, and then a list of those that had recently been subtracted from his life. Amos, Beatrice, Lars, Dolores. All gone.

He sat down on the floor next to her corpse and began to sob.

"I did this . . . ," he repeated through his tears. "It's my fault."

"No, Silas," his great-grandfather said, putting his hand on Silas's shoulder. The old man's tone had changed. Silas could hear the fear in his words. "Grandson, please, listen. We haven't much time. I need you to get up and hear what I have to tell you. There will be time for sorrow later. Please, Silas! Stand up and hear me!"

Silas rose to his feet but couldn't take his eyes off his mother's arm. Augustus Howesman put his fingers on Silas's chin and gently turned his great-grandson's face toward his.

"Listen to me now, Silas. There are things that must be seen to. Your mother is dead, yes, but she is not beyond harm. It is not yet the hour for mourning or for revenge, if it comes to that. Certain rites must be attended to, and your mother has only us to help her. That is unfortunate, because what is required stands outside your knowledge and partially outside of mine. This is not part of the Undertaker's work. This is . . . another tradition. Part of the rites of some of the oldest families of the town. So, we must seek out . . . well, older folk. To my knowledge, even your father never attended a Howesman funeral, or one like it. You will have to trust me. We're going to have to help each other."

Silas breathed in deeply, slowly, trying to gain control of himself, focusing on his great-grandfather's voice. "But why can't I oversee her funeral?"

"For one thing, immediate family should never have to bear that burden unless necessary or asked for by the deceased. For another, as I've said, my side of your family has its own ways of doing things. I need your help, but you'll need to be accommodating here."

"Okay. I trust you," Silas said.

"Are you going to be all right leaving the house? Because you are faster than I am, so you will have to be the one to go for help."

Silas didn't know how to answer. Help from whom? The numbness was ebbing, but now confusion had taken its place.

"Are you sure you're all right?" Augustus Howesman asked again.

"I'm fine. I'm always fine," said Silas, taking a deep breath. "Everyone dies and the world is filled up with terrors that need to be settled and laid to rest, and I am always fine. Don't worry about me, sir. I am the Undertaker. I have stood upon the edge of the abyss and called it home. I. Am. Fine."

"Silas . . . grandson?" The corpse reached out for his shaking hands, but Silas drew them away.

"Great-grandfather, just tell me what I need to do."

"Well, you can start by covering all the mirrors. That should be familiar. We all do that when death comes."

"All right," Silas said, his voice going flat as he opened a deep drawer in the sideboard and took out a stack of linens; several tablecloths and some large white napkins only slightly yellowed from age.

"That's fine," said Augustus Howesman, sitting down. As he spoke, Augustus shifted his chair closer to Dolores. He took her arm, which hung slightly off the table, and drew it up to his chest. Then he stroked her cold hand and gently held it and rocked it back and forth as though he was trying to help her sleep.

While his great-grandfather gave instructions, Silas listened and unfolded the linens, one after another, moving mechanically through the downstairs rooms, covering over all the mirrors. He paused in the foyer at the grandfather clock. Silas opened the cabinet and reached inside, stopping the cold brass pendulum. When he was sure the dial was no longer moving, he covered the clock with a tablecloth.

His great-grandfather called from the dining room. "Did you hear me, Silas? You know where to go?"

"I do," he said, walking back into the doorway of the parlor and calling back to the dining room. "It will all be done just as you've said." Silas already had his jacket on, and he left Temple House without another word.

LEDGER

The funeral rites among families with Restless ancestors and kin remain a subject of mystery, speculation, and general apprehension. The rites, as they are still practiced within the district of Lichport, are certainly very ancient, at least in parts, and are passed from family to family in the manner of the initiations of the mystery schools of old. Portions of these rites may include, as their inspiration or precedents, certain of the more well-known rituals practiced by the ancient Egyptians, for whom the rendering immortal of mortal flesh was a revered specialty of their priests.

Whether the similar traditions among the Restless of Lichport stretch back that far, or merely mimic the elder Nile rites, cannot be known. In either event, the mysteries at work within the bloodlines of Lichport's oldest families remain one of the most strange and frightening of Lichport's many extant funereal eccentricities.

When the inheritors of the great family fortunes left Lichport, those who concealed (for by that point, the Restless were little spoken of except in whispers) "enduring" members of their families sought respectable ways to dispose of them reasonably. Some left the living corpses where they were, either inside their ancestral homes, or within the more recently fashionable tomb houses. Certain of these folk have remained, mostly ignored or forgotten now, within those places.

Other families, particularly those from the old neighborhoods of Queen and Prince Streets (some of the first to leave Lichport) availed themselves of the spacious (and now abandoned) mausolea within Newfield Cemetery. Thus, some of the Restless from those families were placed within the elaborate tombs in the Egyptian style located in that cemetery's old and derelict eastern district. It is known that other families occasionally added to the population of Restless folk within those lotus-columned tombs.

Several of the Restless there are of extreme antiquity, including one venerable lady who claims descent from those ancient Nile folk who were masters of every funerary art. I have twice tried to make enquiry of that lady, but was turned away from the tomb for lack of sufficient blood-relation. It is rumored she was brought to Lichport out of the east by the Brotherhood of the Eastern Temple and that she once formed part of their mysterious oracular rites. Others say she arrived with a circus from the south who considered her to be of "exhibit quality." Though I plan to return, if possible, in the company of my wife's grandfather and enquire further, I do so with trepidation, for it is also known that the Restless of Newfield, stacked and abandoned there by their families, hold little affection for the living.

—From the unpublished manuscript "Notes on the Dispossession of the Restless Since 1900" by Amos Umber

CHAPTER 4

NECESSITIES

THE STREETS OF LICHPORT WERE A GRAY BLUR that mirrored the afternoon sky where a hidden sun hung behind slate clouds. Silas could barely feel the freezing air for all the cold already inside him. There were only the words his great-grandfather had spoken before sending him on his errand. *FOR YOUR MOTHER'S SAKE.* Augustus Howesman's words tumbled through his mind, though Silas could find no comfort in them.

Your mother must not be left alone.

. . . dangerous time for her.

You must trust me.

. . . a bull from Mennever . . . the Peales will know . . .

Do not seek her ghost. . . .

Do not use the watch. . . .

No questions . . .

The Howesman way . . .

. . . what your mother would have wanted.

Trust me. . . .

Our traditions . . . different from the rest of town . . .

Newfield . . . lotus-columned tombs . . . be polite.

. . . dangerous time . . . not left alone . . .

Bring the Book of the Dead, *however you can,*

whatever form it's in . . .

Trust me . . . I'm sorry. I'm sorry.

Do not tarry. . . .
Hurry back. . . .
Midnight may be bad. . . .

There were few people on the streets. On the dark windows he passed, reflections of the bare trees waved Silas away. He put his head down, trying to see the sidewalk in front of him, thinking only of where he needed to go first. Anything more made him want to turn around and go home. There was too much . . . and if he began trying to sort through his feelings now . . . *Keep walking,* he told himself. *Just keep walking. Take the message to Mother Peale. Do that first.*

Silas tuned his mind to the sound of his feet on the cobbles of the street. He'd left his coat open to the cold. There was a wind coming down from the north, and already he couldn't feel his ears. He made no effort to warm them with his hands. He wanted to be numb again.

The lights were already on at the Peales' store. Winter in Lichport seemed to hold the sun at arm's length no matter the hour. It was afternoon, but darkness would come in swiftly enough. As Silas entered, the bells on the door jingled and Mother Peale looked up from behind the counter, where she sat by a small stove with a wool blanket over her lap and another about her shoulders. She shouted, "Close that door! That wind will be the end of me!" As she saw Silas's face, she leapt to her feet.

"Good God, child! You look half-dead!"

"Please don't say that."

"I only mean, gracious, Silas . . . what the devil has happened? What did they do to you out there beyond the marshes?"

He couldn't say the words. He couldn't tell her what had happened to him at the gate, and he certainly wasn't going to share what he had been reading when his mother's corpse was brought home.

His private thoughts, dark as they were, were all Silas had left.

"My great-grandfather has sent me to ask you to send to Mennever Farm . . . for a bull? He said you would understand, and that he 'will bear the cost of everything.'"

Mother Peale's face paled as she put her hands forward on the counter to steady herself. "Silas! By all that's holy, tell me what's happened."

His lips drew tight, and he pushed his tongue against the back of his teeth. Silas shook his head as if refusing to answer her, but finally said, "My mom—"

"Oh, Lord, no!" Mother Peale cried as she quickly came around the counter. "Child, child . . ."

She held out her arms to him but Silas stepped back toward the door. "I have to go. There's more I have to do before it gets dark."

"Where are you going?"

"To Newfield," he said absently, looking away.

"Oh, Gods! Oh! Silas . . ."

As usual, someone else knew as much or more than he did. He didn't want to talk about it or explain or have anything explained to him. His mother was dead. A funeral was to be held. Both of his parents were gone. What else was there to discuss? He needed to keep moving and just get through the blackness of the day to whatever lay on the other side of it. Then he would try to do the same tomorrow and tomorrow and tomorrow. He turned to leave.

"Wait," she said, her voice high and stitched with worry. She went back behind the counter and rummaged in a box below it. "Here," she said, testing and then handing him an old but working flashlight. "You'll need this, I think. It'll be dark soon. Oh, be careful, Silas! Take bread!" She took a fresh loaf from a large basket on the counter and thrust it into his hands. "And take a bottle of milk from the case. I don't know what's best down there. I'll send all requirements to your mother's house directly. Don't fret about that. I'll take care of it all. You come fetch me if there be trouble, or if there's ought else you need."

Without another word, Silas stepped into the street. Behind him, he heard Mother Peale calling for her daughter Joan and delivering a rapid list of instructions as he walked away. "Joanie, get the truck and have them strappin' boys bring around some rope and the big blankets for the beast . . . aye, to Mennever's . . . to the farm . . . No, they'll have the trailer and we'll take it back when all's been done . . . Yes, tonight . . . Take some blinders to cover its eyes . . . must be kept calm . . . I don't care about that . . . you keep that creature *serene*! Tell them lads . . . shift their arses! This is *old-time* business, and we'll do things right or not at all! Tell them *who* it's for!"

As he turned down Coach Street, Silas put the flashlight in his jacket pocket, and the bread and milk into his satchel. Some kind of offerings, he guessed. Just like people used to leave on the porches of the houses on Fort Street. As his hand came out of the satchel, it brushed the death watch. He clutched it out of habit, and the silver case warmed in his grasp. The watch's quick ticking mimicked his own fast-beating heart, which pounded now at the thought of going alone to the derelict lanes of Newfield Cemetery. He had once walked there with Bea, and he remembered nervously how, as evening fell, the dim lamps of the night market, as she had called it, began to glow among the tombs. He could almost hear Bea's words and how they unsettled him then and now. *Haven't you ever lost something? C'mon! Maybe we'll find it. What are you looking for, Silas?*

Looking up, he saw that the sky would soon shift from gray to black. The high wall of Newfield was ahead. Silas shuddered but kept walking as he passed into the long shadows of its gates.

LEDGER

We must, each in our time, master the
Lych Way, become lords of two lands, as
once it was called. Such is our birthright.
It is not enough to open or close the doors
for the dead. We are no mere porters. We
are emanations—shadows and reflections
of the gods. They are mimed in us, in
our deeds and in the obligations of our
undertaking. The Peller's soul is puissant,
for what god's power is not conjurable by
us, should our work require? Yet it is more
than vocation: discovery of the mysteries of
the gods and the inner summoning of our
presiding geniuses—Janus, Jove, Osiris,
Hades, Anubis, Hermes, who you
will—what are these but an Undertaker's
initiation through his own life, from birth unto
his waiting grave, should it come?

—MARGINALIA OF JONAS UMBER

CHAPTER 5

OLD FOLKS' HOME

THE SUN WAS BEGINNING TO SET, but clouds hid the gold of twilight. At the statue of the bronze lion that kept watch over Newfield Cemetery, Silas paused and read out of habit the raised letters of the plaque set into its side.

> Who can stand before the arrows of the sun?
> Or the bright flame of the stalker of the plains?
> Rest in my shadow, Oh, Innocence!
> While the guilty perish by tooth and claw.
> For mine is the undiminished heart of carnelian.

Despite the chill, the bronze was not cold to the touch. Silas put his palm onto the statue, remembering the lion's preserved corpse inside and how, just there between its massive paws, he once sat with Beatrice as she sang to him. He drew back his hand and pressed on, only allowing the memory of Bea to flutter at the margins of his mind, but no closer, not yet. He shouldn't linger. His mother was waiting.

In front of him, Newfield widened out into a vast expanse of fenced plots, mausoleums, and avenues, planted all around with the less auspicious graves of the more common folk. Far in the distance, where some of the older burials ran closer to the cliffs overlooking the sea, Silas could hear dogs barking. He'd heard their howling before, when he'd lived at Temple House and the wild packs would course along the wall in Newfield's northwestern side. He began to walk faster, trying to keep close to the open tombs in case he had to get away from the dogs should they come closer.

In the eastern quarter of Newfield stood the once-fashionable Egyptian tombs. These were separated from the rest of the cemetery by a large wall decorated along its length in the Egyptian revival style, with tall fluted columns and carved capitals in the shape of lotus flowers. Ivy covered most of the walls and hung like a curtain over much of the open archway leading into the avenues.

There was still a little light in the sky as Silas parted the ivy and walked down the path between the mausoleums. Ahead was the pylon-shaped tomb where his great-grandfather told him he would find the *Book of the Dead*. He was cold and nervous now. He had never been in this part of the cemetery, but had once, with Bea, seen strange lights here as darkness fell.

All around him stood sentinel sphinxes and tall statues of Anubis, the jackal-headed funeral god of ancient Egypt. As he passed by, Silas glanced at the ornamental faux-hieroglyphic plaques adorning the doors and walls of the tombs. They bore familiar names—many Howesmans, and other ancestors from his mother's side of the family, and people from the other wealthy families of Lichport with whom the Howesmans generally married. Many of the ornate inscriptions concluded with unsettlingly similar additional dates.

Juliette Howesman-Ellis

Beloved Wife, Mother, and Grandmother

Born   Laid to Rest
1846   1942

Silas saw that as the death dates got later, the "laid to rest" dates began to cluster, as though many of the corpses were finally interred during that more recent period when the bigger families began leaving Lichport. As he peered into some of the tombs, he saw tenantless stone sarcophagi standing upright, others on their sides, their lids askew or broken, the occupants apparently missing. But at the back of many tombs, he could see stairs leading down to chambers below the earth, and it was possible the Restless occupants resided somewhere below.

At the end of the avenue stood the tomb Silas was looking for. Its outer walls were made from carefully dressed stone, and massive columns held up the lintel of the doorway. The entrance stood open, and between the columns, a rectangle of impenetrable black hung like a moonless night.

Silas leaned his head closer to the entrance. He could smell the stale perfume of stone, damp, and mold within.

"Hello?" he whispered to the darkness.

The darkness didn't answer.

Remembering the flashlight Mother Peale had given him, Silas turned it on and pointed it inside, then followed the beam through the doorway.

Within were wonderful things. A large chariot clad in thin sheets of gold stood against the wall nearest the door. There was also a carved wooden bed adorned with finials in the shapes of leopards with eyes of inset lapis lazuli. Numerous sconces stood unlit about the antechamber, but the beam of the flashlight revealed walls painted with detailed murals in the Egyptian style, perhaps copied out of some excavation reports of the last century from sites such as Abydos or Dendereh.

Silas gazed closely at the walls, wondering if their hieroglyphic texts and images held clues to the rites awaiting his mother. The hieroglyphs were indecipherable to him. Yet the carved and painted images were plain enough: The panel scenes depicted the deceased—shown in anachronistic American attire from the turn of the century—being led by Anubis toward a green-skinned god seated upon a dais. That was Osiris, the judge of the dead. At his feet was seated Ammit, the eater of souls, made from the body parts of a lion, hippo, and crocodile, just like the queer trophy-statue in his uncle's house. In the next scene, the deceased had been laid upon a table and was being prepared for interment: wrapped in linens up to his cravat, covered with fragrant oils, a scarab set upon his chest. Then, in the following panel, the corpse was standing, eyes closed, while Anubis inserted a small—was it a sort of little stone crowbar?—into the corpse's mouth. In the final scene, the bandages had been removed from the corpse, who was now departing the *naos*, the funerary sanctuary, on its way back to town, clearly walking up Fairwell Street. Were these the funeral rites of the wealthiest of Lichport's families? Of his mother's people?

As Silas crossed the floor, he saw there were numerous jars and urns as well as many small ivy plants in decorative pots, like those left on the porches of the houses on Fort Street. Most of these were, ironically, dead. There were dusty bottles of wine, pots of perfume, and in the corner, several badly preserved stuffed cranes or ibises wrapped in stained linens. There was also the small, thin corpse of a cat that appeared to have simply curled up in the tomb and died without knowing it was now part of a bizarre funereal tableau.

Against the other walls of the chamber were stacked more pieces of carved furniture, more statuary, and many chests and coffers. Strangely, though, none of its contents had been stolen. Everything was covered with layers of undisturbed dust. Many offerings had once been left, gifts for the dead, but no one had entered this place for some time. As Silas looked at the contents of the tomb, he could not help but wonder what it would feel like to be left here, for family to bring him, at his death, into a chamber like this one, and then to endure beyond death that way: a silent watcher, left behind, surrounded by cut stones and bricks; dust sifting down over his face, his lips becoming tight and dry, eyes closed, dreaming of the world outside that had forgotten him.

A noise drew his attention to the stone steps leading down into the earth. Over the doorway was a carved scarab, much like the gemstone of his ring, set into the keystone. Peering into the passage, Silas could just see a pale light emanating from a chamber far below, and he heard a faint crackling sound.

"Hello?"

Still air closed in behind his words.

He made his way down.

The roof of the passage overhead was painted with ivy vines. Figures on the walls on either side were carrying offering vessels. The air warmed as he descended, and it was scented with smells familiar from his great-grandfather's room in the house on Fort Street: pitch, honey, fragrant preserving oils, and mold.

The stairs ended in a small antechamber perhaps only ten feet long. Carved chairs flanked both sides, giving it the appearance of a waiting room. At its far side, another doorway glowed with a flickering, inconstant light from beyond its threshold. Slowly Silas approached and then walked through.

He entered a deep chamber with rich offerings stacked by both sides of the doorway. There were also numerous large cans of Crisco, some unopened, others empty. He wondered what they could possibly be for. The cans brought back a memory of how his mother would sometimes rub a bit of Crisco into her hands if the skin was dry. She had said her family's kitchen maid had taught her that "ever so long ago."

To his surprise, several electric lamps with tasseled shades diffused a low light about the front of the room. The tomb had been wired for electricity. Their light pulsed, and the crackling sound Silas had heard before came from the old bulbs that hissed and popped, warning that their filaments had nearly expired. An old radio stood in the corner. The far side of the room was cast in shadow.

Along the wall closest to him was a long table covered in games of different kinds: old dice made from jet and ivory, decks of cards, antique backgammon and chess sets, mahjong tiles, a rusted mechanical horse race set. Stacked along the table's side were colorful, worn boxes of board games. Some of the boxes were at least a hundred years old, maybe older. The games had curious names like "The Mansion of Happiness," "Round the World with Nellie Bly," "Advance and Retreat," "Grandmama's Improved Game of Useful Knowledge," and "Mixed Pickles." The box on top of the stack was called "Totem" and bore on its lid a drawing of a bear and a faded quote from Longfellow:

> And they painted on the grave posts
> Of the graves yet unforgotten.
> Each his own ancestral Totem;
> Figures of the Bear and Reindeer,
> Of the Turtle, Crane and Beaver.

The box's side was split open and some small cards with images of animals had fallen out onto the floor.

At the center of the chamber was an enormous stone

sarcophagus, deeply engraved with hieroglyphs on all of its exterior surfaces. Silas walked around it warily. Drawing closer, he put his hands on the edge and looked over. It was empty, but he could see that the inside was also richly inscribed. In Egypt, Silas knew, the oldest books of the dead had been inscribed within and upon the sarcophagi. If that was the case, there was no way to bring this "text" back with him, unless he made rubbings, and his great-grandfather had said nothing about that. The book he was supposed to find must be elsewhere. He walked toward the back of the tomb.

Against the far wall, hidden in shadow that yielded to his light, two well-preserved corpses leaned against each other as though drunkenly passed out. Next to them, so still Silas thought at first she might be a statue, was another corpse sitting in a chair covered with burnished metal. She was much older-looking than the other two. Her black hair was plaited and adorned with small beads of hammered gold, and she wore a pectoral of faience beads worked into the shape of a vulture. Her lips were tightly drawn. Her skin, yellowed but translucent, glowed in the light like citrine. Were they Restless, or merely the tomb's more conventionally deceased occupants?

"Hello?" Silas said softly. "Good evening?"

One the bulbs made a popping sound behind him and went out momentarily. It crackled back to life, but dimmer, its light flashing and intermittent.

Before the corpse of the old lady was a pedestal holding a collection of extremely ancient scrolls. Silas hoped one of these was the *Book of the Dead*. Walking closer to the corpses, watching them out of one eye, Silas reached for the scroll on the top of the stack.

The corpse in the chair shifted and, more quickly than Silas would have thought possible, raised her arm and grasped his wrist.

"Wait!" he said, startled. "Be still! I mean no harm! I have come to—" But as the corpse tightened her grip on his arm, he couldn't finish the sentence. The pain dismembered his thoughts, and his knees began to buckle under him. Jonas Umber's face flashed across his memory. There were ways to stop the Restless. What had Jonas told him? But he couldn't use such terrible words. How could he hurt one of these people? How his Umber ancestor would have been sickened to see him like this, on his knees before one of the living dead that Jonas had so despised.

"Who comes . . . ?" rasped the corpse as she continued to tighten her grip. Silas could smell her breath, thick with the fragrance of desiccating minerals: salt and natron, and the faded essence of flowers and rare oils that still gave off a stale semblance of their former perfumes. The corpse's face held no expression, but her eyes, now open, exerted a terrible compelling force, and he found, trying to pull back, that he couldn't look away from her. Desperately he closed his eyes and tried once more to get away, but her grip was unshakable. With his free hand, he tried to pry hers off, but her fingers, thin and dry as they were, were like the teeth of a trap.

"Please," he said, begging her, "you're breaking my wrist. . . . I am the Janus. . . . I command you to release me." His words sounded hollow and small on the air, and the corpse ignored him. But as he continued to pry at her hand, something caught the corpse's attention and she looked down. She slowly grabbed his clutching hand. She brought it close to her face and stared at the sapphire scarab in his ring. She closed her eyes and spoke.

"Hail to thee, O heart. Hail to thee! O heart which I bore within me upon the earth, do not stand and speak against me in the presence of the Lord of the West . . . Osiris, Lord of the Dead."

Be polite, he remembered his great-grandfather saying. *Be polite to them!*

"Do you . . . like it?" Silas stammered. "My great-grandfather gave me that ring—" Silas said, trying to sound calm.

"What is this? Indeed?" said the corpse, her voice rising as curiosity enlivened her speech.

"Yes. My dad gave it to him. My dad was Amos Umber." And then, thinking fast, he added, "Augustus Howesman is my great-grandfather. He's the one who sent me here to you. But you're hurting me!"

The corpse released his wrist and Silas quickly stepped back beyond her reach.

One of the other corpses leaning against the painted wall flexed his legs and slowly stood upright. The layer of dust covering him slid off his body and onto the floor, making little clouds. He was dressed in a moldy long coat in the style of the last century. The cravat around his neck was loose and stained nearly black with dirt. The corpse drew in a long breath, then seemed to smile, and exhaled a little more quickly, as though he was remembering how to do it. The standing corpse looked at the ring, then at the seated elder, and said, "He is of the blood of the Howe. He walks the paths of the dead."

"Perhaps, but not all the Undertakers have been kind to us," said another corpse, who held an ax of bronze and slowly raised it.

"No," said the eldest, gesturing for the ax-holder to stop. "I have seen. He has brought our kind out of the house of dissolution. He is with us and for us and one of us."

The other corpse dropped the ax, and the bronze blade rang as it struck the stone floor.

"Why has he come? I have not looked, so this I have not seen," said the eldest. Her soft words lilted with an accent shaped by the South.

"Why do they always come?" mused one of the standing corpses.

"For money, I expect," answered the other.

"Oh, no, no. I don't want any money. Here . . . I brought you this," Silas said, remembering the offerings Mother Peale had given him. He took the bread and the glass bottle of milk from his satchel and placed them on the ground before the corpses. "These are for you."

All the corpses' eyes were open now, and as they looked at him a little of the stiffness of their faces seemed to lessen. They smiled. One said, with his mouth moving almost imperceptibly, "That is well. He is not afraid of the old ways."

"Have you come then to leave another of our rank within this place?"

"Yes. Tell us. Who shall come? Who will join us in the sanctuary? I have not looked. I have not seen," said the elder.

"Mother of the *Naos*, who could be left?" said the standing corpse, and he made a deep barking sound like someone with croup.

"Dolores Umber . . . *Howesman* . . . Dolores Howesman is dead." Silas heard himself saying the words. It didn't sound like his voice. When he spoke her name, it felt like he was hearing someone else say it, and he was being forced to listen.

"He has come for the book, then," said one of the corpses quietly, barely moving his mouth.

"Yes," said Silas. "I have come to bring back the *Book of the Dead* for my mother's funeral."

"The *Book of the Dead* may be consulted, though it has been years and years since any have sought it out." She looked at Silas's ring again. "It is your right as both kin of the deceased and Lord of the West to do so, but it may no longer be carried from this place."

"Lord of the West? That is not a title I know."

"You must be satisfied to claim your resonances as well as your relations, child," said the eldest, perhaps smiling at him. "You called yourself 'Janus.' That's not a Howesman name and not a title associated with any of our offices. Not a river name. It's Roman. Newfangled. Frankly, a little tacky. Tell me, where is your father?"

"Dead," answered Silas softly.

"And how did this come to pass?"

"He was killed by his brother."

"You see!" she exclaimed. "Now *that* is *very* Egyptian. For was not Osiris, Lord of the Dead, slain by his own brother? And did not Osiris's own son, Horus, after being reared by Isis, rise up like the sun at dawn and slay his father's killer? Ah! There is only *one* story, but on and on it goes. You are a man to be reckoned with, and you come by your titles honestly—Lord of the West, Lord of the Two Lands. I am glad to meet you, Silas Umber. You may read what is here, if you wish to." She gestured at the *Book of the Dead,* but didn't take her eyes off his face. She was looking at Silas differently than a moment ago, more intently. She was interested in him now, she *knew* who he was.

Silas peered at the partially opened scroll and its many lines of carefully drawn hieroglyphs. The closer he looked, the more frustrated he felt. "I can't read this. And I don't know how it is to be used. My great-grandfather said to bring it back with me. Please! I have come for your help and I think you are obligated to help me prepare my mother for her funeral, aren't you? You have implied I have some authority here. So I am asking you, officially, to help me."

"Child, child, calm yourself. We are just met. Don't spoil such a joyful occasion."

"I am not a child."

"No, indeed." She looked him up and down with an appreciative eye. "I can see you are not. But come closer now, for we are cousins, distant though we may be. Your folk went north while mine favored the lands of the river delta and so stayed in the South until I was brought here by coercion. But that's all ancient history." She stood and held out her arms toward Silas, saying, "Don't make me chase you, child! Come here right now and give me some sugar."

Before Silas knew what was happening, the corpse stepped forward and embraced him and kissed him, placing her dry mouth over his lips. Almost instantly and before he could pull away, he felt something begin to coat his tongue and the back of his throat. Dust. Dust from the corpse had entered his mouth. Silas strained to avoid choking. He glanced in all directions, wondering what to do. The corpse's eyes were closed and she was exhaling into him, more and more dust rising up from the depths of her body and the chambers of her shriveled lungs and past his lips. It was bitter. His eyes welled up with tears, and he couldn't reach up to wipe them or to push her away; her embrace was like being caught between two pillars of stone. His mouth went dry as the dust began to soften and coat his gums and tongue. At the very back of his throat he could feel the dust absorbing his remaining saliva and pooling there. Before he could stop himself, Silas swallowed. A thin stream of mud and grit slid down the walls of his esophagus.

As his body absorbed it, his mind clouded over.

He breathed in deeply through his nose, trying again not to choke.

In his mind, he heard water coursing through shallow cataracts. Behind his eyes he saw a river flowing over a dry desert, past lotus-columned temples and walls deeply carved with animal-headed gods. *I am the river also,* a voice within him said. *I am the black-earthed banks of life-giving loam. I am the reed and the rush. I am the green god who rises up, bringing succor to the dead and peace to all the land.*

Silas saw the world tilt. For a moment he felt himself subsumed below the rapids, but then he heard his name and opened his eyes. He was looking up into the face of the elder ancestress who held him in her arms.

The ancient woman slowly drew back her head and released him. Closing her mouth with her hand, she sat back down in her chair, her eyes still closed. "You know, when I was younger, cousins could court. . . ."

Silas staggered backward until he came up against the wall. "Please, please . . ." He coughed. "I just need the book."

"Child, we are the ever-living. We are the book. Now you carry the book within you." She gestured toward the scroll. "There is no need for that now," she said.

"But I must have it! I need it for my mother's funeral!" said Silas desperately.

"It is redundant."

"I don't understand."

"The book is *in* you. The words of the Lord of the Dead, the Green One of the Two Lands, whose book this is, have always resided in you, in your blood. They've waited in you like seeds. Now we've just made a little garden and watered it, that's all. Just another parcel of your considerable birthright, Silas of the Two Lands."

"One of many, it seems," Silas whispered, wiping his eyes, feeling once again drawn in an unfamiliar direction.

"As a Howesman? As an Umber? Or do you mean as the Undertaker of this town, which I presume you are, since your father is no more?"

"As you wish . . . ," Silas said, turning to go, not answering her question. "So the book is within me? But how can I read it, then? I don't understand."

"Silas Umber, there is no need for such a literal view of the world. Let me show you." The corpse stood up once more, breathed in deeply, and said, "I speak, by the name Nut the bright, the glorious. Who has come?"

Before Silas could think of how to respond, he heard himself begin to speak. The words were foreign to his ears. It was his voice, but in a language he had never heard spoken. It was an ancient tongue, but as he continued and his mind began to rework the words into English, he could smell rich spices and dark loam on his own breath, and the perfume of flowers was all about him. His back went straight and his eyes opened wide and he said in a sure voice, "I must find you, for I am Horus. I am he who shall open your mouth for you, for it is I, your son. I shall not eat. I shall not drink. I was conceived in the long darkness and born into the Abyss. I have come and brought you bread from that place." The words stopped. Astonishment sat on Silas's brow.

"Lady," he asked in a voice now wholly his own again, "who are you?"

"Very few have spoken my true name in this land. I hardly remember it. You may call me Miss Hattie."

"You are not from Lichport, are you, ma'am?"

"No, child. I am from the South, from the lands of the river delta. But I have long been a traveler, sometimes going first-class, other times abiding in steerage. . . ."

The other two corpses laughed at that, but she continued. "I have been carried by generations of my family from one land to another. Twice I was stolen and . . . exhibited. But I have always been recovered. Recovered, it seems, only to be forgotten here."

"You mean you've been here"—Silas looked about the dust-filled chamber—"in this tomb, since coming to Lichport?"

"No, no, child. For many years I was with my family, in our fine houses. We had a place on Fort Street, and a large mansion overlooking the sea on the south side of town. I liked it there, looking over the sea. I could watch the sunrise. How invigorating that was! There was also a townhouse in Kingsport, for the season, you understand, for the nightlife in Lichport has always been below par. But that was long ago. Who knows, maybe some of us are in Kingsport still. Sometimes I had my own room with my things about me. Then later, a small temple house was built for me 'out back,' and I was there, in the quiet of that place, alone with my own thoughts. Then my kin left and I was . . . installed here with some of the others. We have not been invited out in some time. Still, I look well, do I not?" The corpse ran her hand gently past the stiff hair on the side of her head as if to put a loose curl back in place.

"Oh, yes."

"You may one day find that tenacity is a marvelous preservative. Now, aren't you going to give us an official invitation?"

"An invitation? Oh. Sure. Of course. Miss Hattie, my great-grandfather, Augustus Howesman, and I would like you to come, please—all of you here and any others you know—to my mother's funeral." The words caught in Silas's throat. It still hadn't sunk in. When he got home, his mother would be sitting in her parlor as though nothing had changed. But it had. Everything had changed. And he was never going see his mother sitting in her parlor again. He began to cry, but quickly pulled his arms across his face to hide his tears.

"We shall come. Tradition requires it, in any event. There are certain observations that must be attended to, and I am sure no one else—except, now perhaps, you— knows them. We shall oversee the rite together. Silas Umber of the Howesmans of the Mound, I will stand with you at the Great Rite. Many sacred things shall be needed. Were the chests and coffers still there in the upper chamber? We have not been above for some time."

Silas nodded.

"Good. We shall bring what tradition requires. Now, if we may have your blessing, we shall travel faster for it. Haste is necessary. And the manna of kin will be needed for my mind to reach the others. Even with it, and though Temple House is not far—yea, we know it well—we will take some time to reach our destination. Morning will likely greet you before we do."

"Okay . . . ," said Silas hesitantly. "What sort of blessing would you like?"

"Speak the words that even now fill your throat. Speak!"

And Silas spoke again in the voice of the desert, the voice of the *Book of the Dead*.

"May you perform what you desire. Oh, divine souls who reside in your eternal mansions, who hold one foot in the land of the dead and the other in the land of the living, come forth as you may, and swiftly. Ascend to the sky, though you are weak. Climb upon the beams of the sun, though you are old. Be strong within your mansions! Rise up from the earth! Walk now upon the banks of the river in the lands of the dead and the lands of the living! So speaks the Lord of Two Lands."

Silas turned his head to the side, his eyes pinched shut. He breathed in deeply, slowly opening his eyes to look again upon his Restless kin.

The words had immediate effect upon the two "younger" corpses. They both stood more upright and moved their arms freely. They turned and embraced each other, then introduced themselves to Silas. One was his great-great-great-uncle Archie from the Howesman side. The other, Conrad, a cousin several times removed, was the son of a Howesman/Hariot marriage, a match once thought fashionable.

Miss Hattie did not move, but spoke again from her throne.

"You know," she said, smiling absently, "long ago, we might all have been considered gods. Who knows, we might be gods. . . ."

"But now, who would care?" Silas said flatly.

Miss Hattie shook her head, but then spoke to the others.

"Assemble the chariot, please. And, Silas Umber, we shall come to govern over this rite and attend the passage of your mother as befits her name. But now night is falling and you must be home for vigil before midnight, if not well before. That is a dangerous time for your mother. The night before the burial is often difficult. It is wise to be watchful over the dead. More so for your mother than most, I suspect."

There was something very certain in her tone that made Silas nervous. He wanted to ask for more details, when she spoke again, and more sternly.

"Make haste homeward now! Return and watch over your mother. If her corpse comes through the night unharmed, at dawn the Great Rite shall begin."

Silas turned and walked quickly back the way he'd come. Passing the painted and inscribed walls of the stairway and the upper chamber, he found he could read the hieroglyphs. But he did not gaze again among the prayers and charms and hopeful narratives of a glorious afterlife. On Temple Street his mother's corpse lay on the dining room table. Still, things were already changing, or rather, no part of his life was ever allowed to settle, and everything was shifting again, making it harder and harder to find his balance. Everyone he met, living or dead, everywhere he walked, in this world or the other, every rite, the words of the ancient gods themselves—Janus, Osiris—inhered in him and became part of an increasingly complex pattern, like the indelible marks of ink upon vellum that, once made, would remain for centuries. He had become a palimpsest, layer upon layer. Maybe this, and not merely assisting the dead, was what it truly meant to be an Undertaker. If this was so, who was he really? Which name, which formula, which emanation or reflection was Silas Umber? Who was he becoming?

When Silas emerged from the tomb, it was dark. The sky held only thin threads of azure against the wider black. Before him, the avenue of mausoleums was becoming more lively. The once darkened doorways all along the lane leading out of the Egyptian district were lit with pale lights, and he had to pass them all to get out again into the open ground of Newfield.

He could not keep the memory of his previous visit with Bea from his mind, and he grew uncomfortable. Silas disliked how nervous even the memory of the night market still made him. Why should an Undertaker fear such a place? What was he afraid of finding there? Bea had wanted to show him the night market, but he had insisted on leaving as quickly as possible. Now, again, here were the lights of loss . . . of the night market . . . the place where forgotten things might be found. What kind of loss might such a place reveal to him?

The lights flickered from the tombs. He could just discern, at the very edges of his sight, shadows moving along the lanes. A distant and vaguely familiar floral smell was rising on the cold air. He peered down the darkening avenue. He strained to hear the thin sounds of voices. Were they coming from the tombs? Or behind him? Silas felt watched and exposed. At least he had the power to see what was forming in the shadows around him. He took the death watch from his pocket and flicked open the jaw of the small silver skull with his thumb, exposing the dial. From the empty air just in front of him, Silas heard someone say his name. Peering ahead and breathing in sharply to steel his fraying nerves, he stopped the dial of the death watch.

A low mist rose up between the stones of the lane. He walked into it without hesitation, though fear pinched at him. There was a distant song. He matched his steps to the timing of its rise and fall. Many voices. One song. A street song. A market song. Voices bellowed and others sweetly cooed. Footfall on the stones kept time . . . his and the rest.

CHAPTER 6

NIGHT MARKET

COME BUY! THE VOICES SING OUT ALONG THE LANE. *Come buy! Come buy!*

> Lost toys! Lost toys! Once dropped, now found!
> Keys! Keys! By the basketful!
> Innocence! The swiftly spent days of summer? Three
>   a penny!
> Love! Long ago embraces? Secret kisses? Spring
>   assignations? All ripe together!
> Time! Time! Minutes! Hours! Days and years!
>   Come buy! Come buy!
> Youth! Remember when? You can! Come buy!

It is generally known that the night market should not be visited by the sensible. Only lost things adorn its stalls. Only the lost cry out their goods with wide, needy mouths. Only the lost frequent its lanes, filling their baskets with the past, wandering here and there, peering into everything just one last time. The cries of the hawkers—which rise up almost as soon as evening descends—are pathetic, as one would expect. . . .

But you would be wise to keep your pennies in your pocket. It's sometimes best that things go missing. For once they do, we may move on. We stop clinging to the past. We might forget. And some things, once forgotten, are best not remembered. This is why when the youth first sees the lamps of the night market being lit, his heart beats with fear. And so he quickens his pace, moving past the stalls richly hung with wonders slightly stained, a little worn. This is why he only wants to make his way home. For wasn't there someone who was waiting for him? Wasn't there something he needed to do?

You see? Even those who do not willingly attend the night market succumb to the spell of the stalls . . . unable to remember what they've come for or why they should never have come. But there he stands, looking at a bouquet. There are many flowers at the night market, for many folk have lost their bloom. Flowers are for remembrance, and so they always sell well here.

The youth slows his pace, wooed by the perfumed air. And the women with their baskets draw in close to him, holding their flowers up to his face. Remember? Remember? One of the women takes a dried, flat asphodel flower from her skirts and puts it in the youth's hair. Remember, she says. He can smell the hint of perfume clinging to the gray, faded petals.

He closes his eyes.

He sees a meadow covered with flowers. Asphodels bloom all the way to the distant mountains. He sees their buds open like stars, their waving stalks. He hears an infant crying. A man is running through the meadow.

Remember?

Remember?

Then the man is crying too.

His father is crying.

Then his father begins to sing in a broken, desperate voice:

> Hush-a-bye, little one, aye, aye;
> Hush-a-bye, little one, aye.
> The night birds are singing,
> The bells are ringing

And it's time for you now to fly,
Little bird,
It's time for you now to fly.
Fly with me, fly with me, aye, aye;
Fly with me, little bird, aye;
Your parents are waiting,
For ages a-waiting
Little bird, to their waiting arms fly!

The youth opens his eyes.

The women put flowers in his hands, then sift them slowly over him and the stars are falling. Welcome home! one says. In the distance is a small figure who casts no shadow and extends his hand to the youth.

Remember.

The smell of the asphodels is all about him, clinging to his skin and clothes. He wants to lie down in the field, in the street, upon a bed of petals.

Yes! the women chant, Yes! Yes!, upending their baskets over him.

Sleep here among the stalls, among the petals of asphodels. Sleep and dream and remember what was lost, the women sing.

But before he lowers himself to the street, far above the market, a falcon flies in wide circles and quickly stoops to pass lower over the stalls, over the youth's head. The bird screams, its high cry shattering the strains of the women's song. The youth rises. Something in the falcon's cry reminds him of his mother's voice. He sees the falcon fly off, away from the night market, away from the tombs and all the abandoned parcels of the forgotten and the lost. And the dark figure in the distant fields of asphodel draws back his hand and turns away.

Silas found himself staring up at the small slice of empty sky visible above the columns and walls of the mausoleums. All the blue had gone out of the evening, both in the clouds and behind them. There was only the oceanic black of night flowing indiscernible from the dim, unseen sea, and no moon yet. A moment before, he had taken his thumb off the dial, and the death watch began ticking, its tiny mechanical heart leaping again to life. The path through the night market had scraped across his losses, making them raw. His chest felt hollow and the emptiness of it ached. Whatever he'd lost remained apart from him.

He could see movements now within most of the tombs. Granite slabs slid from atop their monuments and sarcophagi. Tomb doors, long closed, were pushed open from the inside. Corpses slowly ascended the steps from lower chambers.

The Restless were coming.

Without looking back, Silas turned on his flashlight and started running down the lane, through the great arch and across the plots, moving swiftly past the overgrown gravestones and out of Newfield, coursing like a small distant comet out of the dark toward Temple House.

CHAPTER 7

RUMORS

THE REMAINING INHABITANTS OF THE HOUSES on the far side of Temple Street have always been a nervous lot. Perhaps it's because they live too close to the walls of Newfield Cemetery. Or perhaps because the houses on that street, while large, are not so large as to be considered fine. So the families of the Temple Street homes close to Coach Street occupied a precarious place within what society remained in Lichport. It is known that those families all made a little money and came up from the Narrows. Not so far that they wouldn't be able to sup with old friends, but not far enough as to be accepted by the Upper Towns folk either. Precarious, nervous types. The sort of folk always looking out their windows and finding fault in what they see.

She'd spied the Umber boy before. More than once. Wandering his way, following some punky lights, far into Newfield. Mrs. Halliwell had seen him with her own eyes, and told a few folks about it. "Leave it be!" they told her. "Them Umbers have their own ways, and those ways ain't our ways, but in a pinch, they're the only thing for it. So let the Undertaker be. His father was a queer one too, and no mistake, but a useful man."

But it wasn't just the Umber boy, it was the whole family. Just last night, hadn't Dolores Umber fallen right down in the street? Then before anyone could be called, the body's gone. Picked up and *carried off* by one of *them*! Mrs. Halliwell couldn't make heads or tails of it. Now, one night later, Silas Umber just walks into Newfield, back straight and determined. What for? His folk are in their own plots on Prince Street and Fairwell, thought Mrs. Halliwell. Yes, he was the Undertaker. Maybe he had business there. But there had been no deaths of regular folk Mrs. Halliwell had heard of, and wasn't the father's body planted on the Beacon? Then, a while later, out comes young Umber running like he's being chased by the devil himself. Then came the lights about the old fancy tombs of those Put Away Folks, moving around on the other side of the wall. Voices. *Old* voices. And the sounds of things being dragged up stairs from who knows where. And the lights. Queer lights seen through holes in the walls. What did he *do* in there?

Upon seeing those lights and strange doings, Mrs. Halliwell closed her curtains on the night and stoked up the fire. A chill had come over her. There was no good in any of it. She could feel that.

Later, she rose from her chair, half-asleep, and parted the curtains for a last look out onto the street. Her mind twisted with fear at what she saw. A procession of corpses slowly made its way toward Temple House. "It is the Umber boy," she muttered to herself. She knew, knew sure as the dead could walk, that Silas Umber had something to do with this. She knew. He was the cause. He would bring evil upon the town. Corpses and corruption, plague and pestilence! It had all happened before. That is why the corpses were put away. That is why they do not live among us anymore!

"Leave the dead where they lie. . . . ," she said, her uneven breath whitening the dark, cold window glass. "Leave them be! God preserve us! God Almighty save us from the Restless dead!"

LEDGER

One for the rook
One for the crow
One will wither
One will grow.

—TRADITIONAL

CHAPTER 8

VIGIL

At the porch stairs, Silas paused.

Temple House was silent, and shadows wound about its columns like creeping vines. A wind had risen, and it bit at Silas's face and hands. At his approach, a bird called desperately from somewhere close by: *cree cree*, and in that sound he heard a warning. High above, he could just see the silhouette of a falcon perched atop one of the chimneys. Before him, a dim glow washed the lower windows that faced the street. Inside the house, candles had been lit. Silas came up the stairs slowly, one at a time, but stopped once more at the front door. Grief held back his hand. He couldn't look at his mother's corpse again. He tried to conjure her in his memory, some moment from their lives together . . . her talking to him, or walking with him, or when he hugged her on Fort Street before his father's funeral. He could see the scenes in his mind, but a veil was always before her face. She was a body with a dark blur about her head that spoke to him, walked with him, but he couldn't really see her.

Silas's hands began to shake and his heart beat into a panic.

The front door opened.

"Good," his great-grandfather said, looking relieved. "Were you able to see to the arrangements?"

Silas stood before the open door but didn't answer.

"Silas!" the corpse said, loud enough to break his wave of panic.

"Yes . . . ," Silas replied. "Yes. They are coming."

Augustus Howesman walked past Silas to the edge of the porch and looked up at the sky, then peered from one end of the street to the other.

"I think it won't be until tomorrow morning that the others arrive from Newfield," said Silas. "They are not moving very quickly and there's much to be seen to."

"It's not them I'm looking for." The corpse looked up once more. "Bad weather tonight. Hopefully, it will break by tomorrow. Let's get inside."

Many candles had been lit and some of the furniture had been moved. Most of the chairs and small settees from the parlor had been turned to look down through the open pocket doors into the dining room, as though an audience might arrive to sit and look at his mother's body. His great-grandfather had been busy. Some of the antiques had been brought back downstairs out of storage, mostly Egyptian things: a black basalt statue of Isis, the infant Horus suckling at her breast. There were also many smaller figurines, Egyptian ushabti, carefully arranged on the mahogany buffet.

Silas looked at all the decorations, the ancient things, and couldn't hold back. "Great-grandfather, I need to know what's happening. I don't think my mother would want anything like this . . . anything so elaborate. She wouldn't want to see these objects. She hated them."

"Not so. These preparations are her express wishes. I understand your concern. For some time, she bore no great love for Lichport or its ways, or even for me. But more recently, she must have had a change of heart, because when last we spoke, we discussed this day in some detail."

"You mean she knew something was going to happen to her?"

"I don't think so . . . but perhaps she had a premonition. Who can say? Silas, surely, here in Lichport, it is no surprise that every third thought of most folks is their graves. In any event, she asked me to be sure that you knew she wanted a funeral in the 'old style,' so that is what she will receive. And you have a very important role to play. You've already begun."

"I will oversee everything. The wake, everything."

"No, grandson. This is different from what you're used to. Far older, I think. The others, when they come, will direct the rite. Be patient. They'll know what to do. For tonight, it's best we just keep our eyes open and watch for trouble. This night, we sit vigil for her, for the winter nights can be long and sometimes the darkness does not stay outside where it belongs . . . ," he whispered. "If all goes well tonight, tomorrow the funeral rite will proceed."

Silas nodded. "Mother Peale sat vigil over my father's body." Augustus Howesman made a small smile, but Silas could see he was nervous, and asked, "What could harm her now?"

"Silas, there are many uses for the dead."

"Are you saying someone would try to *do* something to her?"

"I am saying, particularly for those of our family, the time just after death is a very special time. And it can be a dangerous one. This is what I've heard. I have never sat over a body like this before. But we'll keep a good watch, we will not sleep. We shall be vigilant. We'll watch, and everything, come morning, should be all right."

Silas looked about the room and went to the windows. In the dark glass of the dining room, he saw, softly illuminated, the reflection of his mother's body. Moving closer, peering outside, he saw that the wind moved through the bare trees. Their branches scraped against one another like dry bones, filling the night with rasps and clatterings.

Without looking away from the window, Silas said, "Do I seem sane to you, great-grandfather?"

"Indeed, yes."

"I don't feel sane. It's like I'm trapped in the same dream. Every night it comes. . . . A few faces change, but the story keeps looping back on itself, and someone is always dying."

"Someone *is* always dying."

"And I can't help them."

"Grandson, as I understand it, your job is not to keep people *from* dying, but to help those who don't die well to find peace, and ease the passage for others who ask for it. The world rolls along and does not stop. Not for you, not for anyone."

"It stopped for you."

"Silas, it only looks that way because we're not looking back on it all yet. What I'm saying is just don't you worry too much about your sanity at this very moment, all right? You are the most remarkable person I know," Augustus Howesman said, echoing Silas's own words about him. "Now, perhaps you should light a fire in the fireplaces, here in the parlor and across the hall. I've stacked them with wood. Then we should settle in. It's likely to be a long night. When our dead are close by us, so do our memories press in, and all those folks of the past come back to us, in one form or another. The corpse attracts them. Or maybe it's the mourning of the living that pulls aside the veil. I am no expert, like you, but this is what I've heard and what I feel to be true."

Silas looked down at his mother's corpse.

"Oh, son, this sort of thing is in your blood, whether you're happy about it or not. I see you're uneasy. I am too. Listen, it's the hair of the dog that helps the most. Those things that frighten us, we have to look them in the eye to get past them. Even when they fill our hearts with cold, eh?"

"I'm not scared of ghosts. Not anymore."

"And what if there are worse things than ghosts?" He looked out the window. "I happen to know there are, and I know you do too. The Howesmans are a queer lot, I can tell you. Our successes and prominence made us our share of enemies in life, and our . . . *enduring* bodies have been despised, as you saw at Arvale. And as you can see"—the corpse patted his own chest—"even Death keeps his distance! We have always been fashionable, but not always popular."

The conversation was making Silas uneasy and a little paranoid. As he paced about the floors of the joined rooms—past the corpse of his mother, past the quietly waiting corpse of his great-grandfather—he keenly felt other eyes on him. Decorative carvings followed him with the tiny stare of birds, of griffins, of the lion-headed feet of the mahogany buffet that held the ushabtis. The flat stares of the small statues his great-grandfather had set up were on him. And the Ammit, which had been set on the floor at his mother's feet, followed him with its carnelian eyes. The portraits looked down on him as he walked below them— his grandfather, whose house this had once been; his great-great-grandmother, who had once done her embroidery there in the parlor, Uncle had told him. Silas felt watched and judged. The long wait for morning wasn't calming him.

His great-grandfather sat quietly in his chair a little away from the fire. Every so often, he moved his hand, or tapped his fingers up and down for a moment, but always returned to that preternatural stillness that the condition of death afforded him. This made Silas ever more nervous because he didn't know what to do next.

Finally tired of pacing, he said, "Tell me a story. Distract me, please." Silas was trying to smile. "It makes me edgy when I don't know what's expected of me."

"So like your mother . . . I wish she could have been easier in her mind about life's starts and stops."

"It wasn't in her nature to relax. But tell me anything you like," Silas continued. "A yarn from your side of the family?"

"Did your mother ever tell you Our Old Story?"

"Are you kidding? She never—" Silas began to complain. He looked over at Dolores's body again and swallowed his words. "No, sir. I don't believe she ever did."

"It is an old thing, and has been told by many and not always the same way. The Grimms included a most absurd version in their collections and washed the Howesman name from the tale entirely. It's still accounted fine by those who know it, and I think this is as good a time as any to tell it. At least it will help us pass the bitter hours of the night. Stoke up the fire, grandson, and I'll tell it to you.

"In olden times there was a Howesman man just making his way along the highway, when rather suddenly, a stranger leapt from the hedgerows onto the path before him, shouting, 'Stop! Take not one step farther!'

"'What is this?' said the Howesman man. 'Who are you to speak so to me?'

"'I am Death,' answered the leaper through the hedgerows. 'I rule all. You must obey.'

"Well, that Howesman man refused. You know how we are, eh, Silas? Just someone try to tell us what do! So that Howesman, he grabbed Death by the arm and the wrestling began. It was a terrible fight and the Howesman man had the advantage, being a live man and all, and with a great swing, he knocked Death down by a rock. Death just lay there. And the Howesman man went on his way, leaving Death there on the side of the road, so weak and so weary that the old reaper could not pull himself back up.

"'Well, well,' said Death, trying to catch his breath, 'what shall follow this strange business? If I lie here in the road, no one in the world will die. No, sir! And if they don't die, well then, the world will be too filled up with folk. But if I get up, that Howesman fellow might come back and deal me another blow. No, no. I'll not meet that Howesman man again. No, sir!'

"But as Death lay there talking with himself, another man came down the road. A young man. Spry, of average looks. Just a man. Not a Howesman, but still what might be called strong and healthy. The young man was whistling idly when he saw Death in the road. He looked on Death with compassion and kindness, as though he were simply a tramp stalled on his wanderings. Not knowing who lay there before him, the young man gave Death a drink from his flask, helped him sit up, and waited as Death regained his strength.

"'Do you know, young man, whom you have helped to get back on his feet again?'

"'Just another traveler, down on his luck?' asked the young man.

"'I am Death. It is not in my nature to spare people, and one has already escaped me today. But I do wish to show you some gratitude. So, I make you this oath: I will not come for you without warning. I shall send my messengers to you before I return to take you away.'

"'Well, well,' says the youth. 'That is very well indeed, for then I shall know when you are coming and I may enjoy my life to the fullest until then!' And with that, the youth walked on, whistling an even merrier tune.

"Then, as it befell, the young man and his health soon parted company. Illness came, and pain, and each day was filled with great discomfort. But still, the youth smiled. 'I know that I will not die,' he told himself, 'for Death will first send his messengers. Though these days of illness are grievous, I shall be happy knowing they will end in health once more.'

"And the youth did regain his health and began to live joyfully again. Then one day he felt someone tap him on the shoulder. When he turned around, Death was standing there. 'Come with me now, son. The hour of your demise and departure from this world is here.'

"Surprised and angry that he'd been cheated, the youth said, 'Are you breaking your oath to me? Didn't you promise to send your messengers to me before you'd come to take me away? I have seen no messenger! Not one!'

"'Be silent, man! Be still!' Death said. 'Have I not sent messengers to you already, one after another? Did not Fever come and did not your blood burn and did not your skin grow chilled? Has not Dizziness turned your head from back to front? Has not Gout stabbed you in the toe? Did Darkness not come and draw a veil across your eyes? And, most nights, did not my brother Sleep come to remind you of me and what was coming?'

"The youth could find no words with which to answer Death, and so he gave up his life and followed Death away."

"But what happened to the Howesman man?" asked Silas.

"He is a wanderer still, so it's said. And as for Death? It's told he walks the world as he ever did, but now looks over his shoulder from time to time for fear of being struck down once more by a Howesman!"

Silas looked up to see that his great-grandfather had finished his story and was looking at him for some response. There was something about the story that rang false to Silas. To fight with Death, or try to hold Death at arm's length—this only invited other kinds of troubles. But Silas didn't want to argue about an old family legend. Instead, he said flatly "Oh, thank you, sir. It's a good story. Hopeful in its way, I guess."

The old man slowly cocked his head to the side. "Are you sure you're all right, grandson?"

"No, sir. I am not all right. I have come home and found my mother dead. How am I supposed to feel?"

"No particular one way or another. I'm sorry, Silas, for both of us. I feel your mother was only coming into her own, starting to like her life a little, and then . . . well . . . now this."

"I know who killed her," Silas said, not looking up.

"Silas, how could you know that?"

"Great-grandfather, believe me, I know. I killed her. I brought curses home with me from beyond the marshes and they killed her. If I'd been more careful . . . if I'd known more . . . I might have—"

"Oh, Silas. No more guilt. The troubles of her life, as she once knew it, are over. Don't make yours worse by taking on her problems. And if it was something or someone from that house beyond the marshes that you believe has caused her death, please, let it go! To think on evil calls evil to your side."

"She died so I could live. . . ."

Augustus Howesman was about to speak again, but stopped. After a moment, he said, "Son, what happened to you at that house? Maybe I could help you in some way. Did it happen like in my vision? Were *they* all there?"

Silas nodded, but then said softly, "I don't need any help, sir."

"All right. I understand. You don't want anyone meddling. I respect that."

"Great-grandfather, you don't understand."

"Well, son, I understand that, like your father, you sometimes prefer to keep your own counsel. I also know that when we needed you, you helped me and some of the others most selflessly. And I know that you know that if there was anything I could do for you, all you'd need to do is ask."

Silas's expression softened. "Of course," he said, but quickly looked away. "There are some very terrible things hidden in that place, and I know, somehow, one of them is part of what's happened to my mom. I'm not even sure the place I visited is still there beyond the gates. It's not a place for the living. You know this."

"So it was that bad, eh? I am sorry."

"Not all of it . . . ," Silas started to say, but then Lars's face came into his mind . . . and the pillar of ash that his friend had become when time refused him at Arvale's gate.

"Are you sure you don't want to talk about it, Silas?" asked Augustus Howesman, seeing his great-grandson's face falling. "Was it that you saw someone there you knew? Son, was your father in that house?"

"No," said Silas, looking down into the fire. The mention of his father pushed him over the edge. He turned away from his great-grandfather, trying not to cry.

"I'm sorry, Silas. I just thought perhaps . . . never mind."

"He is doing what he's always done. Taking care of his own business in his own way. I don't know where he is. The people at Arvale were prisoners. They were bound to that house. My father wasn't among them and I am never going back there. For all I know, he could be a prisoner himself somewhere. I have no idea where he went after his funeral, and he has not appeared to me again."

Augustus Howesman stood up and put his hands on Silas's shoulders. A quick wind blew down the chimney and pushed smoke from the fire back into the dining room. He looked up toward the ceiling, as though he could hear something above. "Silas, do you know if all the windows upstairs are closed and locked?"

Turning around, Silas said, "I think so. When I went up there, all the windows on the north wing had been sealed. My mother wouldn't have opened them. Except for her bedroom, she hardly uses the upstairs rooms."

As though roused from sleep, the mantel clock began to stir itself and slowly chime.

"Son, I don't want to frighten you, but I am going to need you to be alert. I can't explain everything you may see tonight. Hell, I don't understand most of it myself. But believe me when I tell you your mother could still be in some danger. She, and those who keep vigil over her."

"Sir, I am not unaccustomed to terrible things. Tell me what might happen."

His great-grandfather stepped up close to Silas, his voice low and wavering. "It's possible that something will come after your mother tonight. Maybe more than one thing. No one's died in our family for some time, at least not in Lichport. But I've been told winter is the worst. The earth is frozen and some clamor and claw for a place to hole up. I am glad you're here, because I'm not really sure what to do if we get into any trouble." He smiled. "There are some problems even a wealthy man can't write a check for."

Silas wasn't distracted by his great-grandfather's forced levity.

"Sir, are you saying something may trouble her ghost?"

"No, no, son . . . it will try to *inhabit* her body. If what I've heard is correct, it will come for her corpse."

CHAPTER 9

FIRESIDE

IT WAS LATE AND THE STORE WAS QUIET.

Mother Peale's daughter, Joan, had taken the truck to the Mennever place for the bull. Lord, but that would be something to see. When was the last bull brought to Lichport? Must have been *years* ago. *What does* that *betoken?* she wondered. Old ways all becoming new again and whatever would folk make of it? Certainly, the town had not grown more accepting in its decrepitude. And poor Silas at the heart of it all, and so likely to catch the blame should there be any trouble. So like his father . . . the boy was a magnet for misfortune, and there'd be more to come, as like as not. And here was a note from *them* on Fort Street to get a bull, then off the boy goes to Newfield to, she suspected, inquire of them even *older* ones. Maybe it's just the way of the rich, old families. Those who were too well off to let go. The rich always have their traditions, and Dolores Umber was one of *them*, even though any money she'd had at the end came from the Umbers. "Well, well," she said, "we will see what's to be seen tomorrow."

Though the fire in the small stove next to her was burning down, she was too comfortable in its lingering heat to brave the cold outside and make her way home. She might just doze in her chair and wait for Joan to come back. She picked a few small pieces of wood from the bucket and used one to open the belly of the stove. The warmth poured out toward her. Inside, the coals glowed like rubies, and tiny flames danced above them, wrapped in smoky veils. Within the wisps of smoke and flickering flames she could feel something coming—a vision lurking within the fire. She closed her eyes for a moment, drew a deep breath, then opened them and looked with intention into the glowing stomach of the stove.

She saw a rider astride a horse of bones. Shadows were before and behind it, and the earth burned and buckled as the horse's hooves struck the ground. A soft whimper escaped her and she sat back in her chair. She was sweating, and her brow was hot to the touch. Her eyes hurt from gazing too close to the fire, and her throat felt dry and sore. She leaned her head back, took a few quick breaths, and then said to the flames, "You horseman, you dark huntsman! You, who I see riding this night, you just pass on. In the name of the Almighty, ride ye on now and pass right on by and do not stop and do not return!"

Even as she spoke, she felt the feebleness of her prayer.

The huntsman was coming.

She quickly shut the front of the stove. Then she rose from her chair and locked the front door. Recrossing the room, she moved her chair closer to the fire, for though her skin was warm to the touch, weren't there suddenly goose bumps rising up and down both her arms, and wasn't she shaking with chills?

She sat down again and leaned her head back.

Tomorrow, she thought, *the soul bell must be rung. For the beloved dead and for the dead that return uninvited to put distress upon the living.* She felt her legs shaking under the blanket, and hoped they'd be up to the long climb to the top of the bell tower.

LEDGER

Unseemly ghost, what dost thou here?
Thou were in hell many a year.
Who has unlocked hell's door
and let thee out?

— FROM "THE PAINS OF HELL," (JESUS COLLEGE MS. 29,
LEAF 271, COLL. 2)

Out of the east we come
with hallows full of dread—
an idol of bronze,
and first-born's blood—
we come to rule the dead.

— CREDO OF THE BROTHERHOOD OF THE EASTERN TEMPLE

THE OLDEST OF THE WANDERING
SPIRITS CAN BE THE WORST OF ALL,
FOR THEY ARE BOUND TO NO SINGLE
PLACE AND THEIR HISTORIES, IF THEY
CAN BE FOUND, ARE BROKEN AT BEST.
THEY COME AND GO LIKE STORMS
AND BRING EVERY MANNER OF ILL IN
THEIR WAKE. AND SHOULD THEY FIND
SOME ARTIFACT CONNECTED TO THEIR
PAST, BOTH THEIR DESIRE TO REMAIN
CLOSE TO IT, AND THEIR HATRED FOR
THE LIVING ARE CONSIDERABLE. CURSES

THEY CALL DOWN AGAINST BOTH KIN
AND ANY WHO RESIDE WITH OR ABOUT
THEM. THOSE OLD SEALED TINS ARE
PACKED WITH SUCH TERRIBLE GHOSTS,
FOR WHO WOULD CLAIM THE WANDERING
SPIRITS OR WISH TO SET THEM FREE,
OR RISK THEIR WRATH? WHO CAN
KNOW THE SORROWS THEY'VE ENDURED,
OR WHAT HORRORS THEY CARRY WITH
THEM AS THEY PASS FROM ONE PLACE
TO ANOTHER?

—MARGINALIA OF AMOS UMBER

CHAPTER 10
WANDERLUST

THE HUNTSMAN HAD LAIN LONG IN THE EARTH.

A broken oath had set him free only to be hunted by the devils of the Summer House. He had known fear, and had fled before them. Now darkness was behind him, and in his heart churned restlessness, wrath, and hatred. Still, his pursuers had lost his trail or had abandoned the chase. The sound of their horns had faded and he was clear of them and wandering.

The night was grown still. He found himself riding on the lych way, a pale ribbon of illumination flowing out across the land. With his pursuit abandoned, he might seek some other place of habitation. And he had quarry of his own to track. The hunt would not be over until the kill was draped over the horse.

He would find the Undertaker. Surely he was dead by now.

With a thin, knotted strip of leather hanging from his rotted sleeve, he whipped the horse until it rose up on its back legs and screamed as it leapt forward.

Memory and pursuit. Past and present. Now all was one.

He remembered coursing through the forest of five hundred years ago. He remembered his daughter running like a frightened doe as he bore down upon her. He remembered the crying of her babe and how his daughter's fear had thrilled him. Those days were gone but not forgotten. His daughter was lost to him. The young Undertaker had put her and her child where he could not harm them, and in return, the huntsman had set a deathly curse upon the Undertaker's arm.

Now his revenge was nearly complete. He needed only the corpse of Silas Umber. And when that was burning within the idol of Moloch and the Undertaker's flesh had fallen into ash, then all would be well done.

The huntsman slowed what was left of his mount. The horse had been fashioned from bones and rotted wood, held together with grim spells, but during the chase, the necromantic vigor had gone out of the beast and the burning coals that were the horse's eyes had nearly been extinguished. *"O felix sonipes, tanti cui frena mereri numinis et sacris licuit seruire lupatis!"* he said in mockery of the horse's wretchedness, for truly, there is no nobility in a broken puppet.

"Take me to the corpse of my enemy," he said to the horse-thing.

The creature threw back its head, unsure where to go.

In the distance, the huntsman could see the glint of metal under the moon.

As he approached the boundary, he summoned in his mind the words that might allow him to pass the gates.

Somewhere in the distance, a marsh bird called out from the water's edge.

As he approached, he could see the gates rising up before him, and that they hung broken on their hinges. The way was *open*.

The huntsman drew the reins back. Silas Umber, Undertaker, Janus of Arvale, keeper of the threshold, had not sealed the gates when he'd passed back into his own country.

The huntsman looked at the land, wondering if the corpse he sought lay hard by. Perhaps the curse had claimed its due before Silas Umber had made it home? But seeing nothing upon the ground, slowly, with some trepidation, the huntsman rode over the boundary and past the gates.

The air changed, and the qualities of the night intensified. Even the flashes of the distant stars were piercing. Stars. He was again moving through a world bound by time. A world in which he might, once more, claim authority.

The horse shook its head, and splinters of bone flew from its neck.

Reaching back with a hand of shriveled flesh and exposed bone, the huntsman struck the horse's flank and shattered the rotten boards that formed its misshapen pelvis. But still it broke into a pathetic gallop, throwing its tortured head from side to side as it ran.

The huntsman was well pleased. The air gave way easily before him. Nothing restrained his progress. The path was unguarded. Old Law held sway. There had been an unpaid debt between himself and the Undertaker, so Silas Umber could work no power against him, not then, and not now that the huntsman's curse had driven the life from him. It would be a pleasure to drag the Undertaker's corpse behind his horse and push it, finally, into Moloch, god of the furnace. And should the Undertaker's ghost rise, he would consign that to oblivion as well. Like the ancients before, the huntsman would sacrifice a firstborn child and receive the gift of life and power over the living and the dead so long denied him.

But before the huntsman could spit the Undertaker's accursed name upon the ground with what remained of his lips, a sound took hold of his attention. Merely a whisper at first, a thin cry muffled by earth and stone, like a memory of a memory, yet it was terrible and familiar and ravishing. A child's cry, then another, and another. And the smell of smoke, of burning flesh, and the sound of lamentations filled his frame with vigor.

In the shadowland of Arvale, the idol of Moloch had been present in his prison house, as it had been present with him in life. Now he could feel with growing certainty, the idol still existed in the world beyond Arvale. His descendants had kept it, or, more likely, the Brothers of the Temple had reclaimed it and taken it someplace where, hidden and safe, it had waited down the centuries. The idol was somewhere very close. Its presence gave off a kind of awful sound that enlivened him. It was the voice of his god. Moloch was calling him!

The huntsman looked about. The lights and shapes of a town were around him: the town into which Silas Umber had fled.

"Here shall be Hinnom!" he cried. "I shall dwell upon the hill of that god who requires only the blood of the firstborn for its beneficence! Moloch, Lord of the Earth! Moloch! Bull of blood! Where are you, Lord? Rise up so that you may receive the sacrifices I am eager to pour out for you!"

Infected with the idol's song, he rode faster. It was *here*. The statue was close but hidden.

The streets of the town were becoming more discernable. To his left and right a house or small manor would rise up, broken, ruinous. The architecture was unfamiliar. He saw the cobbles of the street, briefly revealed like stones upon the shore, only to be swiftly hidden by waves of mist that flowed about him.

The huntsman rode south upon a lane marked "Newfield" until the idol's presence sang out like a mighty chorus within his mind. He turned his limping horse onto another lane and then halted along the side of a columned rotunda. He could feel the bronze god below the earth, waiting, eager to be worshipped. He pulled back quickly on the horse's reins and the beast reared up, flames once more flying from its nostrils and winding through its wild mane. It leapt forward, casting down its head, and as the horse's molten hooves struck the ground, the earth opened up, swallowing horse and rider both.

Again, the huntsman knew darkness.

A moment later he dismounted in a vast underground chamber. The horse shook, trembled, and collapsed into a pile of bones and charred wood. The huntsman barely noticed. He spoke words of conjure, and the sconces on the wall behind him crackled into acrid flame. Before him was a sort of corridor stacked high on both sides with the spoils of pilgrimages and holy wars: Egyptian sarcophagi, Assyrian statuary, every manner of heathendom rendered in bronze and stone and clay, and gold, all stacked and piled up along with some of the crates that once held them to make a sort of high walled lane. On many of the crates and coffers were scrawled the word "Lichport." About him and in the distance, the air churned with echoes of those long-ago and hidden rites: chants and prayers brought from the east, drumming and the clanging of rough bronze bells, the piteous music of the cries of the sacrificed.

He walked slowly, looking about him at the splendors the Brotherhood once amassed, many of the objects familiar to him. Though now covered in dust, perhaps forgotten, he saw the place had once been a tabernacle of the old Knights of the Eastern Temple. In his youth, long ago, he had once carried the banner of that Order. Fascinated, he drifted down the twisting aisles, winding in, then out again. Slowly, drawn on by his god, he made his way, sure-footed as a Theseus, to the center of the labyrinth.

Soon the aisles fell away, and in the middle of the chamber stood his treasure, silent now and waiting. Massive bronze horns rose up into darkness that hung from the ceiling like a canopy.

"Moloch," he whispered to the idol, putting his hands upon its cold bronze belly, "I shall give you life again so that I may live."

A medieval church's wooden rood screen leaned against other

objects nearby, its carefully carved allegorical figures riddled with woodworm. He lifted it and smashed it upon the stone floor, then threw the wood into the hollow body of the idol. He spoke sharp words that worked like flint upon the dry tinder of the wood.

"Soon," the huntsman whispered to the bull-headed god. "Soon, oh Lord, shalt thou be fed, and as your flames rise, so shall my own star ascend into eternity."

First he would find the corpse of Silas Umber and offer it to the flames. Then he would condemn to the fire the firstborn of this town. When the streets were filled with smoke and stench and screams, and if his god was pleased thereby, he might be raised up and govern over this land and hold life and death in his hands as had once long ago been promised to him. Here would rise a New Hinnom, and he would be its king.

As if in answer, the hollow of the idol's stomach began to glow as tongues of fire licked upward into its chest, mouth, and pitiless eye sockets.

The hunter fell to his knees before the idol of Moloch. He shouted praises to that frightful god of the Caananites to whom their children were offered, and to whom the huntsman had in life tried and failed to sacrifice his own child and grandchild. Other curses, habitual, terrible, were spat from his withered lips. Fire. And fever. And that all the firstborn in the land should die and that there should be a great cry heard throughout the world. And it would all begin with the burning of the corpse of Silas Umber.

After a time, he halted his litany of ancient and hysterical hymns. The huntsman rose and said, "Oh, Lord of flame and ashes, there is work to do in thy name. Let all be burned and offered up in fire! Thy kingdom come, thy will be done, on earth as it was in Hinnom! Amen."

He turned to find more wood to feed into the idol and he

saw a chair, partially covered in threadbare carpets. He pulled the carpets away and laughed at what stood revealed: a throne carved of ebony.

"Oh, my Brothers of the Temple," he cried out, "how wondrous were thy gleanings from far distant lands and indeed, from mine own house! How fortunate am I who have found this, the hidden tabernacle of our sacred hoards!"

The huntsman sat upon the throne and closed his eyes and said, "Let us see what we can here accomplish." In the soil beyond the walls he could sense layers of bones stretching away toward both marshes and the sea. The dead piled upon the dead, grave after grave after grave. He felt the churning miasma of their minds and was delighted. Here might be vassals enough upon which to build a kingdom, once the living had been offered up or slain outright.

"Larvae of the bone-choked earth!" he called out "Arise! Come mindless! Come hungry ones with your rasping hands! Come Larvae to blacken the air with malefic vapors! Let the living tremble before the host of the dead!"

As he grew quiet, the huntsman stroked the carved armrests of the throne. "Now," whispered Cabel Umber, "truly I am home."

LEDGER

. . . she is become the habitation of devils,
and the hold of every foul spirit, and a cage
of every unclean and hateful bird.

—REVELATIONS 18:2, MARGINALIA OF JONAS UMBER

The evil ghosts, the evil demons,
   the evil spirits,
Have come forth from the grave.
The evil blasts of wind
Have come forth from the grave,
To demand libations, rites, and hosts,
They have come forth from the grave.
They know not how to stand.
They know not how to sit.
All that is evil in the ground
flies up from the grave like a whirlwind.
Angrily they come.
They want to live again.

—FROM BABYLONIAN TABLET "Y," TRANSLATED FROM
THE CUNEIFORM BY JONAS UMBER

CHAPTER 11

HOSTS

NIGHT HAD BECOME A SHROUD. Every sound in the distant air seemed closer than it was. A chorus of hisses stirred the bare tree branches outside Temple House. The wind wound them up into a howl that buffeted desperately against the outside walls. Somewhere down in the trees of Temple Cemetery, a murder of crows was praying down the darkness in ragged call and response.

All the candles in the dining room had been lit. By the fire, Silas sat vigil with the two corpses.

"Tell me what's coming," he said to his great-grandfather.

Augustus Howesman rose from his chair, put his hand to the side of his head, and closed his eyes, but didn't answer.

"You're frightened, aren't you?"

"No, no, son," the talking corpse said softly, but the old man's voice broke as he spoke.

"If you don't tell me, it's harder for me to help us, if it comes to that."

"I'm not sure. I have never seen happen what I've heard can happen. And I thank God for it!"

Silas helped his great-grandfather back into his chair. Holding his hand, he said, "I'm listening."

"Your mother's corpse . . . something . . . I don't what they are . . . ghosts, I imagine, very terrible ghosts . . . may come to possess your mother's corpse. I have a bad feeling."

"And this has happened before?"

"I have only heard of it occurring at the funerals of some members of the older families." As August Howesman spoke, his back straightened and his voice cleared. "It's more common in the older lines. Families of quality. Those that have stood the test of time. The ones that sometimes come back."

"And what comes for them, is it just one or is it many? Do they also attack the living?"

"It was described to me as a host of terrible spirits. And only the corpse is troubled. It is as though they cannot discern the presence of the living."

Silas nodded. "Larvae. That is what such things are called. I've read about them. They are a kind of Wandering Spirit, the ghosts of those who die a violent death, or those for whom no funeral rites were held. In ancient texts, they were often met on the road, as the ghosts of those who perished in the wilderness. They have been forgotten by their kin. Their condition causes madness, and when they group together, they are especially furious. They have little mind left to them, only enough to hunger for what they lack: life and place. That is why they come for corpses to possess. I suspect they haunt the funerals of the Howesmans and the other families that host Restless kin because of the . . . enduring quality of their corpses. I'm guessing."

"Yes . . . and I now think it is very bad luck that I brought your mother back to this house. Nothing for it now but to wait it out and see what, if anything, comes. Let's try not to borrow trouble. As I said, none of this has happened for a very long time."

Silas was quiet, thinking about the house they were both sitting in. His great-grandfather was probably right, yet he was wishing they were back at his place, with Mrs. Bowe close by. Who knew how many mass graves there were in Temple Cemetery, or how many bodies his uncle had dumped in there over the years. It was one of the oldest cemeteries in town, and its connection to Temple House made Silas increasingly uneasy. If there was one cemetery in Lichport likely to give rise to corpse-hungry spirits, Silas felt sure it would be the one at the end of Temple Street. He wondered if all the complex sigils inscribed on the door and floors of the Camera Obscura might have been used to keep things *out* as well as *in*. What of Temple House's grounds? There may even be unmarked burials *on* his uncle's property, or under the newer parts of house. And now it was winter . . . and the night seemed preternaturally black.

Augustus Howesman was rocking back and forth in his chair. Silas knew they needed to keep the conversation going. Both of them were inclined toward grim thoughts.

"But there is no guarantee it will happen, right? Why didn't the Larvae appear at your funeral?"

"I was fortunate, I'm told. I died at dawn and rose almost immediately. My funeral, which had been planned for, was held then and there, in the morning, which I understand is also a boon. Nothing troubled me that I am aware of. And of course you know that people in the better families try never to die during winter. It's so common. And if the winter is bad and the ground frozen solid? The poor corpse has to wait around for burial. And for *us*, well, spring is the preferred season of death. Ironic, I suppose, but more elegant in its way, more poetic. But this was all long ago. Who thinks of such things now when so many of the old ways have fallen out of fashion? And these are bad times. Few, if any, folk in older families endure beyond their deaths. Whatever's out there hasn't had this chance for a while now, and it is likely to be . . . hungrier for what it wants."

Augustus Howesman looked at Dolores's body on the table. "Where is she now, I wonder?"

"I don't know . . . wait." Silas closed his eyes. "She is not in this room. I'd feel her here. I know I would. No, unless she is in some sphere, some distant shadow of this place, I do not believe she is inside this house with us. In any event, she is not now within her body. I am sure of it."

Outside, the wind rose up again, angrily coming against the house on one side, then another. Branches struck the exterior walls at chaotic intervals. Each one made Augustus Howesman's body go taut.

"I hope her spirit has not traveled too far," said Silas's great-grandfather.

"Sometimes a spirit wanders for a time after the moment of death. That may be the case. But we both know that much of her life wasn't very happy . . . so she could be in some other place, a place she can't get out of. I don't know. . . . You told me to trust you."

"I think if we get through the night, grandson, all will be well."

"Do you think it, or know it?"

"I hope that it shall be the case, grandson. Truly I do."

Silas had never seen the Larvae, but what he'd read about them made him worry not only for his mother, but for his great-grandfather, too. And Silas was unsure how to best defend against them. He knew he might avail himself of powerful words that might be effective against any spirit, but Silas didn't know what effect those words might have on his great-grandfather. If a formula could banish a ghost, could it also drive the spirit from his great-grandfather's corpse? How securely was Augustus's spirit bound to his body? He didn't think such a question would bring his great-grandfather any comfort, so he kept it to himself.

Silas listened to the increasing hostility of the winds outside. The doors and windows rattled. Beyond the gusts and billows came less natural sounds: the distortion of a raven's call, something like but not quite the low hooting of owls, and the mock-cries of other night-birds, all woven with the gibbering of once-human madness.

"There are voices in the wind, great-grandfather."

"I hear them."

Silas rose and went to the chimney. He turned his ear to the hearth to better hear the sounds coming from outside. He heard the cry of a hawk or falcon, high-pitched and terrified. There was a flapping sound in the flue, and for an instant Silas thought the bird might try to fly down into the house to escape the growing tempest outside. The bird cried again, but the descending *cree cree cree* was quickly obliterated by the winds and other sounds, as though the bird were flying from its chimney perch and away.

There was a roaring then, like a train passing over the house, and Silas stepped back quickly from the fireplace.

His great-grandfather moved his chair closer to Dolores's body.

A sound like a hammer rang against the far side of the house.

"Just a bird," Silas said quickly, trying to keep his great-grandfather from panicking. "They must be having a terrible time out there tonight with all the wind." But he knew it was no bird. Silas listened again. The noise outside had already lessened. Something out there was waiting, drawing in its breath. Every hair on Silas's arms was standing up. He took out the death watch and, holding it ready in his hand, walked slowly to the front door.

"Good God, Silas! Don't go out there!"

"I need to see what's coming."

Silas slowly opened the iron door. A gust of wind whipped bits of debris past his face into the foyer. He stepped across the threshold into blackness. Night clutched at Temple House, and for a moment he could barely see the street. As Silas's eyes adjusted, he moved slowly to the end of the porch and looked past the columns, toward Temple Cemetery.

Less than half a block away, he looked into a scene like the end of the world. Darkness churned there, more than night, more than mere murk. He pushed at the darkness with his will and could just see a vapor, like coal smoke, pouring out of some of the graves, turning the air about the cemetery into a miasma.

With more fascination than fear, Silas slowly came down the front steps, never taking his eyes off the end of the street. The moment he walked into the yard for a better view, he felt exposed. There were no walls here, no door, no ceiling above him, nor any visible boundaries he could compel with ritual words. At Arvale there was a threshold and the limbus stone to hold or banish the dead. But here he had only himself. His work as Undertaker was about reason and compassion, about bringing the dead to accept their condition. How could you reason with a mass of madness?

A rising cry reached his ears. At first it was not unlike the wail of a hungry child, but as it rang in his head, the sound became more desperate, more terrible. In those shrill howls was every kind of loss, and the night was torn like the ragged shreds of a mourner's cloth. He needed to *see* what he was facing. The death watch was still in his hand. Silas stopped the dial. He felt a heaving in his chest as though his body were a train that had been called too quickly to a halt. When he looked up from the death watch, the sight before him made Silas want more than dark, open sky above him. He turned quickly and ran back up the stairs to get under the cover of the porch.

From the raging sky, shadows loosed themselves from the mass and came flying toward Temple House. Thrashing like bucketed eels, the Larvae grasped and scrabbled through the thickening air. They screamed above the street, ripping rotten leaves and bits of ice and snow up from the ground as they flew. The closer the spirits came to the house, the more discernable they became. Silas's vision was filled with the hateful composites of carrion birds—crows, vultures, ravens—carved out of the night and twisted into malformed, partly human shapes. Each was terrible and unique but for two shared traits: All flew with hungry distorted beaklike mouths gaping wide, vast, snapping open and closed as the Larvae came on, flying at the house and madly about its roof and walls. And none of them had eyes.

Silas awaited the onslaught, but the Larvae turned just before him and flew up, hurtling against the windows. They tore furiously at the roof and at the brickwork and tiles, trying to claw their way closer to the empty corpse inside, whose very presence called them on like the smell of raw meat to ravening hounds.

For Silas, fresh from Arvale's horrors, the mindless Larvae felt too familiar. Silas shouted at the shadows but they would not heed him. It was as useless as trying to stop the waves on the shore. There was nothing within the Larvae for his words to appeal to. He tried again.

From the top of the porch stairs, he shouted the formal Latin query into the house-hating storm.

"Nomen? Causam? Remedium?"

The spell was meant to force a ghost to speak, but the effect it had upon the flock was awful and made Silas back up and crouch closer to the door. No longer able to speak as humans, some of the Larvae cawed and cried their answers incomprehensibly, screaming with the throats of tortured birds, all humanity wrung from their words. Others only sobbed shards of their half-remembered names, creating an unintelligible chorus of horror and sorrow. Most, unable to see or hear Silas through their own madness, flew past him, untouched by the spell's questions. Had they heard the spell properly, it might have allowed them to find peaceful remedy in revealing their identities and the particulars of their pain. But they were no longer individuals; they were a mass, a cancer, a hunger.

Silas trembled, not at the dark, contorted visages moving past him to swarm the house, but at the Larvae's terrible deliberateness. He had seen this with the ghost-girl at Arvale before he'd learned her name, and it meant there would be no reasoning, no peaceful resolution with the spirits that had come for his mother. In the past, when he used the death watch, a ghost would become almost immediately aware of his presence. The demonic Larvae did not see him or did not care. They were rabid dogs that no command could bring to heel.

Silas looked frantically around to each side of the house, where the Larvae scraped at the walls, wanting only to get inside to his mother's vacant body. It was as though Dolores's corpse was a kind of beacon, calling them on and on. Those souls, lingering long beyond the dissolution of their own corpses, wanted to move again, to feel the weight and lively presence only the flesh could bestow. The air stank with their desperation, their corpse-hunger. In the wind that buffeted the house, Silas could smell the moldy soil of their recently abandoned graves.

He turned and ran through the front door, slamming it shut behind him.

The moment he was back in the house, he felt some relief. Inside was better. Even inside Temple House. Here were walls and doors, borders and boundaries. Things that might be warded with words. But as his mind expanded to become part of the place, he could feel its gaps: spaces under doors, old ill-fitted windows, crawlspaces leading to vents leading to grates leading to outside and open air. And all the chimneys. Temple House had well over twenty that Silas had seen, and there were others in corners of the house he'd never gotten to.

"Silas!" his great-grandfather cried from the dining room. "What is it?"

"Nothing is getting in this house!"

"What should we do?"

"I'm thinking. I know a way, something I learned, but I am worried it might hurt you if I do it . . . certain words of compulsion . . . but they are very old . . . very dangerous . . ."

But Silas couldn't finish the thought. Outside the front windows, something was scratching and tearing, trying to claw its way through the walls.

Silas ran quickly toward the front of the parlor.

"Close the curtains!" his great-grandfather called.

"No! I need to be able to see outside." Silas blew out the candles closest to the windows.

"Do you think looking twice at whatever's out there will make it any better?"

Silas didn't answer, but went to stand before the front door.

Augustus Howesman shouted, "Don't open the door again, whatever you do!"

"I'm not opening it, I'm sealing it. Maybe the front door will stand for all."

Silas put his hand on the cold metal of the enormous iron door. He drew in breath and, slowly exhaling, put his intention into the door, through the hinges, out, into the walls and floors of Temple House, sending it up, beyond the ceilings of the lower floor, up through the beams, into halls and chambers, attics and bedrooms, around window frames and into all the brickwork and wood. He focused his mind upon the door, upon the thick forged might of its bolts and hinges. He closed his eyes and spoke.

"Let nothing come against this house. May no harm come to those within. The door is closed against the night. Let bolts and locks and hinges hold fast. I close this door and seal it in the name of Undertaker and Janus, and may these words hold fast, through night, through day, over water, in this world and in all others!" Silas opened his eyes. In the pit of his stomach was the gnawing fear that words like that only really worked in Arvale or in the shadowlands. He needed to know if they held weight in all worlds. He was sickeningly sure he was about to find out. Before he drew his hand away, he felt the door vibrate as something scraped against it from the outside. Then a shock shot across his hand, as though a great wave had struck the door and now the force of water poured against it. But the door held fast.

As Silas walked back to the dining room, his great-grandfather said, "Good. That's something, anyway." But the corpse looked at the fireplace, where a rustling noise could be heard somewhere up the flue. "How many fireplaces are there here, Silas?"

Silas heard the noise too, and he paused. It was some kind of scrabbling along the roof. He knew Temple House too well to dismiss its night noises, and now who knew what might be up there. There were too many hearths, he thought, way too many to secure them all individually. If something was going to use the chimneys to get into Temple House, there would be no way to close and bind them all in time.

"Silas? How many chimneys, son?"

"A lot. One in every bedroom, the foyer, the kitchen, the study. There's a huge fireplace in the rotunda, and I have no idea if it's open or sealed . . . and . . . too many."

"Never mind. Too late for that. I'm sure what you've done will suffice." But the corpse did not look so sure, and muttered, "I cannot understand why your mother chose to remain in this house. I have always considered this one of the worst parts of town. It has a penchant for attracting trouble. Why did I carry her here instead of Fort Street?"

"Don't blame yourself. This had become her place. She made her own decision to stay here. But no, I agree with you, this is never going to be my favorite house in Lichport."

The wind howled in the chimneys and rushed down the fireplace, blowing hot embers, ash, and soot into the room. As he moved about the room making sure none of the embers were still burning, he admitted to himself that this was never going to work. There were too many ways into this house, more than he even knew of. It would be impossible to seal the house with any method available to him. He considered trying to seal off the dining room, but even this room had two fireplaces, large windows, and several doors. Then there was the basement below with its coal scuttle, storm doors, and who knew what else.

He was counting the possible entryways here and in the adjoining rooms when something caught his attention. On the dining room buffet next to his mother's corpse, dozens of ancient figurines stared at him with open vacant eyes. They were ushabti figures, once placed in Egyptian tombs to serve the dead in the afterlife. These had been part of his uncle's collection. His great-grandfather had found them and set them up while Silas was at Newfield. Here was something. The ushabti were interred as servants: servants for the dead. Any unpleasant task, the ushabti would willingly perform. The statues ranged in size, some as small as a couple of inches, others a foot tall. Some were made of bright blue-green faience, others of terra-cotta, some carved of alabaster. Most of them gripped tools in their hands, ready for tasks that awaited them. Silas thought about all the fireplaces in the houses, all of them opening out to the furious night. And without thinking, Silas's mouth began to move with the elder words growing from the blackened earth he'd swallowed, words copied down from the walls of tombs out of the *Book of the Dead*. Silas spoke quickly as his great-grandfather watched, unable at first to understand what his grandson was saying. Silas closed his eyes and, raising the hand that bore the blue scarab ring, framed the spell to his need in his own tongue.

"O Ushabti, residing in the tomb house of my mother, any work that falls upon me, you must do as well. Any task that must be done, it shall be allotted to you, servants of the dead. Be watchful and cast down any obstacles before you. And now I, as the living Osiris, call upon you to stand against those that come against this house. Stand up! Stand up! Stand up and serve and say 'I am here!'"

He opened his eyes to look at the ushabti again. Very softly at first, voices rose in his ears, words rounded in smooth clay syllables and bright as faience and polished stone. Once, twice, three times the voices of the figures, all speaking in unison said, "I am here!"

Silas spoke again. "Servants of the deceased of this house, rise up now and serve at every hearth. Stand and protect this house from any night terror, from any pestilence, from any harm. Should any evil enter the tomb house, raise up your arms and fight! Let nothing harmful enter the rooms of this house. Let no harm come to the dead within it!"

A fine dust, like a mist made of their faience and terracotta and alabaster, began to flow about the figures and spill onto the floor. Small figures of vapor, reflections of their statue forms, moved through the air in all directions, some passing through doorways toward the back of the house. Others traveled up the staircase and into the galleries and rooms of the upper floors.

From all over the house, noises leapt up: the slamming of flues and window shutters. Doors all over the house were being closed in such quick succession that it sounded like clapping.

The fire iron still lay on the floor where Silas had dropped it when he first saw his mother's body. He bent to pick it up. The cold iron felt good in his hand. As he rose, Silas looked at his mother's face and his breath caught in his throat. Death sat so lightly on her that for an instant, Silas was tempted to say her name to wake her. Instead, he turned away from the corpse and steadied himself for whatever came next.

The glassy eyes of the Ammit statue, positioned at his mother's feet, glinted with reflected fire.

Augustus Howesman was wide-eyed, riveted, watching the small shadows move out of their statues. He stammered, "Son . . . son . . . what is all this?"

"I am trying to protect this house."

"It felt right to place them here, near the corpse. Was it helpful?"

"Yes. Thank you! I don't know. I hope so. I feel like everything I do is guesswork, like every time I find my footing, the floor drops out of the world again. The world of the dead is so much wider and more various than I ever thought possible. It feels like I'm never going to understand it all so long as I'm alive."

Augustus Howesman looked down at his own hands uncomfortably. "Grandson, do you think it's possible that a spirit could be forced from its body?"

"Great-grandfather, don't worry. Nothing is coming in this house."

"But what you've just done—is it that easy to pull a soul from its housing?

"No. At least, I don't think so. That was different." But was it? Silas thought. "I can't swear to much one way or another anymore, and we don't have time to speculate now. But I will swear to this: Nothing in this world or any other is going to hurt you or Mom if I can help it." Silas saw his great-grandfather smile thinly, trying to hide his fear. "Just stay close to Mom, okay? You watch over her, and I'll watch over you both." He put his hands on the old man's shoulders.

From above came the sound of an explosion, like someone had driven a train down the chimney on the upstairs landing. Silas ran to the bottom of the stairs. From just out of sight on the upper floor came the sounds of contention. The air rang with desperate cries, and on the floor, objects thumped and crashed, knocked from their shelves.

Back in the dining room came sounds of cracking and of clay shattering. Running back from the foyer, he saw some of the ushabti's statues breaking to pieces, their spirits fallen to whatever force was pushing its way into the house. More in his mind than in his ears, Silas heard small screams; distant, low, torn from throats of chalk. They faded quickly and Silas realized that not all the ushabti were meant for this purpose. They were household servants, not warriors. They could briefly delay, but not detain or destroy. Outside had pushed its way in.

"Silas? Silas? Please! What is happening?" Ausgust Howesman yelled. Silas was unnerved at the desperation in his great-grandfather's voice. He quickly returned to the foyer, where he could better hear what was happening in other parts of the house. Silas looked up the stairs and began to move quickly backward. Furious shadows poured down the staircase like a black and churning river. Silas held up his hands to shield his eyes from the dust and ash that flew at his face.

Through his fingers, he could see the stone of his ring giving off a pale light. It burned the finger and the part of his face where it touched the skin. His father's writings filled his mind, and he remembered that the ring granted safe passage and protection from evil. Silas could see the words of the ledger in his mind's eye: "Even the fearful demons who haunt the plains of Caanan and the lands of the sons of Ammon could be struck down should Pharaoh raise his hand against them and utter the words inscribed upon the stone. And of his travels, perfect memory was granted also by the might of this stone always." Even as he wondered how to direct the ring's power, words from the *Book of the Dead*, words from the land of the scarab's making, pushed aside all other thoughts, and Silas's voice called out into the tumultuous air of the house:

> "May the river of the night seek another course.
> May the devils of the air be put down into the earth.
> Get back! You who come to snatch away the coffer
>   of the heart.
> You hear these words. You fall into the earth.
> You shall not wound any here!
> Obey me, you serpents of the grave!
> Get back! Retreat!
> Go back to your place of putrefaction
>   below the earth!
> I shall suffer no defeat, for my words
>   are the words of truth."

His incantation rang like a pure bell upon the air, but again, for such words to work, the dead must comprehend, and the spirits that assaulted his mother's house had little if any of their minds left. Some dropped out of the air, tangled into a mist, and then vanished, but others had already flown past him and into the dining room. The only thing they could discern was the corpse's vacancy. Nothing else existed for them.

Silas heard his great-grandfather's voice rising in panic. He ran back to the dining room.

Augustus Howesman lay over the corpse of Silas's mother, using his own weight to keep Dolores's body on the table. All about him, the writhing Larvae grappled at Dolores's limbs, trying to pull her away. Portions of the Larval mass boiled up to the ceiling—the chandelier swinging madly like a pendulum around them—only to fly back down at Dolores's face, trying to seek entry into her body. Silas's great-grandfather had clapped his large hand over her mouth even as the spirits swarmed about his own face. The old man was clenching his jaw, and all the muscles of his face distorted in fear as he pressed his lips and eyes closed so tightly that Silas could see the skin cracking.

Silas did not pause as he entered the room. He knew he was out of options and would have to risk the use of stronger words. Most of the candles had been blown out, but where they had dripped soft wax on the tables and pedestals, Silas gathered it up. He ran to his great-grandfather's side and said, "Do not ask questions. Put this in your ears and do not take it out until I tell you."

Eyes still closed, Augustus Howesman nodded furiously. Silas took some wax and pressed it into his mother's ears. Then, before doing the same to his great-grandfather, he said, "Do not hear my words. Do not!"

The thought of what he was about to do sickened him, but he called up the words of judgment and destruction he'd used at Arvale, and behind them, that simple formula that wreaked such havoc upon the dead. He had no idea if it held any power so far from the Limbus stone of Arvale, but even as he thought the words, Silas could feel a static rising in the air of the room and throughout the house.

"Now I speak my judgment against the Larvae, against the hungering dead. Here and now, they shall depart, shall be as if they never were, and shall never again trouble the living or the dead!"

Instantly, the flood of spirits hung still and ceased their churning of the air. Many still opened and closed their mouths, blindly trying to find the corpse. Beyond the windows, it was the same. The Larvae could no longer move forward or backward, up or down. Then, as he had done once before, Silas pitched his voice into a roar.

"*Cedo nulli!*" he shouted. His words rattled the house and boomed outward through wall and floor, door and window.

At once spirits fell away from the two corpses and onto the floor. The room grew still. Nothing moved against the walls, or raked against the bricks of the chimneys outside. The floors of the house were covered with maggots that slowly, pathetically, turned themselves once, twice, and then did not stir. Their white bodies dissolved in a mist that instantly sank through floorboards and carpets, and back down into the quiet earth below the house, leaving only the reek of mold behind.

Silas's whole body was shaking.

The room was recast in a predawn grayness. In the fading shadows, the jaws of the Ammit seemed to gape slightly.

Many of the ushabti on the sideboard were broken, a few were still intact. Silas passed his hand over them, saying without thinking, "You have served the tomb house with honor. Thanks be given to those who cross the night and step once more unto the western riverbank at dawn."

By the table, August Howesman stood over Dolores's corpse,

his eyes still closed. Silas put a hand over his. The old man opened his eyes and looked frantically about the room. Silas nodded, and reached up to pick the wax from his great-grandfather's ears. Cold and solid, it came away mostly in a large piece, molded in the shape of the corpse's ear canal.

"I think it's over," Silas said, but before he could tell his great-grandfather anything more, another light came flooding into the room: crimson and yellow, as though the sun had risen in the south and was shining into the front windows of Temple House, though that was impossible. Hadn't the spell banished all?

Something outside was burning.

Silas ran to the large front windows of the parlor and looked out onto Temple Street, where what looked like a bonfire had been lit. Flames rose off the street and licked at the gray sky. In the midst of the conflagration, a shadow stood and turned its head to look at where Silas was watching. At first, the flames seemed to subside. The shadow within them coalesced into the shape of large man, portions of his skull gleaming through the dark skin of his head and a coronet of silver upon his brow. The specter wore the clothes of a hunter, a black leather jerkin with ragged sleeves that dipped and waved, unconsumed as they passed through the flames. This was not one of the Larvae, but some other Wandering Spirit. Had it sent them? Or was this another graveless ghost also come for his mother's corpse?

Silas shouted back into the dining room, "Cover your ears again! Cover them!"

Locking eyes with the spirit in the street outside, Silas yelled, "*Cedo nulli!*" once more.

The spirit remained.

Low laughter rose in the cold air beyond the window, and the glass trembled.

Silas's mouth went dry. Words coursed across his mind, but if that spell had no effect on the ghost, what else would work? "Let nothing come against this house, let nothing come against this house," he repeated to himself, but then cried out in pain. The skin where the curse-wound had been bristled and burned beneath his shirt.

Outside, a voice rose out of the flames. Silas instantly feared it, even as he strained to hear it better.

"Old Law holds true," it growled. "Even though you yet live!"

The glass was growing warm. Sheets of ice were sliding from the roof of Temple House and crashing on the steps. From the dining room, his great-grandfather was calling nervously, wanting to know what was happening. The house noise muddied the clarity of the words coming from outside, making it hard for Silas to hear them.

Never taking its eyes from the window where Silas stood, the fiery specter raised its arms and stretched its mouth into a howl. Though the words came raggedly to Silas's ears, they set his teeth on edge.

". . . let all be done . . . now . . . all receive at last the profits of their sowing . . . and all debts . . . paid. What is . . . shall be mine. And it . . . end in fire . . . by the kingdoms of infernal rule . . . by Styx . . . Acheron . . . by the fiery lake of ever-burning Phlegethon . . . and by my god's ever burning . . . I swear . . ."

Silas strained to make out the words that only he could hear. The glass was fogging up, and Silas wiped at it quickly with his sleeve. Sweat was dripping into his eyes as desperate, ineffectual words fell from his mouth. "Whether thou art from out of the earth, or one that lieth upon the earth, or are a ghost unburied, or one forgotten, you shall not come against this house, you shall not come against this house . . . you shall not."

But through the clear parts of the window, around the ghostly conflagration, Silas saw other figures were approaching, oblivious to the spectral fire in the middle of Temple Street. They moved slowly but deliberately toward Temple House. A moment later he heard loud, crushing footfalls on the porch.

Silas turned quickly toward the foyer, but the flames out on the street flared up, and Silas could feel their heat through the glass. He looked back out the window.

The ghost in the flames turned its head from side to side. Was it afraid of the shambling figures on the street, or perhaps the rising light in the east was abhorrent to it? The ghost quickly put its stare on Silas once more, even as it became indiscernible from the fire. All at once, both flames and spirit sank down into the earth and were gone. In that instant, Silas felt nausea wash over him and he clutched at his stomach. Not wanting to see any more, his stiff, aching fingers released the dial of the death watch.

As the proper light of the rising dawn spilled into the house, a tremendous booming sounded from the foyer.

Something very strong was beating on the front door.

LEDGER

THREE SORROWS

WHEN I THINK ON THESE THINGS THREE
NEVER MAY I HAPPY BE:
THE ONE IS THAT I MUST AWAY,
THE OTHER: I KNOW NOT THE DAY.
THE THIRD THOUGHT IS MY CHIEFEST CARE:
I KNOW NOT WHITHER I SHALL FARE.

—TRANSLATED FROM MIDDLE ENGLISH BY AMOS UMBER

CHAPTER 12

FLOW

EACH BLOW TO THE DOOR REVERBERATED through the front rooms of Temple House. Silas Umber wet the inside of his dry mouth with his tongue, tasting the acrid words of power, preparing to shout down whatever else might come against his mother's house. He made a fist with the hand bearing the scarab ring. With his other hand, Silas opened the door.

The dead were there, and nothing more.

All the Restless had arrived. Corpses paced along the porch and milled about the lawn. On the path leading from the street, the two younger corpses from Newfield held aloft a decorative bier on which Miss Hattie sat in her golden chair. Silas looked past the small throng on the porch and standing in the yard, to where Joan Peale had just arrived. She was easing a large bull out of the back of a trailer. Visibly nervous and without a word, she handed the neck rope to one of the Restless near the bier and got back in her truck. She saw Silas and half raised her hand, then rolled up the window of the truck and drove off down Temple Street towing the trailer. The corpse walked the bull through the yard to the bottom of the stairs and waited there. The bull was extraordinary, the cleanest animal Silas had ever seen, lean and muscled, with beautiful markings. It had been pampered and very well treated. Its horns had been burnished with gold foil and seemed to glow and flash as it moved its head, even in the low light.

Miss Hattie's bier was carried up the stairs. The bearers paused before the door of Temple House.

"Child? Aren't you going to invite us in?"

"Of course," said Silas. "Please, be welcome in my mother's house."

"Dear?" Miss Hattie asked patiently, shaking her head a little, "We cannot enter. You have bound this threshold against the passage of the dead. Where's your hospitality, child?"

"Sorry." Silas looked down. Then, as he had done at Arvale, he threw his hands wide in the gesture of opening. The door of Temple House shook on its hinges.

"There, now, that's *fine*," said Miss Hattie, as her bier was carried over the threshold and into the house.

Her chair was placed in the parlor by the fireplace as the other Restless of Lichport came in. Miss Hattie sat watching the others assemble in the parlor and flank the entrance to the dining room where Dolores Umber's body lay in state. Silas was absolutely sure that behind Miss Hattie's eyes, dead as stone, an ancient but agile mind was thinking, waiting. Looking at her, he could feel her deliberateness, a mighty but unmoving presence in the room. This was not a social call.

Among the Restless he recognized the group that had been summoned against their will to Arvale. These, he guessed, were from Fort Street. As they walked past Silas into the house, some whispered "Thank you" while others touched his shoulder or briefly held his hand in appreciation.

The corpses from Newfield accompanying Miss Hattie immediately set about their work, slowly moving ornate chests from the sides and back of the litter on the porch into the house. They set up tall bronze braziers and set coals alight within them. Over these they spread dried resins and herbs. As the coals grew hot, thin ribbons of smoke began to rise. The smell was strangely familiar to Silas, and that portion of his mind that held open the *Book of the Dead* whispered, "*Kapet* . . . pine resin, camel grass, mint, mastic, sweet flag, cinnamon, wine, raisins, honey, to hallow the temple . . ." He inhaled deeply.

As the rich incense spread through the air of the rooms, Silas noticed the Restless began to move more easily, the stiffness of their condition lessening as more and more smoke came from the braziers, clouding the room. Looking over, Silas saw his great-grandfather inhale deeply and then quickly stand up, turning his head from side to side, stretching.

A wreath of dried flowers had been hung about the neck of the Ammit statue.

A box of small stone relics—ancient iron, alabaster, and quartz—was opened like a surgeon's tools and set out on the dining room table next to his mother's corpse.

Unsure of what he was supposed to do, Silas asked Miss Hattie, "Are we ready to begin?" He was not eager to conduct his mother's funeral, but the longer she lay there on the table—a spectacle he knew she would never have approved of—the sadder and more nervous Silas felt. He welcomed the focus that conducting the ritual would bring.

Miss Hattie lifted her head, as though she had been listening to something far off. She tapped her finger on the gilt arm of her chair, then slowly rose and walked to Dolores's body. She held her hand over the corpse and touched Dolores's mouth. Then she turned back toward Silas and said, shaking her head, "No, child. We may not proceed. We have come too late. Her soul has fled." She looked at her assistants and said softly with real sorrow in her voice, "There shall be no rite. Prepare our daughter for the fire."

"Wait!" Silas said, standing beside his mother's body and putting his hand on her arm. "You can't burn her! There must be a funeral. There must be words and a wake. She's not some candle that got blown out."

"That is not our way," said Miss Hattie.

"Well, this is not *my* way."

"The corpse is like a child, like a baby. It requires care and is in a state of extraordinary delicacy. The newly dead spirit, even more so. I don't have to tell you this, Silas Umber. Sometimes, and even if you watch over the body very dutifully, as I know you have, sometimes . . . well, there are complications. The soul knows best its own mind."

Miss Hattie slowly passed her hand over the corpse again. "It is no matter now. Her spirit has fled the house of eternity. She is gone. No demon or ghost has defiled her body, but her sorrows and fear have carried her off." She gestured to the others to collect the corpse.

Silas moved to stand between his mother's body and the other Restless.

"Stop! Wait. I can help. I will call her spirit now. We will have the wake. I can give her the waters of Lethe, and then we can bury her properly."

"Oh, my. No, no, no," said Miss Hattie firmly. "We do not partake of that tradition. Neither will she come. She will not hear you. She is not present in this place. Even now"—she lifted her head as though watching something pass overhead—"she makes her way to the dark land on the far bank of the river. She will pass into the realms of night and will reside in the shadows and shall not return. I am sorry, child. Her *Ba*, her soul, has fled."

"I will bring her back."

Some of the Restless began to murmur and speak, words of

dissent and concern, but Miss Hattie raised her arm, her golden bracelets catching the light of the candles burning about the corpse.

"So be it. Try if you like." To quiet the others she added, "Silas is Undertaker here. And he is the son. It is his right. So be it. The sun shall journey through the world below and the realm of night. Where will you look for her in the Tuat?"

Silas knew the term immediately, for it was recorded many times in the *Book of the Dead*, and the very word summoned frightening images from tomb walls and scrolls. Monsters and fearsome beasts that would lie in wait for the dead, for the lost. The Tuat was the shadowland, but an old name, a primal name, a terrible name.

Miss Hattie saw the blush of worry on his face and spoke again.

"So be it. Bring her back and we will perform our traditional rites, or, if you fail, if she has gone to her second death, we shall make preparations to burn the corpse so that none other shall occupy it or cause her harm, as is our custom."

Silas didn't answer.

He walked toward the door and then called to his great-grandfather.

"Was my mother's body brought through this door into the house after her death?"

"Yes. I carried her into this house myself."

"Good," Silas said, "if a corpse has passed over the threshold, then it's lych and holds the memory of her passing."

"Lych?" said his great-grandfather.

"A lych way, a road of the dead. Once a corpse is carried over a path, that way is forever hallowed. Lichport is covered with them, but because her corpse came into the house this way, it's easier for me to enter the shadowland and follow her from here. Please do not close this door until I return."

Augustus Howesman moved to stand by the front door of Temple House and said, "Silas, I swear to you, no one will touch this door while you're gone." Then, remembering, he spoke again. "Silas, I don't know if this is helpful to you, but when your mother was a child, she used to play along the riverbank. She loved it and would spend hours there. When she was older, she would walk there by herself, I think, when she wanted a little peace. Love of the river was in her blood. We were, long ago, river people—"

"Oh, my yes, child," Miss Hattie continued. "We steered our long, lean ships up the river valley, along the black-earthed lands on either side. From Alexandria down into the lower cataracts. Then, more recent ancestors took our people out across the seas and we again found the river, following it up into strange lands where we settled and traded, when the others came. But your great-grandfather is right, child. She will go to the river and follow it into the nightland. That is our common road."

"Have bodies ever been brought along the River Branch? Into or out of Lichport?" Silas asked them both.

"Not recently, but yes. Bodies used to come into Lichport for burial by barge from the inland towns, especially during wartime," said Augustus Howesman.

"Then the river here is lych too. I will use the river to find her."

Silas touched his great-grandfather's shoulder and then put his hand on the front door. He took the death watch from his pocket once more, and opening the skull, wound string around the dial to hold it fast. It was still warm. Beyond the door, like a tide, the mist came in. Silas turned back once more to look through the parlor entrance at his mother's body beyond.

Already the house voices were fading.

"Now the weighing of our sister's heart begins," Miss Hattie said to the assembled. And where it sat, loyally waiting by the corpse, Silas was sure the Ammit stirred, shifted its weight slightly, eagerly, from one mismatched foot to another.

Outside the door, an unnatural night had followed in the mist, draping over the morning.

Thinking of the river and holding a portrait of his mother's once living face in his mind, Silas stepped from Temple House and into shadowland. He felt numb. His dad was cold in the ground. His mom lay dead on the table.

Time to go to work.

LEDGER

"LONELINESS IS THE FIRST THING
WHICH GOD'S EYE NAMED NOT GOOD."
— JOHN MILTON, MARGINALIA OF AMOS UMBER

"O thou goddess Isis, whose
mouth knows well how to
chant and speak in spells
and charms, your son shall
travel without harm. No
illness, no pestilence or
poison shall injure your
son, for in the boat of the
god of the sun, there is
health and well-being. I
have come today by the boat
of the solar disk to the place
where yesterday we stood.
When darkness rises, when
night puts on its crown,
light shall vanquish shadow,
for the sake of the son, for
the sake of Isis, his mother."

—FROM THE *WANDERINGS AND SORROWS OF ISIS*,

TRANSLATED BY SILAS UMBER

I have risen up from the
     chamber of beginnings.
I fly and circle in the air
     like a falcon.

I have risen. I have
gathered my soul
as a falcon.
I have come forth from the
Night Boat . . .

—FROM "THE CHAPTER OF CHANGING INTO A DIVINE
FALCON," BOOK OF THE DEAD, TRANSLATED
BY SILAS UMBER

CHAPTER 13
RIVER CRUISE

THE YOUTH HOLDS IN HIS MIND the image of his mother. Her face. Her eyes. The down-turning of her mouth and her rare smile. Then he conjures more familiarity: a smell of fine perfume she wore only on special evenings, or on the more frequent occasions when she just needed to feel special. The more of her he recalls, the closer to her ghost he will come.

In the distance, he can smell the river, too; the deep water and everything it holds. Once, as a small child, he had seen three dead deer that, while in rut, had locked their antlers together and, still connected, drowned in a pathetic triskelion. The stags, waterlogged and stiff, spun slowly like a pinwheel in the larger eddies near the riverbank before their joined corpses were carried downriver.

There is the smell of smoke suddenly, and the earth warms as the youth walks. There are fires below the ground. He has felt them before. But the youth keeps his mind on the water and the ghost he is looking for. He does not want to think of fires, of things burning. *Let the earth be cold*, he thinks, and the acrid smell fades.

He can hear the water, the slush and churn of the river ahead. He does not look back.

Ahead, a voice emerges from the reeds along the riverbank. It says his name.

An old woman in a faded dress of calico pulls a long, thin skiff out from the rushes. A boat made of reeds.

The youth can see the river now. Black, it flows swiftly as though in a hurry to get away.

"We are going upstream, I think," says Mrs. Grey. She bows to him. Deeply. Reverently.

"I am surprised to see you here," says the youth, returning the bow, but not so deeply.

"Shouldn't be. We are both waiting for the same thing, I reckon."

"Why should you wait for my mother?"

"When the Howesmans came down the river, I was here. They built their great mounds there, beyond the marshes. They felled the trees and made ships and sent them up and down the coasts and grew prosperous. Great houses they built overlooking the sea. As a favor to your father and his father, I have watched over your mother since she returned here to her own land. Now my sister needs to make her final journey upriver to the headwaters, and I will take her, though her passage may be perilous."

"Why you, Mrs. Grey? Who are you to her?"

"Her Death," says Mrs. Grey, reaching out a hand to help the youth into the boat. "Nothing more."

"Do you know when she'll be here?" asks the youth, carefully stepping aboard.

"She is here now."

And the youth turns toward the prow. His mother stands there, looking forward and away.

The youth asks the ghost to come with him. "Return," he says. "Mom, come back with me."

"She will not," says Mrs. Grey. "And she cannot hear you. But you may travel with her, if that is your wish."

The youth nods.

The ghost does not look backward as the youth takes his place. The ghost looks not to either side. Only ahead holds any interest. There is no other thing except what lies before the boat. And seeing the waters before her, the ghost begins to weep silently. Her tears fall past the prow of woven reeds and into the river, making tiny eddies that unwind themselves into larger ripples and then make quick rapids, memories that will carry the bark upriver toward the long forgotten headwaters, through the nightlands.

The youth touches her shoulder. She does not move. He speaks her name. She does not answer.

On both banks of the river, voices whisper and call, drawn up from mist and the dark undulations of the land, just there among the reeds. And flickering images, reflections of the past, shine in the sheets of ice that break free from the shoreline as they pass. All about the boat, the past casts a glow over the water.

A birthing room in one of the great houses. A baby girl is born and handed to her mother. There is a throng about the bed. Grandparents, a few siblings and cousins, and the dead. Several corpses smile and coo over the baby girl. She turns her head and seems to look at one of the corpses, a stately man who wears a cravat. He insists on holding her and the mother, reticently, hands the baby to the corpse. Child, child, the corpse says lovingly. The baby opens her eyes and the first face she looks into is that of a corpse. Someone hastily tells the mother, perhaps to comfort her, that the baby can't really see yet. The baby begins to cry softly and the corpse hands the tiny girl, his granddaughter, back to her mother.

The little girl is perhaps seven years old and she is screaming in the street. Her mother pulls her arm. Both are dressed in fine clothes.

They are to make a visit. The mother stops pulling, slaps the girl. The girl relents and walks ahead of her mother up the steps leading to the mansion's front door. They go inside and ascend the staircase to an upper gallery. Every step the girl takes is slower than the last. They enter a room where a corpse with a cravat sits in a carved chair. Slowly the corpse rises and raises its arms affectionately. The little girl turns to run, but her mother hisses her name, and she turns back and walks to the corpse, who embraces her. Still caught in the tender hug, she cranes her head around the corpse's body to stare at her mother. The girl appears ready to burst into tears. Her mother takes a piece of candy from a bowl on a table near the door and looks sharply at her daughter. The little girl nods and holds back her tears. A little while later, as they descend the staircase once more, the mother offers the candy to the girl, who refuses it. You saw me buy it to bring here last time, says the mother sharply. She pushes the piece of candy into the girl's mouth and waits for her to swallow it. When they pass the front door and come down into the yard, the girl runs to the bushes and vomits.

A repeating scene: the girl alone in her room. She has many dolls, many toys. Often, shadows lengthen along the floor and walls, and spirits move close to her, stand about her, fascinated by the presence of living kin. Her parents don't let her talk about it. They open the door to her room, look in, smile, close the door again. When she cries, the ghosts of women of the family, living in the walls of the old great house, come to her, flock about her. Soon they follow her outside her room, through the galleries of the large house, sometimes on the streets. Only when she is alone. When the ghosts come to her, she cries because their presence upsets her. Yet when they leave, she cries more because she is left alone again.

◆ ◆ ◆

The girl is in her teens. She stands looking at the wreckage of a motor-boat that has washed up on the shore. The driver had been her boy-friend. They cannot find him. They cannot find his body. The sea has gone silent. Three days later, at sunset, the young man comes home. His ghost stands outside the girl's window. Every night he comes to her. Her family sends for help. Another young man arrives. He is quiet and som-ber and tall. He brushes his dark hair out of his eyes every few moments. He takes out a pocket watch and asks the family to wait in the drawing room. He goes upstairs to the girl's room. The family hears voices. He is talking to the ghost. A short time later, the young man comes downstairs and says the ghost is at peace and not to worry. Her parents thank him. She thanks him. He looks at her and tells the parents he does not need to be paid. She watches him as he puts on his coat. She smiles a little as he leaves.

The young man with the dark hair comes back to the girl's house. They walk about the town, talking in whispers. When he walks her home, the girl says, Stay with me. I won't leave you, the young man says. He is in love with her already. They are a handsome couple. She holds him tight, and he begins to sing, so softly, the sound barely stirring the air. "Dolores holds my heart in thrall. She holds my life and liberty, for love is lord of all." And by the river they kiss and when they walk from the water, they hold each other's hands.

They are together in a house, some years later. Things have changed. The woman wears loneliness like a housecoat. He is very good at his work. His needful work. He works most nights. One night after another, he leaves the house, closes the door. She sits below the low light of a lamp. She watches the door. Waits and waits for it to open. Some nights he does not come home. His work. His needful work. She begins to hate the door, hate both its opening and closing, hate the man who passes back and forth over its threshold. Even when he is home, he is quiet, his mind elsewhere, someplace she cannot go, does not want to go.

At first the youth feels pity to see the sorrow of his mother's childhood. Then his heart swells to see his parents fall in love. To watch them, the same age as himself, growing closer, walking hand in hand. But soon the light of the scenes begins to darken as past regrets spill into later episodes. The youth has seen enough. They are floating on a river of self-indulgence, and where once pity filled his heart, now there is anger seeping in.

"Enough," he says to the ghost of his mother, who has closed her eyes again. "Look! You must look! This is what *has* happened. It's not happening anymore! These scenes have gone out of the world. Only in your mind do they endure. Look at them! Mom! Look at them and let them go."

The bark turns, following the river's course. About them, creatures swim just below the surface, their movements churning the dark water. The ghost does not stir, but ahead of the boat, a scene takes on light and presence.

From the reeds along the riverbank, walls waver and rise. A room in a common house. A midwife stands beside a silent mother who lies on the bed in labor.

At the front of the boat, the ghost clutches her fists.

As the birth continues, she becomes more and more agitated at the vision before them, though her eyes remain closed. The youth's father joins the phantom scene on the shore. His face is pale as all men's faces are pale when they are in the presence of the mysteries of women's bodies.

The baby is coming.

"There is a caul," the father says, and steps back.

The midwife holds up the child and hands it to the father.

The father draws aside the caul and moans. He says it will be all right.

The new mother says, "Show me the baby!" But then she cries out, "Bring home the child!"

Back on the boat, the youth says, "Good God. Good God," and cannot look away.

Something in his voice has changed. The scene has him now, has set its teeth in him, and he can't hear anything but weeping from the birth room. He sits down in the boat and looks at the shore. He whimpers and begins to cry.

A shiver of powerful maternity passes through the ghost, still standing at the prow, and passes down through the boat and into the water. She hears her son crying. And wakes.

The ghost of Dolores Umber turns back, leans over, and covers her son's eyes.

The air about the shore wavers.

"Come away!" the ghost says to him. "Do not look! Do not see this! Silas, close your eyes now, right now!"

The youth looks away from the scene, his mother's voice the only thing he hears, and his attention loosens and slips from the shore. He looks into her face, and the land goes quiet again. His mother's eyes are open and dry. She sees him and he knows it, can feel her recognition, and her rising confusion and then sorrow as she realizes, or remembers, her condition.

He sees the ghost's eyes, dark and present. The youth stands up and says to her without thinking, "Will you take the water of peace and forgetfulness that I can offer you?"

"Silas!" Dolores says, almost beginning to laugh. "Don't be stupid. You know I gave up drinking." Dolores looks at the light of distant street lamps beginning to glow beyond the river.

"Do you want to come back with me? To Lichport?" Silas asks.

"Is that where you're going, Si?"

"Yes. And no other place."

"Then that's where I want to go."

Without a word, Mrs. Grey turns the boat and steers back the way they've come, and the water flows so gently beneath them that the river seems to be asleep.

O Proud Memphis! Great
city who keeps the God!
Osiris! Apis! Earth and
Bull, Below and Above!
Now, glorious Serapis! You,
who carry the dead upon
your back into the Lands
of the West! You, who were
conceived by lightning!
Now wondrous bull, die for
us, and we shall live!

— FROM *THE COFFIN TEXTS*, TRANSLATED BY SILAS UMBER

Most wretched are the abominable Restless
of Lichport and their stolen Nile Rites.
For in their vile imitation of life, they mock
both the living and the wisdom handed
down from the past, even claiming a direct
descent, an undiluted stream of practice,
from that ancient time unto our own; a
claim that can only be accounted absurd.
They worship Serapis in his many
forms, that composite god of Alexandria
whom the Ptolomies adored and who
may have somehow derived his name from

ASERAPIS, a pairing of the name of Osiris and Apis, the Bull god of Memphis ... two deities closely associated with regeneration and vitality. Or, more likely, the name was aped or stolen outright from the term _Serapsi_, the honorific of the elder god Ea of ancient Babylon. "Serapis" will be a title not unfamiliar to any Undertaker familiar with our traditions, for that honorific has been sometimes used by generations of Undertakers who may be often called not only _Janus_, but _Lords of the Deep_, which is the meaning of the name _Serapis_ when Englished.

— MARGINALIA OF JONAS UMBER

CHAPTER 14

A WAKE

THE MASSIVE OPEN DOOR OF TEMPLE HOUSE stood in the distance as Silas came away from the river. He could feel his mother's ghost close by him. As he walked toward the door, he heard his great-grandfather calling out.

"Is all well among the living and the dead?"

The voice sounded far off.

"Yes," Silas answered. "I think all's well."

Silas crossed the threshold. It was nearly dusk.

Inside the house, bright embers burned in their braziers and incense swam through all the rooms of the ground floor. Even though Silas had released the dial of the death watch, his mind still clung to the movements of the river, and the voices of the past buzzed about his ears like marsh flies. The boundaries remained blurred in him. He was constant to no single sphere, and it seemed that each time he used the death watch, one foot stayed more firmly planted in the shadowlands after he returned to his own time and place.

Looking about the rooms, he could see that more additions had been made in his absence. His mother's house had become a temple in more than name.

The dining room table had been pushed to the wall, and his mother's corpse had been stood up and wrapped in a linen sheet with her arms straight down at her sides. Behind her was a life-size statue of Osiris carved of black stone. Silas hadn't seen this one in his uncle's collection, so it had either been brought out of storage from someplace in the house, or the Restless had carried it with them out of Newfield. It appeared to be truly ancient, for the patina of age had softened its surface, and the weight of time and long veneration came off it like a heat. The god of the dead wore a tall crown. An actual withered sheaf of wheat had, at some time, been tied to it. *God of the dead, and god of fertility both*, Silas thought. *Life and death, or life in death?* As he looked at the statue standing guard over his mom, he realized that preparations had been set in place that he had not approved of, and he was not in control of what was happening. He wanted to bring this around to something he felt he could handle, something he knew. He didn't want anything going wrong he couldn't fix. It was his job, his obligation, to conduct his mother's funeral now that her spirit had been found, and to preside over her wake. Silas turned to his great-grandfather. "Sir, I would like to begin."

"Oh, Silas. I thought you understood. You and I will participate, but the Undertaker does not preside over certain funerals among the Howesmans and some of the other families. Now don't take this the wrong way. You have a part to play, as the son, and your father was always, always very helpful to us, but we have our own customs, and it is important that we stay true to them when they are required. I know only what I've heard. So let's you and me just try to be useful. As I understand it, we are not entirely out of the woods."

Silas was about to protest, but Miss Hattie rose from her throne. "Bring in the god," she said formally, her voice rasping against the bottom of its register.

One of the Restless went outside to lead in the bull. As the great creature came through the parlor and into the dining room, it bowed its head so its long, high horns did not scrape the door frame. A ring of flowers had been hung about the animal's neck. The bull came to stand facing Silas's mother's body on a large piece of canvas, on which also sat a massive wooden tub. Silas couldn't help but stare at the bull. It was not the strange sight of it indoors that captured his attention, but the beauty of the animal itself. The bull was black except for two patterns of white hair: a diamond on its forehead and an elegant bird's wing shape on its back. The bull was utterly serene as it stood before the corpse, surrounded by the Restless. Its nostrils flared as it breathed, and it slowly rolled its eyes to look about the room, but otherwise did not move.

From one of the carved crates now stacked along the wall, one of Miss Hattie's assistants drew out a long ornate sword with a curved blade. Its edge was so sharp that Silas had to squint to see where the sword stopped and the air began. The corpse handed the sword to Augustus Howesman and rasped something into his ears. Augustus Howesman nodded and turned to Silas.

"You see, son? I told you we had important work to do."

"Yes?"

"The bull is to be sacrificed."

Silas looked at the bull and back at the sword.

"You don't mean right now! Here?"

"Indeed I do. I think it's best if we don't overthink this. Better to get it over with."

"This is not what my mother would have wanted."

"Your mother made her wishes clear on her last visit to see me. She wished to observe the most prestigious of our family's traditions. I promise you, grandson, as foreign as this may seem, none of this would have shocked her. Besides, is it really so strange? You eat meat, don't you?"

"Yeah, but I don't sacrifice it."

"But it is a sacrifice nonetheless. It is killed for you. Surely this isn't so much different from the funeral rites you know or have studied? There are offerings, prayers. . . . Isn't it all one, really?"

Silas looked about the room again at the corpses, the bull, the statues of ancient gods, and said, "It's not its strangeness. I have read of such rites in books. It's that I like to know what's happening. Part of being an Undertaker is being prepared for anything that might occur, and to be able to help the dead as required. It's hard for me to feel prepared if I don't know what's next."

"Well, next comes the sacrifice. If the god, any god, gives its life for the assembled, then that is a sacrifice. It's like that in church."

"I wouldn't know."

"Is food ever given to the dead when you're running a funeral?"

"Yes. Sometimes bread is placed on the body—"

"A loaf of bread, a good steak, or a good god, it's all one in the belly. All are sustenance. A life is given so your life might continue. Oh, it's not spoken of in *just* this way, but you should accommodate yourself to the truth of how you eat, of the animals whose lives are taken and given to you. If you eat it, or use it, you should be man enough to kill it yourself, at least once in your life. Anyway, this is a requirement of the rite and it's up to us to do it. So, Silas, pick up the sword and do what must be done, and let's have no more small talk about it. It's for your mother, remember. I'll help you. I'm sure you can't take off its head cleanly by yourself, and the creature should not be made to suffer."

The bull stood before the corpse of Dolores Umber. It continued to breathe easily, as though it knew what was to happen and it didn't seem to care, as though the bull better understood the nature of sacrifice than Silas did.

"All right," Silas relented. "I guess it's best to cut its throat?"

"In a manner of speaking, I suppose that's right."

Without a word, Augustus Howesman took Silas's hands in his. Together they grasped the sword hilt, stacking their hands, alternating them along its length. Standing side by side, they lifted the sword over their heads. Silas could feel his great-grandfather's determination through the metal of the sword and the skin of his hands. They were one person now, one machine, ready to deal out death to the animal that stood quietly in front of Dolores's body. No hand held the bull's neck-rope now, but the animal bowed its head slightly and the sword swung down with the supernatural force that August Howesman's enduring condition bestowed. Silas relaxed and moved in concert with his great-grandfather, and faster than the eye could follow, the sword whipped through the animal's neck, past sinew and bone, and struck the floor below, digging deep into the floorboard. The bull's head fell away from its body, and into the wooden tub. Blood sprayed from its exposed neck and over the corpse, making Dolores Umber glisten as though she were a statue carved of garnet. The body of the bull fell over with a crash, and for several moments, the crystals of the chandelier shook and chimed.

Miss Hattie walked forward and dipped her tight-skinned hand into the tub, then reached up and gently smeared more blood on Dolores's lips.

"Dolores stands before you, you, who destroy destruction. The door has been opened and the son has brought home the mother to the house of her eternity. See? Oh, ever-living folk, how the mother of the son returns to you! Now let her sinews be knit up, her bones made firm. May all corruption be taken away from her. Now we take hold of her hand and say: Here is the Living One! May she live forever!"

Miss Hattie turned to Silas but spoke outward to the assembled Restless. "We normally take no food, for we draw sustenance from our offerings, but when the god is present, we dine. This is a blessing upon all of us. Y'all come on now." And Miss Hattie reached down and tore a warm, fist-size piece of flesh from the bull's neck, raised it to her mouth, and ate.

Silas stepped back as the other Restless came forward and fell upon the bull's body. His great-grandfather pulled one of the legs from the animal and then tore it in two. The lower half he handed to another. The upper part of the leg he stripped of skin. "Silas, there's good meat here. If you prefer, I'll take this through to the kitchen and you can prepare it for yourself as you like, but, son, I do think, to be polite, you ought to have some as it is."

Silas didn't answer. The thick incense was making him dizzy, and the room had grown hot from the fire, the braziers, all the candles, and the now fading body heat of the bull. He was sweating and his hair was in his eyes. The smell of blood was everywhere, and that newly awakened part of him that held the *Book of the Dead* roused itself and Silas's instinct with it. So, with no more thought, he reached out and took the raw meat his great-grandfather offered. He held it to his mouth and tore it with his teeth, smearing blood across the lower part of his face. The meat *felt* good in his mouth. The taste of warm, salty blood stirred his appetite. He kept eating. As his stomach filled with the flesh of the god, he felt suffused with strength and presence. Though in the short time he'd lived in Lichport, he had chafed at the sharp facets of his personae—son, great-grandson, boyfriend, Undertaker, Janus, Osiris, child, friend, man—now he felt the almost electric charge of the bull's life force moving though his body, rounding out the edges, making him feel whole and calm, not striving between being one thing or another, simply *being. One life given so others might live. Blood and salt and flesh,* he thought. *Here is the taste of sacrifice and acceptance. And it is good.*

As Silas reveled in the primitive feast, Miss Hattie directed one of the Restless to stack some of the meat on the altar in front of Dolores.

Drowsy with eating, but suddenly more aware of where he was, Silas recalled the days with Charles Umber here at Temple House and, for once, smiled at the memory. How displeased Uncle would have been to see so much fresh food served in the dining room.

The Restless had finished with the sacrifice. There was very little left of the bull. Bones and shreds of fat and sinew were scraped together and placed reverently into the wooden tub holding the bull's head. Several of the Restless folded up the edges of the canvas, carefully tucking them into the tub as well, and carried the whole thing outside, along with the bloodstained linen sheet that had been used to wrap Dolores's body. With a soft piece of cloth, Miss Hattie herself wiped Dolores Umber's skin, removing any trace of blood from her face, neck, and arms. Yet, even before she'd started, there was strangely little blood left on the body, as though Dolores's corpse had absorbed it.

"Beloved, Osiris—" Miss Hattie began, but then smiled, looked over, and said, "Beloved, O *Silas*—Lordy, but what a day we've had!" She touched his shoulder as she continued. "With your help we shall complete the funeral rite, and then we can call our good work done. What follows is very important and most sacred. I believe you are the only living man in Lichport to have seen this part. Usually, the living family members are curtained away. But times change and it seems inappropriate for you not to conduct this portion of the rite. Indeed, I believe it has been apportioned to you from the very beginning."

Miss Hattie led Silas to the altar and passed her fingers over the implements.

"With these, the Opening of the Mouth is accomplished."

She pointed to a carved wooden handle with a metal blade lashed to it. "The adze, and these," she said, picking up two small curved blades, "are made from the iron that falls to earth. Their shape is that of the two fingers of the midwife, she who welcomes the child into the world by sweeping its mouth to clear the baby's airway. With these, we'll likewise welcome your mother into the Afterlife."

Miss Hattie touched the knives to either side of Dolores's mouth, then handed the adze to Silas and nodded that he should do the same.

As he raised the adze to the level of his mother's face, he recalled a distant familiarity in the action. The words came easily as the age-polished handle of the adze moved against the skin of his hand.

"We shall open your mouth and the gods of your place shall loosen the bindings of your jaw. Let us fill you with words of power and untie the fetters of your speech. Let those who would bind you be cast down."

Led by Miss Hattie, Silas put the iron adze to his mother's mouth and gently pushed her lips apart with it. He continued, "Then, with the same iron that opened the mouths of the gods, let your mouth be—"

But his words faltered. As Silas looked at his mom, her mouth now slightly agape, she seemed more dead than she had been a moment before. Not asleep, but stopped, as if life had fled out of her mouth and left the door open behind it. All the doors were open now. His heart clutched in his chest as he looked at his mom, and his sorrow for her and his own loss became too much to keep buried inside. Silas's throat thickened and he began to cry.

Augustus Howesman stepped forward and put his arm around

him. "That's all right, grandson. It's too much for even you to hold by yourself."

"Did she tell you? It was just getting better between us. It had been bad for such a long time, and I wasn't any help. I saw her nearly every day of my life, and I don't think I knew her very well at all." He reached up and softly touched her cheek, whispering, "I'm so sorry, Mom. I am so, so sorry."

Miss Hattie brushed her dry hand over Silas's hair, combing it from his eyes with her long fingers. Then she finished the words of the Opening of the Mouth for him, quietly, solemnly, saying to the corpse, "Let your mouth be open." As she said the words, the air in the house stirred as though a breeze had drifted from some open window or down the chimney.

"Silas, child," said Miss Hattie, "there is just one more thing and then, I pray, your mother will be at peace." She took from her own neck a pendant, a scarab, as large as the palm of a hand, carved of deep blue lapis lazuli. "Take this now," she said, passing it to Silas. "Place this on her breast, child, and all shall be done."

Silas turned the scarab over in his hands, running his finger over the lines of hieroglyphic inscription beneath it.

"You know this symbol," she said. It was not a question.

"Yes," said Silas, holding up his ring.

"What is it?"

"It is a scarab, the sign of life eternal. The Egyptians believed—"

"*Believe,*" Miss Hattie said, correcting him.

"The Egyptians believe the beetle who rolled a ball of dung across the ground was the emblem of the sun, making his passage across the sky."

"Yes. A maker of roads. A passageway into life eternal."

"The lych way . . . ," Silas said to himself.

"What's that?"

"An old name for the paths the dead are carried over and that the dead follow."

"The living and the dead walk hand in hand," she said.

"Life and Death are one," Silas replied, like a catechism.

Miss Hattie smiled and nodded. "Now, child, repeat after me—"

"It's all right, Miss Hattie," said Silas, gently interrupting her. "I have read them. I know what to say. . . ."

Silas took the pendant and looked once more at its inscription. Then he passed the gold chain over his mother's head and placed the scarab above her heart. He did not draw his arms away, but instead hugged her and put his cheek to her cheek. His eyes wet with tears, he spoke the spell of the scarab's inscription into his mother's ear, saying the words only to her.

"My heart of my mother. My heart of my mother. You are the protector of life. Let no one stand against you. Let no one drive you from the house of eternity. Wherever you go, you shall walk in joy. When your words are weighed, let them measure out contentment. Let there be joy in your heart and joy in the hearts of those who travel with you. Great shall you be when you rise up in triumph."

Silas kissed her face.

"I love you, Mom. Always."

As he finished the incantation, both candle flame and hearth fire flashed and then flickered and burned with a blue incandescence. The corpse shifted and, worried he was about to unbalance his mother's standing body and pull it over, Silas stepped back, ready to steady her. But she did not fall.

The corpse of Dolores Umber slowly, deeply drew in breath. She opened her mouth and spoke, and the first word she spoke was her son's name.

LEDGER

I am the blue lotus rising from the dim primordial waters of Nun. O, Nuit, Lady who is the arc of heaven and queen of the chorus of stars, O, you who made me, know that I am here: The great ruler of That Once Was has risen from the depths. . . .

— SPELL 42, FROM THE *BOOK OF THE DEAD*, TRANSLATED BY SILAS UMBER

DOLORES UMBER SLOWLY TURNED HER HEAD and looked at the corpses who filled the dining room and parlor of her house.

"Silas? What the *hell* is going on?"

He couldn't move his mouth.

Dolores looked at the altar in front of her, at the blue-flamed candles, and, turning her head again, saw the dark statue of the god of the dead behind her. She saw Miss Hattie seated in a carved golden chair and Augustus Howesman staring. Dolores lifted her hand to her chest and, finding the scarab there, held it briefly. She shook her head. "For Christ's sake . . . ," she said, with more annoyance or disappointment than awe. Then very tentatively she stepped to the mirror on the dining room wall and drew its veil away. She stared at herself for many moments, then held up her hands, opening and closing them, scrutinizing the taut skin. She turned her head left, then right, gazing at each side of her pale face.

No one in the room spoke. Silas barely drew breath. All eyes were on Dolores. Silas could see her face and its expression reflected in the mirror. She looked more lively now than she had in years, younger, more beautiful. The lines of worry and anger that life had inscribed upon her had all nearly vanished, and the smallest smile began to form at the corners of her mouth.

"All right," she finally said. "There is no need to gawk. I am here. That's all. Silas, don't stare so. We've never exactly been a conventional family." She turned back to the room and passed her hand over the head of the Ammit, saying, "It might have been worse." She walked slowly back to her son, meeting his eyes.

"My son has brought me back."

"Mom, I'm sorry. I didn't mean for this to happen."

"Don't be sorry, Si. This was inevitable. I can see that now. It was going to happen whether I wanted it to or not. Don't take so much on yourself. Some things just have to go their own way, and I am one of them. But, Silas, can you love me now? As I am?"

At first he didn't answer. He just stared at his mom's face. Though she seemed strangely improved, there was no question she was dead. It showed mostly in her eyes, which had taken on a flatness. She was present, but not all there. When she'd spoken, Silas felt like he was having a heart attack. The world had stopped when she'd said his name. There was no gravity. Then the more she talked, the more she moved, it all seemed horribly obvious. Silas's chest ached and he felt as though he was being pulled in four directions as once. Should he still mourn her? Did he still need to feel guilty about her death? Was relief appropriate? Was it okay to feel happy about her return? He felt portions of all those things. But even as his mind spilled over with mixed emotions, detachment darkened the edges of his thoughts. His mother was another of the dead things in Lichport. As awkward as their relationship had often been, she had been an anchor of normalcy for him. She was the one who fought against the strangeness of their new home, the one who wanted to protect him from Lichport's occult side. Now she had utterly succumbed to it. Silas felt the land tilt beneath him, as though he was standing again on the little boat of reeds. The river was flowing forward once more into the shadows. There could be no looking back now. Not for her. Not for him.

"Si?" Dolores said, breaking in on Silas's thoughts.

He wondered how much, if anything, she remembered about the river. He put his arms around his mother and said, "Nothing's changed, I promise."

Dolores shook her head. "Oh, Si, a very great deal has changed, but I will never change again, it seems."

The dead milled about the dining room and leaned against the walls of the hallway and foyer. Augustus Howesman looked delighted, utterly in his element, and he walked among kin and neighbor, playing the host, introducing Silas to long-absent relatives.

Silas could see his mother was uncomfortable, most likely with seeing her house in such a state, filled with what were, for her, uninvited guests. So, as politely as he could, he thought he would draw the evening to a close. No matter what had occurred, it was still his mother's house, and he knew she would prefer more quiet than company.

"Thank you all for coming," Silas said. "You have honored us with your presence and assistance. But now, or as soon as you like, you may return to your homes."

He noticed his great-grandfather was watching him speak to the others.

"You are all welcome here anytime. But it's been a hard day, perhaps we should all think of making our ways home." He meant this kindly and sincerely, and in truth, he was exhausted.

As Silas spoke the words of departure, some of the Restless looked confused or surprised, as though something in their world had just changed drastically, but they weren't sure what. One said, "Do you mean we are welcome to return to our tombs?"

"No, no! Not at all. I mean, sure, if you like. But please, return to wherever you want. To your houses. To your families."

"You mean to where we once lived?" asked one of the Restless, his mouth hanging slightly to the side.

Silas thought of all those Restless he'd seen in Newfield in their dark, lonely tombs. Then he looked at his mother, surrounded by family, smiling at him, looking more alive and at home in death than ever before. "Yes. Sure," said Silas. "Go to wherever you will be happy. Rejoin your kin. Live again, if you wish, as you once did. Or back to your tombs if you prefer. Let it be as you desire. Go to where your hearts wish to take you."

Many of the Restless began to smile. Some, of course, had homes to return to, crumbling though they might have been. Others had long ago been put away by the living: in tombs, in tomb houses behind the houses their families had abandoned, or in some cases, where their descendants still resided. And now, the Undertaker, the embodiment of the Lord of the Dead, had told them they could "go home." Silas's words emboldened and delighted them. Slowly, taking their time, the Restless began to make their farewells as Silas took to the settee next to where his mother stood, unable or unwilling to sit down.

Before she left, Miss Hattie approached him, no longer needing her chair for balance.

"No, dear child, don't get up!" She took his hand. "Thank you, Silas, for all your good work. Your mother is the happier for it, I am sure. Oh, goodness, aren't we all!" And the Restless did look different now, more lively. They were moving more easily and naturally. A few looked merely elderly once more, much of their corpse's pallor having been driven away by the funeral rites and the sacrificial meal.

"A good death is always enlivening, child, to the dead and the living both, especially among family." Mrs. Hattie began to lean in for a kiss, but then patted his hand and smiled at him. "You take care now, Silas Umber. You promise me you'll do that?"

"Yes, ma'am," said Silas, getting up to walk with her to the door.

"Good. You come by and visit sometime, all right? Don't be a stranger. The tombs of Newfield are always open to you."

She turned to Dolores. "Welcome home, sister." Dolores nodded indulgently. She clearly did not enjoy being outranked in her own home.

Miss Hattie whispered instructions to some of the men in the line of Restless leaving the house. They carried away many of the boxes and coffers of funeral instruments and placed everything back on the bier. As Silas stood at the entrance to the parlor, shaking hands and bidding farewell to the guests, he imagined the pageant of the dead, wandering home, up Fairwell back to Fort Street, across Temple and through Newfield, back to their tombs—smaller versions of the temples of Memphis or Abydos—which soon would be standing in the morning sun. What would the townsfolk make of such a procession?

His great-grandfather was the last to leave. Silas saw him speaking with his mother and then embracing her. He winked at Silas as he left to make his way back to Fort Street.

After all the Restless had gone, Silas wondered how long tradition required him to stay. He didn't think he should leave his mother. But other parts of Lichport, where he still had work to do, called to him. Bea was there, below the millpond, waiting. He wanted to save her. He was desperate to go to her, to try and get her back, but he didn't feel right just leaving. And the rite had taken the life right out of him. Silas could barely keep his eyes open. He reclined on the settee and waited for his mother to finish her good-byes.

A little while later, his mother approached and stood over

him. He raised his head and shoulders to make room for her, and as she sat down, she took his head in her lap and tenderly stroked his hair. "It's not as strange as it seems," she said.

"Seems? Nothing seems. Things are what they are."

"It'll be all right, Si. I promise. Now I can look after you a bit. You rest and we'll chat a little more tomorrow."

Dolores felt something against her fingers and she paused running her hand through Silas's hair. She pulled a small dried flower from the locks above his temple.

"Where have you been wandering, my son?" Dolores whispered.

But Silas was already drifting off. He nodded slightly as sleep came over him, and the living corpse of his mother bent down and gently kissed his eyes.

Dolores briefly considered singing Silas a lullaby, but then thought better of it and went to change into something a little nicer.

Dolores Umber walked to the front windows and opened the curtains wide. She had nothing to hide, nothing to be ashamed of. Outside, the clouds had thinned and gaped, revealing glimpses of the moon. In the streets, she could see the Restless milling about, walking on their way to the various districts of Lichport. Many had been exiles for years and years, sent away to now forgotten tombs or abandoned houses to live alone, without the company and comfort of loved ones. But now her son, the Undertaker, had told them it was time to go home, and they were going to do just that.

LEDGER

"Life is a dream wandering, death is homecoming."
— CHINESE PROVERB

He hath need of warmth, who now is come,
numbed with cold to the knee;
comfort and company the wanderer craves
who has walked o'er the rimy world.

. . .

The pine tree wastes, alone on the hill,
neither bark nor needles shelter it;
such is the man whom none doth love;
for what should he longer live?

— FROM THE *ELDER EDDA*, TRANSLATED BY AMOS UMBER

Among the most important obligations of the Undertaker are the rites of Separation and Isolation. Namely, the keeping of the dead in the ground, by force, if necessary. Should the dead arise, the sanity of the vicinity is threatened. Pestilence often follows in the wake of the dead should they come to walk. If this basic task is not attended to, the hallowed office of

Undertaker shall know shame, and those that once venerated the Undertaker shall hate and despise him.

—MARGINALIA OF JONAS UMBER

CHAPTER 16

COLD COMFORT

THE RESTLESS WERE GOING HOME.

For some, like Augustus Howesman, the journey was habitual and simple. They merely returned to Fort Street where they'd lived, alone, since their families had left them behind. For them, the journey ended as it had begun, with the opening and closing of a familiar door. Crossing the thresholds of their homes, they returned to their favorite chairs, their bodies slowing, their minds pondering the recent events, the more distant past, and what might follow now that some of their traditional rites had been rekindled by the death and return of Dolores Umber.

The oldest and most resigned of the Restless returned to where they'd been put: So Miss Hattie and most of her retinue returned to the Egyptian ghetto of the dead at Newfield, to the elaborate but largely forgotten tombs where they had long resided.

But others had been emboldened by Silas's words about going home and, filled with hope, followed their hearts back to long lost places of comfort. Some had taken Silas's parting words as a sort of blessing and had been enlivened. A few of the Restless still had family—living descendants—residing in Lichport. Some had former houses that had not fallen to ruin. So, with the encouragement of the Undertaker, they were going back to the places where they had once lived, and where those previous lives had come to their ends.

◆ ◆ ◆

One man, who had once lived in a fine mansion on Coach Street, returned home to find his house had all but fallen to the ground. The nature of the ruin told the tale well enough: The deeply carved stonework had been pulled off and the copper gutters as well. Anything of value had been stripped from the outside, and water had come in through the cracks. Finally, the roof had fallen, along with most of the walls. Here and there, tall trees now grew up from the pile. He could remember building every part of that house. Each new profitable venture had led to more and more ornate improvements. He thought of the tomb house behind the home of his great-great-grandchildren, where he had more recently resided. He was not supposed to leave it, for his appearance was found to be distressing. His descendants had not seen him leave for the funeral on Temple Street, but if they learned he was gone, there would be harsh words. Had he endured so long to be spoken to in that fashion by his children's children's children? Or to hear the sound of their laughter, the music of their daily lives at a distance, from the margins? And after the fine company of the funeral, the thought of going back to the lonely tomb house brought him little comfort. He walked away from the ruin of his former house and down toward the sea. Making his way awkwardly over sand, he continued, moving into the small, cold waves, letting the sea take him where there would be no more sound to trouble him and where he would trouble no one.

Two of the Restless, husband and wife, long entombed together at the Garden Plot Cemetery on Prince Street, thought fondly about evenings by the hearth of their old house south on Queen Street, overlooking the sea, and so headed there. When they arrived, the house still stood, though it had no lights in the windows and looked to be abandoned. After slowly ascending the long stairs up to the entrance, they knocked on the door. When there was no answer, one of the couple tried the handle and, finding the door open, the two corpses walked inside and to their old parlor. They found two chairs still by the hearth, and using some matches and scraps of wood he found on the floor, the husband lit a little fire. There they sat in the dark, and closed their eyes, and were content.

Some time later, the occupant of the house, an elderly man who had inherited it from an aunt, came downstairs to find two corpses sitting in his dilapidated parlor by a dying fire. As the man began to scream, the corpses rose and, without word or ceremony, went back to the front door and left their former home once more. As they descended the stairs, the corpse of the old woman slipped and fell to the street, tumbling and turning over and over on her way down. Being dead, she felt no pain, but most of the bones of her legs and hips were shattered. Her husband tried to help her stand, but it could not be done. And so he tenderly lifted his broken wife up into his arms, and carried her back to their cold tomb.

Juliette Howesman-Ellis turned her back on Newfield and walked home to the family she herself had raised and to the house where she had raised them. She had not been dead so long as most of the others, and her daughter and grandchildren were all still alive and in Lichport, though they mostly kept to themselves and spent much time in Kingsport at another house. She put on no airs, did not bother to fix up her hair into the tight bun she wore in life, but rang the bell of her former house on Cedar Street. Her daughter answered the door, but quickly slammed it shut. A tiny ornate hinged peephole set in the door opened.

"What do you want?" the living woman said, her voice a mix of fear and anger.

"It's me, your mother," the corpse said to her elderly daughter. "I've come home."

"My mother is dead," said the daughter from the darkness behind the door.

"I *am* your mother," the Restless corpse said again.

"You *were* my mother," the daughter said, closing the peep-hole cover abruptly and walking back into the belly of the house.

Other Restless were also turned away over the next few days. Some by family. Some by strangers. None gently. Some, struck with renewed grief and rekindled sorrows, simply stopped moving, frozen on the streets and sidewalks where misery held them fast. Standing in the cold, those silent Restless looked like newly placed memorials, reminders to Lichport's living residents of both their own mortality and the shameful treatment of their deceased kin.

Of course, the people of Lichport were no strangers to wonders and terrors. Ghosts were common and trouble enough, but compared to the irrefutable and physical presence of a living corpse, a specter, now seemed somehow less terrible. A ghost did not usually sit, eyes wide, and stare at you for hours as you watched television, or while you slept. A ghost did not usually give you advice on how to raise your children or what to do with your finances. A corpse raised fears of sickness and contagion. A corpse was a curse.

There was talk of a fever. Rumors rose almost as soon as the first corpse knocked on a door, and fearful whispers and accusations ran rampant through the town as people looked upon the lingering dead on the streets of Lichport. Some called the corpses' return a plague and, as happens during plague-times historically, people began to look about for something or someone to blame.

LEDGER

Though you are young and I am old,
Though your veins hot and my blood cold,
Though youth is moist and age is dry,
Yet embers live when flames do die.

—Thomas Campion (1567–1620). Marginalia of
    Amos Umber

CHAPTER 17

BRUNCH

SILAS AWOKE LATE IN HIS OLD BED in Temple House. His broken memories of the previous night were waiting for him. His stomach still felt full, which confirmed some of his stranger recollections. He remembered standing in the parlor, watching the Restless slowly pack up the temple relics, many of them smiling as they prepared to make their way back to their homes and not-so-final resting places. He would never forget that moment when his mother's corpse opened her eyes and said his name. He wasn't sure how to feel about her death now. She had died. Now she was . . . not alive . . . but back. There had been a funeral, but by the end, it had become more of a birthday party. Despite his mom's very real and renewed presence, he could not help feeling that he still should be mourning her. Even as he'd looked into her eyes last night, and felt her brush his hair with her dead hand, he'd felt an awful sense of loss.

Work was easier than trying to sort out his feelings. It brought focus, and his participation in the funeral, his speaking words from the ancient *Book of the Dead* had made him feel a little more competent, having used another, older rite related to the Undertaking. Now, rested but still tired, the funeral over, his role completed, the bindings on his sorrows had come loose again, and he could no longer keep his feelings from bleeding into one another. His mother's death. Bea's absence. Lars's death. His dad's. The harm he'd brought to Maud in trying to help Alysoun and her poor baby. And in helping mother and child, he'd broken a vow and set Cabel Umber free from his prison house. No action in his life was discrete from any other now. All the edges blurred into a wound of obligation, guilt, and aggravation that he could not get to heal properly or avoid making worse.

He'd slept in his clothes and couldn't remember how he'd gotten upstairs. He wanted to talk with his mom, but there was no hurry. Not anymore. His mother wasn't going anywhere. But the more he thought about the events of the last two days, the more he just wanted to go home. He needed some quiet. As he prepared to go downstairs into the rooms where his mother had risen from the dead, an anomalous thought broke in: He idly considered what others his age might be thinking as they prepared to take their morning meal. He found himself wondering what it might have been like to go away to college: to wake up some morning and go to a lecture, to eat with people his own age, to worry about an upcoming exam and no other thing. What would it be like to have a real girlfriend, to date, to ask her if she'd marry him? To have children and raise a family? He pushed those thoughts from his mind. What was the point? If that world could ever have existed for him, it was a million miles away now. Silas's stomach tightened as his thoughts unraveled into the reality of his life. His actual life. He had a girlfriend. She was dead and lay imprisoned beneath the ice. She was dead and waiting for him. More than anything, he wanted Bea back, and he needed a moment to himself to sort out how he was going to get her.

The upper galleries of Temple House were quiet. Letting his memories of Bea flood everything else from his mind, he returned briefly to the little study off the Camera Obscura. Nothing had been moved since the other night when he'd searched for spells to summon the spirits of the dead. Books lay open on the desk just where he'd left them. He ran a finger idly down an open volume. "Ye Darke Call" was written in red ink across the vellum page. A marker still lay in the book's gutter. Not his. Uncle's. His uncle had once used this spell. Silas could almost smell the residue of the words from the book sunk into the wood of the walls and floor. Maybe, he thought again, Charles Umber had used them to hold Adam's spirit in his corpse. Or on the poor woman whose hand he'd robbed out of a grave in Newfield.

Silas looked away from the book and past the open door leading into the Camera. A room of wonders, Uncle had told him. Empty now. What wonders would it hold next? Silas scanned the lines of the book again. He took a clean sheet of paper from the desk and carefully wrote out the dire words of the spell, reading them once to compare them against the original. He knew these words already, for Cabel Umber had whispered almost the exact same formula into Silas's ear in the sunken mansion at Arvale. Heard once. Read once. All that remained was to speak them. *Soon,* he told himself. *Soon.*

He folded the paper and thrust it into his pocket. He closed the book and left the room, passing once more through Uncle's empty bedroom and out into the long hall of the north wing.

As he approached the hall overlooking the foyer, Silas heard music. The cheerful tune floated about in stark contrast to his mood. Even though he could hear his mother walking about the house below, he felt sure that when he went downstairs, he would still see her corpse lying on the dining room table. His head hurt and he felt sore all over. The stresses of the previous day still sat heavily on him. He was beyond trying to sort out his tumultuous feelings. Anger, grief, weariness, and longing were the four horses still drawing and pulling at him. The strain showed on his face. He looked into a mirror near the top of the stairs. His eyes were swollen and his skin looked pale and splotchy. He should have stayed in bed.

Words of a song from the old Victrola downstairs pulled his attention from his pallor. *Didn't we have a lovely evening. . . .* It was Bing Crosby's voice, one of his mother's favorites. She used to listen to his records in Saltsbridge on her cheerful, not-quite-too-much-to-drink nights. He hadn't heard this song in years, and it gave him an uneasy, displaced feeling, as though he might go down the stairs and into a moment long gone from the world. A time before last night's funeral. A time before both his parents' deaths. And couldn't such a time still exist somewhere, out there, in the mist?

> *They didn't leave a scrap for Rover*
> *We ought to feel real proud*
> *And mighty glad the darn thing's over . . .*

As he stood at the top of the stairs, the music sang out on the scratchy recording, filling the house . . . *Sure was a hungry crowd . . .* Silas could smell tuberoses; perhaps the fragrance of some perfume Uncle had given his mother after they'd arrived in Lichport.

He could see the night had not ended when he'd fallen asleep. His mother had been busy. More statuary had been hauled out of storage and carefully arranged. It was not the museum it had been when Uncle was alive, but the rooms of the lower floors now seemed a sort of salon. Fresh flowers had been delivered and stood in vases and urns all about the room. Mostly roses and chrysanthemums, their perfume was slight, as they'd surely come from a hothouse, perhaps in Kingsport. And the room was immaculate. There was not a drop of blood or dust on the floor anywhere.

"Did you sleep well, Silas?" said his mother's voice from the dining room, rising over the music just as the song came to an end. She stood dramatically in the doorway with her hands clasped lightly before her waist, more portrait of a mother than a mom. She wore a leopard-print turban and a black dress with more leopard print on the collar and cuffs. As she stepped toward him, the dozens of bangles and charms on her wrist chimed with the sound of tiny bells. Around her neck was a heavy gold chain. The heart scarab hung from it, resting on the upper part of her chest. Her skin was pale and smooth, her lips reddened, and there was the smallest touch of rouge on her cheeks. For a corpse, she looked good, Silas thought. Even the thick black eye makeup—right off a 1950s Italian movie set—suited her. It made her eyes look large and luminous, and when she looked at Silas, he could not look away from her.

Except for the fact that she looked better than ever, it was as though nothing had changed.

She took a seat at the dining room table and gestured for him to join her. "Brunch! It's Mother's Day, Si!"

"Um. It's not Mother's Day yet, Mom."

"It is Mother's Day *for me.*"

He nodded and walked through the open pocket doors. The scene was surreal yet utterly common. If he had not known his mother was a walking corpse, he wouldn't have even blinked at the sight of her sitting at the table waiting for him to come and eat. There was fruit and some cheese. Juice had been poured for him into a wineglass.

Dolores repeated the question. "How'd you sleep, Si?"

"Not well. I must have kicked like a rabbit all night. My legs are sore."

"It was a long day for you. Maybe a warm bath later.

Tonight you should take a little drink before bed."

He stared at her.

"Don't look at me like that. I'm not saying you should get drunk. I am suggesting a nightcap to help you sleep. A hot toddy, maybe. I'll make you one."

"I need to get back to my house. I want to sleep in my own bed."

"Of course, I just thought . . . well, that you might like to stay here for a while. You'd like it here now. See? I even brought a few of the finer objects out of storage. I was going to sell them, but now, I think, they rather suit the house and I know how you love such things."

"I can't stay. I need my own—"

"And I wouldn't smother you like Mrs. Bowe."

Silas didn't answer.

"Of course. Don't worry. I am very self-sufficient. More so now than ever. You'll see. I just think life would be easier for both of us if we were closer."

Silas realized she probably meant that literally. His great-grandfather benefited enormously from their time together. Even his pace had quickened after Silas's numerous visits. He under-stood that spending time with the living gave the Restless a kind of charge. Company was manna to them. Without the attentions of the living, they slowed, and began to move less and less. If left alone long enough, Silas imagined they could become statues, their minds looking out through their hardened, immobile human remains. Without the love and remembrance of kin, the Restless could endure, but not pleasantly. Silas knew then that he would be paying his mother a lot of visits. "Don't worry, Mom. I'll be back. I just have work to see to, that's all."

"Well, now. That is familiar, I must say. More and more like your father every day."

"We have both benefited from those similarities, you know."

"Of course, of course. I meant it as a compliment, I promise. I suppose I understand it all a little better now . . . your father's sense of commitment to his work. Much of it is still a mystery to me, though less so now. I suspect I'll never really understand your father's ways."

"Except through me. It's my work now."

"Yes. Your work. Certainly. I mean, of course, I am appreciative of your help. But it's a son's job to help his mother now and again." She smiled briefly, but then the corners of her mouth pulled down slightly as she continued. "It's just that there's no point in it, really. Trying to help all those *other* people. As though you could put a stopper in the miseries of the world. I need you. Isn't that enough?" She poured him more juice.

"But I have helped people. Helped some so much I haven't been able to do anything for myself. "

"I know. I'm not denying that. But that's my point. I'm saying it can't make much of a dent. And of course, out there"—she turned her head toward the window—"they just keep dying and dying, and most of them aren't too happy about it. How in the world do you expect to fix *all that*?"

Silas paused. She wasn't entirely wrong. It felt good to help people, and he had taken to the work. He knew it was what he was supposed to be doing. But where would it end? His mom was right. It was a war of attrition. And for everything he'd done, here he still was, surrounded by the dead, and the only ghost he wanted to see was trapped and waiting.

"Maybe it's not about winning or losing, Mom," Silas said. "Maybe it's just about being useful. Maybe it's about working with your gifts. And there is no doubt this is my work. I can't explain that, but when I am walking the lych way, I can *feel* what to do, where to go. And the dead can feel that too. Don't worry. I will visit you. Every day, if you say it would make you happy." He sighed. "There's enough of me to go around." But he didn't believe the words even as he said them. He felt stretched thin as a wire already.

Perhaps sensing this, Dolores looked at him hard and said, "But, Silas, your whole life could just be eaten up by those people who've already lived their lives, wasted them. They've made their own beds."

"You're mostly talking about our friends and neighbors, you know."

"Friends and neighbors . . . hmmm . . . friends and neighbors," Dolores said as though she'd forgotten the meaning of the words.

"You remember? All those people who came to Dad's funeral?"

"I do remember. Tell me, Si, how many of them came to mine?" She didn't wait for him to answer. "Ah. You see? They fear us already. That is so *common*. They'll love you like family one minute, but the next, you're worse than a stranger. Just wait and see, son. Step out of line, they'll turn on you, too. They liked your father when he helped them and not much longer than it took to do it. Even those few who loved him right along, believe me, they feared him too. I once saw a man cross the street to avoid brushing arms with your dad, and the previous week, your father had helped that same man bring peace to his grandfather's ghost. Your work upsets people, Si. Yes. Even those who ask you for help. They hate themselves for needing to ask, and so before too long they—"

"Well, even if that's all true," Silas interrupted, "if I stopped now, if I turned aside my work and ignored them, I would be no better than them, and my life would end like theirs: in regret and sorrow and confusion. I think it's already moving in that direction anyway, so it's better that I have something to focus on."

He looked away, but then reached across the table and held his mother's hand.

"Then why not focus on family? There's an investment with a likely return," Dolores said. "I'm thinking of putting in a projection room, for films. Wouldn't that be fun? Going to the cinema in our house?"

Silas breathed in deeply. "I understand. You want me to be happy. I want to be happy too, but maybe not everyone gets to be happy, Mom. I'm not sure happiness is part of the road I seem to be on. I promise you I'll try . . . try not to do too much. What if I only worry about my job? How would that be? You worry about your life. I'll worry about mine. And you can leave our people, our friends and neighbors, to me."

"And who, exactly, are 'our people'? It's a fine thought, Si. But I suspect that once one heads down that path you've chosen, the choices get fewer and fewer, that there are more and more distractions. Look at you now! After just one funeral. Your face, Si! You need more rest. Go back upstairs." Dolores paused, looked as though she was weighing whether or not to say more, then she rose.

"But let's not worry about all that now. We can at least think of this as a new beginning for us, can't we? Let's face it, we've both had a hard time of it."

"Okay."

Dolores paused, rethinking, stepping back from something she was about to say. "It hasn't been easy coming here. I know it's always been hard for you. Saltsbridge. School. All of it."

She picked up a parcel of brown paper and handed it to him.

"Speaking of a fresh start, here."

"What it is?"

"Just some things of your dad's. More old stuff. His wallet. Some papers. Amos was a scribbler. Nothing of value. You can open it when you get home. Nothing that won't keep. Just a few more relics of the past. It's all done with. . . . I'm done with that now, so take them if you want them. I don't think there is any point in keeping such things from you. So take this with you. I suspect you've already been through many of your father's notebooks and papers."

"Some. There's lots in my house. The desk is filled with them. I haven't had time to go through everything."

"Well, you know what I'd recommend?"

"Burn the lot?"

"Yes. Let the past go. Forward! That's my motto."

"I know it is." He looked at her, so mobile and lively, when only yesterday she had lain cold on the table awaiting burial.

Silas took a few bites of his food, then got up from the table.

"So soon?

He nodded.

"Where are you off to, looking so intent and forlorn?"

"You know."

"Silas—"

"Mom, I don't know what else to do. I love her."

"You can't think of what to do because you don't know anyone else. That is the problem, Si, with being antisocial. You have no society. Believe me, I know. All those years with your father . . . we ended up living like recluses in Saltsbridge. But even back in our Lichport days, after our marriage, how many parties do you think your father and I got invited to?"

"I don't know."

"It was a rhetorical question, Silas. But I'm not going to tell you whom to love and not love. My infatuations never led me anywhere too grand, mind you, but everyone has to choose for themselves. And then they've got to be prepared to live with the consequences. Besides, I'm hardly in the position now to tell you not to love the dead, am I?"

"I can't let her go. She was the first good thing I found here. I can't think properly anymore because everything leads back to her. When I came back from Arvale, I thought I had lost her, but then . . . then things turned. And she's down there, trapped, because of something you and the others did—"

"They told me you were in danger."

"Okay."

"Silas, you know me. I'm not a meddler. I thought something was going to hurt you."

"I can feel her, sometimes, under the water. It makes my skin crawl."

"It's all right, Si. You can blame me if you want."

"I'm not blaming you. I'm not blaming anyone."

"It's all right. I'm your mother. You're supposed to blame me for everything. One day, you'll get married. Then you can blame your wife for everything, but until then, I'll take it."

Dolores smiled.

"Well, then, I'd like to ask you something."

Dolores slowly crossed her legs, leaned back, and put her chin on the back of her hand. "I have all the time in the world."

"All those years we spent in Saltsbridge and you never spoke of *any* of this. You let Dad lie to me about his work and never spoke about your family or anyone else here in Lichport. As it turns out, there was a whole other world on the opposite side of the marshes, and I barely knew anything about it. Why didn't you tell me?"

"Maternal instinct."

"C'mon . . ."

"You're asking me why I didn't tell a child that a few miles away was a dragon waiting to eat him? Si, please."

"Okay, but when I was a little older . . . you might have told me something."

"Walk with me," she said, rising from her chair. "I want to stretch my legs."

Silas and his mother walked from the parlor, past the portico leading into the long hall, and a few moments later entered the rotunda. Silas was surprised to find that great chamber warm, even with all its marble and the cold outside. The tiles of the floor felt as though they'd been heated from below.

"I couldn't begin to tell you how the thermostat in this house works. I'll call someone. No need to heat this part of the house," said Dolores.

The rotunda's fireplace was empty and clean of ash. The carvings on its massive mantel looked gothic, deeply worked with images of coiled dragons and leaf-headed wildmen.

Walking slowly about the room, Dolores said, "Did you know, Silas, that it wasn't my idea, at first, to take you from Lichport? Oh, I was ready to go, make no mistake about that, but it was your father who first suggested we should bring you away."

"I never knew that."

Dolores looked at the unopened package still in Silas's hand and continued.

"Your father spoke of the ghost of the millpond. Oh, yes. More than once. I think he was a little . . . fascinated with her. And I think she has been aware of you for some time. He told me that when you were very young, and we still lived in Lichport, a spirit would follow you. You were an infant. Your father would take you out in the carriage. He loved to parade you around, and sometimes, he claimed, a young woman would appear and fix her gaze upon you, watching you pass by. Then, when your father turned around, she'd be gone. Happened more than once. I was quickly sick of hearing about what I joked was your father's little spectral paramour. But now I know it wasn't your father the girl was interested in."

"Where did this happen? When would she appear?"

"Most often when your father was on the north side of town, close to the millpond, of course, but also when he'd take you around what was left of the 'new' town square. There were still a few shops open then. Your father told me she walked out of a theater doorway to watch him pass by with you. Strange, because it was still boarded up. Amos thought maybe someone had gotten the money together to pursue the old theater's renovation, but when he inquired, turned out no. Never happened. I asked him, 'What kind of girl lingers around a ruined theater?' He didn't answer. But now we know what kind of girl, don't we, Silas?"

Silas nodded. He wasn't sure if his mother was mocking him or trying to be understanding. Maybe it was all one with her.

"Silas, if you think her freedom will play a part in your happiness, then by all means, go pull her out of the pool. If you're that sure you want her, then you call her to your side and never look back. I can't judge you anymore. You're a man. You'll have to do what you feel is best, regardless of what I think. Life is so short, so very short. But death is long, and one should take steps to be happy or . . . what comes after . . . might be a miserable thing. Go to her. But go without expectation, Silas. She is not really present, as present as her ghost might feel. She is all shadow and little substance. Yet the heart wants what it wants, so follow yours, but do not look too far ahead or hope for too much. That's your dead mother's best advice."

Strangely, her words were a comfort to him. Maybe it was

just hearing someone say he could do what he wanted. But it was not so easy. He could not just reach down and help Bea from the water. Mrs. Bowe and his mother had seen to that.

"Do you think the binding can be broken easily?"

"No," said Dolores matter-of-factly. "You will have to apply some cleverness, I suspect."

"But you're saying it can be done?"

"I suppose so, somehow. I am no expert. You have several things working against it, though."

"Please tell me."

"The easiest way to break it would require the people who set it to untie it. "

"And you were there—"

"Yes, Si, I was. But I am not now as I was then. So, already, I think you will have to find another way to break it. I told you, I am no expert."

"I could summon her. I could use something of hers and call her back."

"By force? Son, I suspect she would find that . . . stressful."

"I don't want to cause her any more pain."

Dolores took his hand, and walked back with her son toward the main house.

"Silas, if your father had to find a ghost, what would he do? When you were looking for Amos, when you were looking for *me*, how did you go about it? How would her losses be staged? Where? Where did you last see her? Where did Amos last see her?"

"But I know where she is now."

"You know where her spirit is trapped. But how do you know that's the only place she's gotten hung up? She's had a busy time of it, both before and after her death, haunting many others since she died. Every house has more than one door. Of course the mill-pond holds her, but she has left her mark on many places about town . . . are there any other places that might still hold a portion of her, or that might lead to her? Perhaps one with a door that Mrs. Bowe may have forgotten to lock?"

ffor the playhouses, or theaters, be naught but temples to lascivious behavior to capture the hearts of goodlie folk and lure them to ruination. And what is playacted upon the stage shalle soone be acted in the streets of the town, for the playhouse is the verie tabernacle of contagion. Beware the playhouse, then! ffor there is limbo for the once hardworking citizen, who, casting aside hys respectable trade, becomes enslaved to every kind of lewdness and spectacle. Then, at play's end, the wretch who hath but paid to watch, his pockets full-filled with Sin, shalle wander back into the world, squinting at the sun, and seeking only the tavern and the company of other wretches with whom to share his day's profit."

—FROM THE SIXTEENTH-CENTURY PAMPHLET "HERE IS THE
    PLAYHOUSE AND HELL BESIDES"

ALL LOVE STORIES SHARE A BORDER
WITH THIS PLACE. UNREQUITED LOVE
LINGERS HERE LIKE A FOG, AND THOSE
SOULS SEPARATED BY TRAGEDY OR APATHY
WANDER THE AISLES AND LOBBY. ONCE
SET IN THEIR FORLORN ROLES, SUCH
GHOSTS BECOME "TYPE-CAST," UNABLE
TO ESCAPE THE DRAMA THEY'VE WRITTEN
FOR THEMSELVES, AS THOUGH THE PAIN
OF LOVE FORSAKEN, OR UNREQUITED, OR
SOME SUCH LOSS WAS MORE COMFORT
THAN THE RISK OF HAVING LOVED, OR

EVER TRYING TO LOVE AGAIN. THE
SHADOWLAND OF **THE THEATER OF LOVE**
CONFOUNDED IS A CROSSROADS AND ITS
ROWS OF SEATS, BALCONIES, PROSCENIUM,
MANY SETS, ETC., SHARE FRONTIERS
WITH OTHER OF LICHPORT'S MIST HOMES
WHERE LOST LOVERS FIRST LOST SIGHT
OF THEIR PARAMOURS.

—MARGINALIA OF AMOS UMBER

Theatre to Close Following Tragedies

After only two performances of their much-
anticipated *Romeo and Juliet*, the Queen's Company
Acting Troupe is to leave Lichport and return
to England following the suicide of their stage
manager Alexander Burrage. Plans for next
season's local production of *Hamlet* have also been
suspended pending further investigations of the
disappearance of Miss Annabelle Phelps, who was
to play Ophelia. Miss Phelps was last seen walking
past the millpond at the edge of the marshes and
is assumed drowned pending the findings of a
continuing investigation. The theatre will remain
closed until further notice. Refunds to be given for
all ticket holders for canceled performances.

—CUTTING FROM THE *LICHPORT CROW* NEWSPAPER, 1939

CHAPTER 18

PLAY

THE THEATER WAS A SHADOWLAND FOR LOVERS, who, Silas remembered, had played at love and lost. He remembered seeing the image of the playhouse stitched in the red silk at the house of the three. His father had walked there before. Now he would follow again in his father's footsteps. There he might discover some forgotten scene or trapdoor into Bea's shadowland, or find another way to bring her home, a way that wouldn't harm her any further.

He had loved Bea and lost her. So maybe even shadows of their own story would draw aside and reveal a path to her. Maybe a glimpse of Bea would still be there, in the moment of their last parting, and if he could find her before the curtain on that scene closed, maybe he could just call out and bring her back. All the shadowlands and lych ways were permeable landscapes. Silas and Bea had both loved, and in Lichport. Could the place of her imprisonment share a frontier with the theater? And wasn't his own longing for Bea quickly becoming a sort of living limbo itself?

As Silas took the death watch from his pocket, he saw ahead of him a strange scene. In the yard of a house, one of the Restless stood. In the driveway next to the corpse, a man and woman were quickly packing a car with suitcases and other belongings.

"No, Grandma!" the woman said to the corpse. You can't come with us! God Almighty!"

The man kept packing and didn't look up.

As Silas passed by, the woman turned toward him with pleading eyes. Her husband said, "Get in the car!" She did. The corpse stood motionless a few feet away as the engine started up.

As Silas walked up to the corpse, the car began to leave the driveway. The corpse hung her head.

The man rolled down the window and stared at Silas. With a sneer, the driver spit on the ground. The car pulled away.

The corpse looked up and watched the car drive off. She said, "You told us to go home. You said we could go home. . . ."

"I am so sorry. Listen, please, go to Fort Street. Go to my great-grandfather's house. He can help you. There are empty homes on Fort Street. He can tell you which ones. Tell him I'll come soon and we'll sort it out together. Can you do that?"

The old woman nodded.

Silas walked with her a little way until she turned the corner to make her way toward Fort Street.

He paused and looked at the death watch in his hand. A little more eager to be gone than a moment ago, Silas opened the skull and stopped the dial.

Fires burn in large oil drums on each corner of the town square.

Outside the theater, just before the large doors that tilt at angles from their shattered hinges, wide, stained advertisements of past diversions still hang from the beams of the entry courtyard. One, from some long-forgotten commedia, depicts Time with his titanic scythe, threatening three young women who kneel and weep and beg for pity, minutes, hours, and days. Under Time's foot the traveler may discern some paraphernalia of the arts in a heap—a viol, a papier-mâché crown, a mask, a script, a tin horn—all crushed, bent, and shattered, and so bespeaking the true value of earthly indulgences.

As he enters the theater lobby, the youth sees an elaborate puppet stage, stained and old, the worn wood still offering glimpses of gold leaf. Its curtains are torn. Its carved arch depicts little plain houses, all in a row, each the same. Three large forms are painted on the front of the theater: a father, a mother, a child. The familiar but cartoonish figures wave blindly at an audience that has long ago departed.

A man emerges from behind the puppet stage. He is dressed in what seems to be a bit of everything: pieces of costume taken from years of productions. A doublet of velvet, coarse cotton pants, a sash of satin. Everything worn and thin.

"Auditions are over," the stage manager says.

"That's okay," says the youth. "I'm not here to audition. I am looking for someone I love. I lost her. Is she here, in the wings?" Then, trying to shape the scene to his need, he says, "I know a play, it begins by the millpond. . . ."

But no. The stage manager cannot be budged.

"Nay, sir, nay. That play is done. As I've said, all the actors but you have gone to their restitution, and what's left of the scenery is not so fine. You'd find the conditions of the stage distressing. All the bladders have burst, and it's a bloody mess back there."

"But I'm not one of the actors. I am here looking for someone!"

The stage manager smiles in incredulity. "Not an actor! By my troth, sir, you jest!"

"It's true. I'm no actor."

"An inactor then? Oh, sir, are they not all the same come performance day? Cannot the inactor play the bawd or the melancholic or the wretch as well as the thespian? Does not your talk, of this and that, declare the nature of your disposition? Does not everyone take that part which is proper to his kind? Ask anyone, actor or inactor, if in the laying out of their parts they choose not those characters which are most agreeing to their inclination, and that they can best discharge believably to a crowd? Oh, sir. All the world's a stage, or so some have said!"

"If that's so, I'd like to wait in the wings, and see something of the production," says the youth.

"I tell you, the show run's over! All the principals have flown excepting your good self. Only the rudest of the mechanicals remain. There is only the epilogue, and it is very small spectacle, I swear."

But the curious youth moves past the stage manager and puts his head beyond the arch of the doorway to see what might be seen on the large main stage below.

On the stage stands a child with an absurdly overdecorated Valentine's Day card. There is white paper glued about the edge in something almost like lace. The word "LOVE" is written in shaky script across the paper heart, and the child looks to the side of the stage for Love's entrance. Briskly, in walks his fourth-grade teacher. Her low heels clip across the wooden boards, and the child smiles, but looks down. As the teacher approaches him, he raises his arms slightly, elevating the heart to the height of his head. He is offering it to her.

"An old tale!" jeers someone in the shadow-strewn stalls. "Give 'er a kiss, if you love her so!"

The teacher walks past the boy without noticing the paper heart. She sits at her desk and busies herself. The school day is nearly done.

The boy with the heart waits a moment, unsure if he should approach. But then he walks up to her desk and holds his heart out to her.

She laughs. "This is sweet," she says. "Oh, Silas. For me?"

The child nods.

She takes the heart and sets it on a pile of paper on the very edge of her desk.

As the boy walks back to his seat, a bell rings. All the children run from the room. The boy follows them. Outside, he sits by a tree, waiting for one of his parents to come and take him home.

Offstage: the sound of birdcall made with a device.

Light laughter from the audience.

The boy watches the teacher come out of the classroom. She is hold-ing her purse and a stack of papers. She pauses to wave to a colleague. The boy's paper heart slips from the stack and floats to the ground behind her. She does not see that it has fallen. The boy already knows that when she gets home and puts the papers on the table, she will not notice the heart is gone.

The boy sees his heart on the ground. He presses his face into his knees and covers his head with his hands.

More laughter from the audience.

The youth has seen enough of the play, but before he can turn back to the stage manager, he hears a scratching sound, a tearing at the floor-boards somewhere past the door, farther down among the distant rows.

"What was that?"

"Well, sir. You know how it flies with such as them. The folk of few words will always grub about for more lines, and then go mad with hunger between seasons."

Down in the darkening theater, the remaining floor lights go out. Growls come crawling from among the empty seats, and worse and louder cries leap up from the orchestra pit.

The youth steps back from the doorway where the carpet runs red and down the aisle.

"Come back to the lobby, sir, I pray you. There awaits diversion in keeping with your station. There'll be a bit of farce left, I warrant you! We're done with historicals and comedicals. Why not a bit of farce, then, before we shut our doors and go home to our own tragedies, eh?"

Behind him, the youth hears the sound of the swazzle growing louder like the approach of locusts. As the noise becomes a din, he raises his hands to his ears to block it out. But then the awful noise crests and swings into a singing voice, a buzzing, jovial, mocking song.

The youth returns to the puppet stage. The thin walls shake from motion within. Two puppets rise up and jerk this way and that, finally turning out to the audience.

The Judy puppet, wearing a necklace of little paste pearls, holds a tiny parcel, their baby. She shakes the baby frantically and screams.

"What's all this, then?" cries Punch, swinging a pocket watch too casually.

"Something's happened to the ba-beeeeeee!" screams Judy, flinging the child at Punch, who catches it awkwardly.

"He won't laugh," says Judy.

"Babies don't." Punch laughs. "He's fine as a fiddle."

"All right," says Judy, instantly recovered. "I'll go shopping, then!" She drops below the stage and emerges a moment later carrying a large purse.

Punch stands there holding the baby. "Who'll watch the child while you're away, missus?" asks Punch, his dangling legs clacking. He looks at the baby and says, "Quiet down, you! Quit your chirping!"

Punch sings a song.

Hush-a-bye, little brat, aye, aye;
Hush-a-bye, little brat, aye.

But before Punch can finish his tune, a crowd of ghosts appears from the side of the stage. They cry "BOO!" frightening Punch, who throws the baby out the window.

Judy returns, her arms filled with boxes, and asks, "Where is the baby?"

Punch sings, "That bird has flown!"

A small bird on a wire drops from the top of the stage and flits about their heads. Punch checks the time on his pocket watch. Dashes offstage and gets a net. He tries to catch the bird. He knocks Judy down. He runs back and forth, but finally catches the bird in his net.

"There's your nestling, missus!" cries Punch, showing Judy the *captured bird struggling in the net. He hands her the net.*

Judy carefully takes out the little bird and looks it over.

"Them's no babe in arms!" she cries, handing it back to Punch.

"It is if you holds it, deario!" says Punch, who throws the bird back to her. "Now you rears it up proper! For here's our little bird come back to the nest once more!"

The ghosts gather again, now at both sides of the stage, beckoning to Punch, who has started singing, "Rum ti tum ti iddity um. Pop goes—"

"BOO!" shout the ghosts.

Punch chases them. As he passes, Punch leans over the edge of the stage, bowing. "Now I must away, to earn our crust, or hell's to pay," he sings. Judy bows. The ghosts return and bow. All the puppets drop below and the little curtain draws shut.

The youth, slightly pale now, looks to the stage manager and says, "If my love isn't here, I have to go."

"You are welcome back for the season, sir!" replies the stage manager distractedly, eager for home or a drink at some public house. Then he bows reverently to the youth, once, twice, three times. He rises, but does not look into the youth's eyes. "Death is always welcome, sir. Think of our little playhouse of life's longings as your home away from home . . . as your summer cottage. Love and Death are old friends, sir. Why, they're lovers, as you know well, sir. Oh, how they tussle and tup. But Death is always on top. Every time. If we could only fall in love with Death, then, oh, how long and majestical our play might be. . . . Death loves us, oh most certainly, most deeply and sincerely, but ever and ever, his love is unrequited . . . how we do fight him! So, Death gives us back the blow and does not even close our eyes or kiss our cheek after he lays us low, you see, because we've broken his heart so many times."

The youth cannot hear any more. The youth cries out, "Cedo Nulli! Nulli! Fall away from the earth, all of you!"

All the footlights go dark, but the youth hears a trapdoor being thrown open and the awful sucking sound of air and souls being drawn swiftly into the traproom, into the abyss. In the midst of this lamentable third act, the youth takes his leave of the playhouse and walks until the air grows moist, where tall reeds stand stiff with frost and sorrow at the edges of the millpond.

. . . they see imprisoned in the transparent stone
the lonely water which winter did not freeze.
Placing their thirsty lips upon the dry crystal
they press useless kisses on that icy stone
that holds within the waters that are their chief desire.
—CLAUDIAN, FROM "ON A CRYSTAL ENCLOSING A DROP
OF WATER," TRANSLATED BY AMOS UMBER

Who calls the dead
from quiet sleep
Shall the huntsman's
vengeance reap.
— FROM *CHILDREN'S RHYMES AND TALES FROM
THE LICHPORT NARROWS*, BY RICHARD UMBER

MORNING AND MIDNIGHT BOTH DID FIND
THIS KNIGHT AT HUNTING. FROM CHASE
OF EVERY CREATURE, OR OF POOR
MAIDENS, ONDINES, AND MOSS LADIES,
HE DID NOT CEASE. HE LIVED FOR
NOTHING BUT CAPTURE AND KILL, AND
FOR THE BLOOD OF HIS ENEMIES, HE
WAS MOST RELENTLESS. AS OLD AGE
BEGAN ITS APPROACH, THE KNIGHT FOR
A MOMENT SLOWED HIS HORSE. HE
LOOKED TO HEAVEN AND PRAYED ALOUD.
"LORD," HE DEMANDED, "LET ME HUNT
UNTIL THE DAY OF JUDGMENT COMES!"
SILENCE FELL UPON THE FOREST,

AND THE KNIGHT SPURRED HIS HORSE ON AND EVER ON, AND WHEN DEATH CAME FOR HIM, THE HUNTSMAN PAUSED HARDLY AT ALL, BUT SOON ROSE UP FROM HIS TOMB AND SET OUT ONCE MORE UPON HIS TERRIBLE PURSUITS. AND BY THIS, GOODE READER, KNOW 'TWAS THE DEVIL, AND NOT GOD, HAD GRANTED THE HUNTSMAN'S PRAYER.

—TRANSCRIBED BY AMOS UMBER FROM THE BOOK
THE DARK AND DIABOLICAL HUNTSMAN, HIS KITH AND KIN,
BY JOHN BROMYARD (CIRCA FIFTEENTH CENTURY)

CHAPTER 19

FIRE AND WATER

THE MILLPOND LAY FROZEN AND GLISTENING under a watching moon.

The quiet of the place put a loneliness on Silas heavy as iron and dagger-sharp. Beyond the pond, even the marshes were silent. No birdcall broke the silence winter had settled on the land. Each reed stood separate from its neighbor. When Silas shifted his weight, his shoes grated against the icebound edge of the pond, but even that sound seemed faint and distant.

Silas could feel Beatrice somewhere below. The longer he stood quietly among the sharp reeds, the more he thought he could hear her crying.

He looked about. Cold land under a cold moon. Nothing more. Even with the death watch stopped, the landscape was totally familiar. Except for the ice, it was no different from the millpond he had visited before. Again, the boundaries had blurred. His world, the otherworld: indistinguishable.

Silas stepped onto the ice. The surface of the pond was frozen completely solid. He knelt down and listened. About the pond, trees bent and moaned with the weight of snow on their branches. With each gust of wind came the sound of grating and cracking as reeds stirred and splintered the ice clinging to their stalks. He leaned over and brushed the scattered snow away from the surface. Blue-green glass shone up and caught his reflection.

Below, something whimpered and cried. Had it said his name? Silas leaned closer and looked through the ice.

There was only darkness beneath the surface at first, but he moved aside, and moonlight fell through the ice. Ripples of water below, like quick fish, flashed in the pale light.

He pressed his face against the surface, as though his warm, unkissed cheek alone might melt it. Maybe the closeness of his affection could summon the girl's ghost. He could feel the thickness of the ice pressing back. He set his hand to it and felt his skin briefly freeze to the surface. As he looked down, he thought he could discern something else moving below. No mere play of moonlight, something was stirring up the mud. He struck the ice with his fist. It was heavy and solid. He would never be able to break through it. Not even with an ax.

And what of the binding? Three women he loved wove the spell . . . three strong women. Even if he could loosen or break their binding, what would happen to them?

The more he looked at the cold, ironclad surface of the pond, the more he allowed its solidity to weaken his faith in himself.

Silas rose, standing on the ice.

The fact was, the state of the pond was a different kind of reality from the spell that was holding Bea. They were not the same, although those two realities had become bound together and certainly the ice was deliberately made part of the binding, a condition of the spell. If he waited until the spring thaw, he believed he would have less trouble releasing Bea. But he didn't want to wait anymore.

When Bea had drowned here, that tragedy, her corpse sinking to the bottom, had made the pond lych, hallowed by the presence of her corpse. Her bones remained at the bottom. The pond was then especially subject to his power as Undertaker, and as Janus, guardian of the thresholds of the dead. And now he could, if he wished, call upon other, even more ancient names. He'd been thinking too literally about the problem. Instead, he'd open a door for her. He didn't have to dig her out, or break the spell in a conventional way. He would open the lych way *through* the pond, through the binding, and bring her to him.

"I open the door. Let this way be open to me and to any I call. I, Janus of the threshold, open the door!" And he threw both his arms wide as he'd done at Arvale. The air seemed to condense over the millpond, and a crack formed at the center of its surface. Swiftly water welled up and began to freeze again. But from across the ice, flickers of cold blue fire rose, and pale shadows lengthened below the moon. Perhaps others had died here. Silas looked at the rising veils of mist and could barely discern their faces, but his heart told him Bea was not among them. She was still down there, held by the binding, by the formidable wills of the three strongest women he knew. But those women did not love her, and he did. In his memory, she was still free. He could see clearly with his heart: their walks through the town and among the graves of the past . . . he could hear her voice, singing to him.

He put aside the words of formality and compulsion. He didn't need to summon her. They were bound with something stronger than fear, something more enduring.

He leaned down and whispered to the frozen water.

"Beatrice, please come back to me. Don't stay here, love, in this cold place, alone. I have not forgotten you. I have felt you in my dreams. Reach up now and take my hand and we'll go home together. Beatrice, my love, my love, come back to me."

A cloud flew across the moon, and for an instant the land was completely dark.

"Come to me, Beatrice, please!"

Before him and a little away, mist came up from the ice. Silas's heart jumped.

Beatrice's ghost hung in the air above the millpond, her eyes closed and her lips quivering.

"My love left me here. . . . ," she whispered.

"No, Bea. I *am* here. Come to me!" Silas implored and held out his arms. "Please, come."

Beatrice opened her eyes and raised her hand, pointing one slim finger toward Silas. Was it recognition or indictment? Silas couldn't tell. As he held out his hands to her, Bea's eyes opened wider, and she trembled above the ice.

"Come to me . . . ," Silas implored.

From behind him, a familiar voice cracked the air like the firing of a cannon. Silas felt a blast of heat singe his neck.

"Enough, Silas Umber. I am come. Shout again, and you might wake the dead!"

Silas turned around. He held his arm in front of his face to shield it from the conflagration swirling about the ghost of Cabel Umber, who was seated on top of a horse made all of burning wood and bones. As the ghost laughed, the horse reared its head, screamed, and threw its flaming mane from side to side.

He knew now, without question, that this was the fiery specter he'd seen at Temple Street. Silas shouted, "Cabel Umber, stop!"

Before Silas could say more, Cabel Umber continued, his words wrapped in smoke and disdain as he spoke them.

"You see, Silas Umber? We are met again, just as I foretold."

Silas stared but took a few steps back, trying to get closer to Bea. Despite the heat pouring off Cabel's ghost, Silas could not look away from him. His thoughts turned several ways at once, each a dead end. He could work no spell against the ghost of Cabel Umber, because behind Silas, Beatrice stood newly risen from the waters. He could not run, because he was standing on the ice and the fiery ghost blocked the homeward path. How could he protect Bea, when the last time he'd met Cabel Umber, he'd not even been able to protect himself?

"What is this? No greeting for your kin? This is cold comfort indeed, sir. But, as I have traveled only to see you, let me be brief. You are in debt to me, Silas Umber. You cannot deny this. We had a bargain and you have broken it. In truth, I think this was for the best. For now I am here and may make of this new world what I will. Also this: All of what is yours is mine. You were warned when last we spoke, were you not?"

Silas ignored the speech. Instead, he held his ground, and trying to be as specific as possible, spat words meant to work upon the fiery spirit and no other.

"Cabel Umber of Arvale, you are not welcome here. Go now! Go back to that place where once you were imprisoned. Do not return here. I, the Undertaker of Lichport and Janus of Arvale, command and compel you! Crawl back to where you were before! Go now!"

The wind rose and whipped the snow up from the pond's surface and into the air about them.

Cabel Umber sat upon his horse, unmoved, a corona of scarlet fire about his head.

"Stirring words, little cousin. You might have been a troubadour with your fine voice. But I pray you, play us another tune."

Reaching down into his mind for more and elder words of power, spells older than Cabel Umber, Silas shouted lines from the *Book of the Dead*, "You are the snake that hides in the marshes. Return now to your black cavern. Go below the waters. Do not breathe the air. Do not return. Do not see the sky again. It is the Lord of the West who speaks these words."

The ghost's horse shuddered and reared. Cabel Umber turned and looked at Silas with surprise. "Now, Silas Umber, that is old magic indeed. I reckon, if it were not as it is between us, I should even now be finding some dark hole to lie up in. But, if we are done with playacting, let me speak to you a few needful words. There is nothing you can do to bind or harm me. Nothing. This is Old Law. Your unpaid debt renders you ineffectual where I am concerned. Shout what you will. Curse me, if you like. It will come to naught. While I do not know how you slipped the noose of the curse I set upon you, rest assured your being yet alive only compounds the debt owed to me. Had you only died, why, then, I might never have come unto this place. I thank you."

Silas turned his head and whispered frantically to Bea, "Go back, Beatrice. Or go to my house. Hide, please. Hide!" Her eyes were blank and her whole body shook into a blur.

Cabel Umber smiled with the half of his face still capable of a grin.

"Now it is my turn to show how it shall be between us. What is yours is *mine*."

Cabel Umber raised his arm in threat and spurred his horse forward into the air between them, casting sparks and embers across the surface of the millpond as it landed. Silas jumped to the side to avoid being struck and fell hard on the ice. Cabel did not stop but drove his horse directly into Bea. Smoke enveloped them, and an instant later, when the air blew clear, Beatrice had been pulled up and across the front of the horse. She lay over the creature's fiery mane, Cabel's hand pressed down on her back. Her eyes were closed, and flames spread hungrily over her body.

"Stop! Stop!" Silas screamed. "I'll give you anything you want! Anything!"

"I know you will," said Cabel with a sneer. "There is only one more thing I desire from you, and now I shall have that, too! No need for you to make a gift of what I am owed already and can take easily enough." From the horse's side, Cabel Umber drew up a bar of iron, hot and burning red as an ingot fresh from the forge.

"Please, just let her go when it's done, okay? She is nothing to you."

"Don't be absurd. She is something to you, and that makes

her demise, even as she is, marvelous to my eyes." He stroked her hair, which steamed below his hands. "Besides, she reminds me of someone I lost long ago . . . a child who ran from me, a daughter who, with your help, fled that most just punishment she might have received from her father's hands."

The horse walked toward Silas, and Cabel raised his arm above his head, preparing to strike.

Silas closed his eyes, but the blow did not come.

The spectral horse moaned and moved backward, farther out onto the ice. Cabel Umber shouted, "Hold! Hold, damn you!"

A strange and graceful harmony began to cut through the cold air. Music was drifting across the reeds. The specter's horse stopped, suddenly incapable of motion. The flames circling Cabel's head lessened. Everything about the ghost seemed to fray as the music rose louder. Above, the stars brightened, and in their light, the edges of Cabel Umber's ghost began to thin. Through Cabel's body, and his horse's, Silas could now just make out the steeples of Lichport in the distance. In what remained of Cabel's eyes, Silas could see fear. The music and its effect had caught him off guard. Silas moved across the ice toward them, hoping he might be able to draw Bea away.

The music was unlike anything Silas had ever heard. It was both soft and sharp at once, and composed of celestial grace. It held a harmony beyond earthly things.

Cabel Umber had heard enough. He swung the horse about and, holding Bea tightly with one hand, pulled back sharply on the reins with the other. The horse kicked its back legs, sending burning shards of bone into the air, then leapt up, coming down on the ice close by the shoreline. Cabel shouted something in a language Silas did not know, and the earth tore open. The horse, the huntsmen, and his quarry crashed down into the darkness.

Clouds of steam flew up hissing, but the spectral fires were gone, and Silas was alone once more among the cold, brown reeds. The massive hole filled up with mossy water and immediately began to freeze.

"Beatrice!" Silas cried, jumping toward the edge of the millpond, but she was nowhere to be seen. Except for the fragments of bone and ash strewn across the ground and still floating in the air, it was as though the ghost of Cabel Umber had never been there. Mist turned and drifted on the icy surface of the pond. He could see nothing below the surface.

Silas sat on the ice. He was freezing and exhausted, and the only things he knew with any certainty were there was nothing more he could do tonight, and that now matters were worse. Before he'd summoned Bea, at least he knew where she was. Now she might be anywhere. Silas unbound the hand of the death watch and pushed it into his pocket.

With the death watch ticking once more, Silas was surprised to hear the unearthly music continue. It grew louder and filled his mind with its harmonies. Silas looked up, trying to see where it might be coming from. The stars were brilliant in the winter sky, and he thought for a moment, perhaps affected by the cold, that the music was somehow descending from the spheres above and drifting down to the earth.

He stood up.

He tried to think of what he was going to do next, how he might find Bea, but the music was all about him. His thoughts were thin and would not hold together. He relented and allowed the music to wash over him. He could not do otherwise. So the song of the stars was in his ears and in his eyes, and it drew him away from the millpond.

Pluto is represented as the grim, stern ruler over hell. He is also called Hades and Orcus. He has a throne of sulfur. He is described as being well qualified for his position, being inexorable and deaf to supplications, and an object of aversion to both gods and men. From his realm, there is no return, and all mankind, sooner or later, are sure to be gathered into his kingdom. As none of the goddesses would marry the stern, gloomy god, he seized Persephone . . . and opened the earth and carried her through into his dominion.

—FROM *THE MUSEUM OF ANTIQUITY*, BY L. W. YAGGY AND
T. L. HAINES, 1883

The swift necessity of the Undertaker's task
be chiefly this: Dissolution. The longer
a ghost remains in this circle of the world,
the longer a spirit may be left to harass the
living, the more mightie it may then become
and the harder it shalle be to finally put
it down. Those ghosts, left to haunt their
ancient piles, retain and darken the habitual
thoughts and ways they worked in life.
And so the ghost of a prince, or a master

of slaves, or a huntsman shalle, in death,
hold scepter, whip, and chase over any lesser
spirits about them, and shall much annoy the
unfortunate living with whom they share a
habitation.

— JONAS UMBER, FROM HIS TRACT "PUT THEM DOWNE
 WITH SPEEDE"

CHAPTER 20

A WORD OF WELCOME

CABEL UMBER HAD NEVER HEARD MUSIC like that before.

The terrible sounds had thrown the light of the stars into his face like broken shards of glass and had driven him back down into the earth, where mud and rock and soil muffled the awful music of the spheres.

But his quarry was still over the saddle. So enough. Time for more mischief later. Why not pause and take a moment and examine his prize?

The girl was lovely. So young. And there was a knowingness in her face. She was willful, he could tell. How her father must have hated her.

She sobbed. But that was nothing. She did not yet know what wonders lay in store.

"Be collected, child," Cabel said to her. "Listen only to my voice."

Fear drew over her face like a ragged veil.

"Beatrice . . . Beatrice . . . Beatrice." Saying her name was part of the spell. Now she could not depart. With her name, with his voice, he bound her to this place.

"Just us now, Beatrice. No more worries. I shall keep you here with me."

Softly, as though for the first time, Bea spoke. "I am longing to be elsewhere, where my love is hid."

"But you are on the doorstep of your new home. Be collected. Be all within. Dry your eyes. You are where you must be."

She looked around, at the statues of the monstrous gods of the earth and sunken places. She wept louder and cried, "Where are we?"

"Hush, child, hush," he said, grinding his teeth between the words.

"Please . . . what is this place?" Her words were soft, weak, and barely held the air.

Cabel Umber lifted up her face by the chin and showed his teeth. "The new hell," he said, laughing, "but you may call it 'home.'"

CHAPTER 21

LAMENT

BEATRICE STOOD, UNABLE TO MOVE. Fire was before and behind her.

Her mind was smoke.

There was nothing to hold on to.

She closed her eyes but could still feel the flames. Not only their heat, but their hunger. She spoke to herself. She made words in her mind to keep herself from falling to pieces, to keep the flames away.

Where are the things that are mine?
The white things
in the water
are far from me

I cannot be.
I cannot be
here

Where is solace?
Where is my thyme?
The time he gave to me?

I cannot be
Here

It laughs at me
through the darkness

Let love come for me
Let love carry me
Let my love come back for me

How will he find me
My love?

I am not there
with the white things that are mine
I am in the burning place
Let my love come for me
through the fire
through the flames

Let me be
Let me be
Let me be

BUT THE SPIRIT OF THE LORD
DEPARTED FROM SAUL, AND AN EVIL
SPIRIT FROM THE LORD TROUBLED HIM.
AND SAUL'S SERVANTS SAID UNTO
HIM, BEHOLD NOW, AN EVIL SPIRIT
FROM GOD TROUBLETH THEE. LET OUR
LORD NOW COMMAND THY SERVANTS,
WHICH ARE BEFORE THEE, TO SEEK
OUT A MAN, WHO IS A CUNNING
PLAYER ON AN HARP: AND IT SHALL
COME TO PASS, WHEN THE EVIL SPIRIT
FROM GOD IS UPON THEE, THAT HE
SHALL PLAY WITH HIS HAND, AND THOU
SHALT BE WELL.

—I SAMUEL, 16:14–16. MARGINALIA OF AMOS UMBER

COME, CHEERFUL DAY, PART OF MY LIFE, TO ME;
FOR WHILE THOU VIEW'ST ME WITH THY FADING LIGHT,
PART OF MY LIFE DOTH STILL DEPART WITH THEE,
AND I STILL ONWARD HASTE TO MY LAST NIGHT.
TIME'S FATAL WINGS DO EVER FORWARD FLY,
SO EVERY DAY WE LIVE A DAY WE DIE.
BUT, O YE NIGHTS, ORDAINED FOR BARREN REST,
HOW ARE MY DAYS DEPRIVED OF LIFE IN YOU;
WHEN HEAVY SLEEP MY SOUL HATH DISPOSSESSED
BY FEIGNED DEATH LIFE SWEETLY TO RENEW.
PART OF MY LIFE IN THAT YOU LIFE DENY;
SO EVERY DAY WE LIVE A DAY WE DIE.

—THOMAS CAMPION (1567–1620). MARGINALIA OF
AMOS UMBER

CHAPTER 22

HARMONIES

DESPITE THE COLD, MRS. BOWE'S WINDOW was open, and music poured from her parlor and into the street. Silas could hear no other sound, and nothing he saw on the street distracted him from following the music to its source: not the locking of doors, not the drawing of curtains as he passed. The crack of the breaking of ice, the chaotic clamor of the ghostly rider, all previous frights had been suppressed in his mind, or rather dissolved. Even his fear for Bea was softened by what he heard. He followed the music like a spell—those beautiful and unearthly sounds—right up to Mrs. Bowe's front door.

Before he could knock, he heard her familiar voice.

"Come through," Mrs. Bowe called out to him.

As he opened the door, the music was all about him. He walked slowly toward the parlor and saw Mrs. Bowe standing before a strange device; like a lathe, but on the long iron spindle that ran its length, bowls of glass had been threaded, largest to smallest. On the end was a wooden wheel attached by a cord to a pedal that Mrs. Bowe pumped with her foot, making the bowls spin. She dipped her fingers in a small dish of water and then pressed them to the various bowls. The glass sang.

Not looking up, Mrs. Bowe said, "A glass armonica. This one belonged to my mother. I believe it was the wizard Ben Franklin who made the first on these shores—one of his many and excellent petty sorceries." Mrs. Bowe closed her eyes and kept playing.

"The music of the spheres," said Silas, barely speaking out loud.

"Yes," said Mrs. Bowe.

"Celestial harmonies."

"Indeed."

"All from friction."

"Always. On earth as it is in heaven, music restores order. No chaos, nor evil . . . nor cruelty may endure in the presence of such music as this," Mrs. Bowe said.

On the table close to the mantel, a crystal ball sat with a candle burning by it, its flame wavering in the cold draft from the open window. But there was a great fire on the hearth, and the room was comfortable and warm enough. Seeing the crystal, Silas knew she'd been watching him from a distance. But instead of feeling intruded upon, he was glad. Her careful watch had most likely saved his life at the millpond.

"I am so sorry, Mrs. Bowe. I should never have raised my voice to you before."

"Bless you for saying it, Silas."

"You were playing to help me just now, weren't you?"

"Partly, yes."

"You saw him, then?"

Mrs. Bowe stopped playing. "I did," she said, crossing herself.

"I can't fight him, as things are," said Silas. "I left Arvale in such a way, well . . . nothing I do has any effect on this spirit. Maybe you know some way to bind him, or banish him?"

"Oh, Silas. Whoever or whatever he was in life, that ghost is an old thing. Terrible and mighty he is. Your father would have found him challenging. Against such a malediction, I can be of little help, beyond what I have done. But I fear for you, too. Why did the spirit go to the millpond?"

"To hurt me . . . to kill me."

"But the spirit took her and here you are. So it seems the ghost's intention is to bring you harm by harming others."

"He tried to kill me before, as I left Arvale. There was nothing I could do against him, because . . . I broke a vow to him."

Mrs. Bowe nodded slowly. "So it is as I've said. You are at a stalemate, but he has the advantage: He is here, in your home, among those people and places you love. There is much evil he can work. We have driven him off, but for only a moment. In any event, no one expects the glass armonica. . . . Well, what I could do, I have done. Music is a great power against evil, I believe. Anger is a fire in the heart. Music can wash it away. Fury is cacophony. Music puts all to harmony again. At least for those in whose heart love still resides. That ghost bears no portion of love—that is easy to see—and so the music was anathema to him—painful, I suspect. But it will not surprise him again. This time, by the Heavenly Mother, we were fortunate."

It was too much to think about. Silas had no idea how to get Cabel Umber out of Lichport, or how to destroy him. He might return to Arvale, but who there could help him now? And Silas had no idea if the house was even accessible to him anymore. More importantly, he didn't want to go back there. At least in Lichport, Silas felt he had some advantage because this was a place Cabel did not know. He began to wonder if there might be something more in his uncle's collection of books that might be consulted. Fight fire with fire?

Mrs. Bowe began playing again, and all dark thoughts fled his mind. Silas closed his eyes and asked, "What are you playing now?"

"Just an old parting song, the sort of thing we might play at the end of a gathering if we were feeling wonderfully maudlin. Sometimes, where my family comes from, it would be played at wakes. Would you like to hear some of the words?"

"Please."

In a soft voice, Mrs. Bowe sang.

> *Of all the money e'er I had, I spent it in good company.*
> *And all the harm I've ever done, alas it was to none but me.*
> *And all I've done for want of wit, to mem'ry now I can't recall.*
> *So fill to me the parting glass. Good night and joy be with you all.*
> *Oh, all the comrades e'er I had, they're sorry for my going away,*
> *And all the sweethearts e'er I had, they'd wish me one more day to stay,*
> *But since it falls unto my lot, that I should rise and you should not,*
> *I gently rise and softly call, good night and joy be with you all.* . . .

Mrs. Bowe's voice trailed off, and she brought her fingers away from the glass bowls of the armonica.

"In memory of your mother," Mrs. Bowe said. "She once favored such airs. I am sorry I couldn't attend the funeral, Silas."

"It would have been good to have you there."

"I think you know my feelings on such matters as relate to those folk of your mother's family that go *that way*. There would have been no need for my services in any event. Occasions such as that are not really appropriate for the living, I believe."

"I attended."

"I know you did, dear."

"I was only saying it would have been good to have you with me."

Mrs. Bowe wetted her finger, about to play again, but then paused and asked, "Is your mother truly among *them* now?"

"She is."

Mrs. Bowe gently shook her head. In acceptance or disapproval, Silas couldn't tell.

"And you? Are you well pleased to have her with you still, or does it . . . trouble you?"

"I don't know how to feel, really. I'm trying not to think about it."

Mrs. Bowe pursed her lips slightly. "I miss my father and mother. Their deaths were sad to me, but not mysterious. I love them very much. Love and longing go side by side in death, if all goes as it should. But now—"

"Now I can't mourn her death, can I? I saw her lying dead on the table. So that is in my head. Then I saw her get up. And, of course, we've spoken. She is as she was—mentally, I mean. Better, maybe. More reasonable. So, partly, it's like nothing has happened. But things *have* happened. I saw them. So now what?"

"Dear God, your poor heart, Silas."

"Maybe it's not for me to judge. It is what it is. She is still here. I mean, I don't want her gone. . . . I think she is happy, in her way."

"That does not surprise me. Anyway, it is very hard to avoid family traditions. Sometimes they simply must be accepted as part of ourselves."

Silas nodded. She would know that, of course. As a wailing woman, much of her life had been dictated to her by custom and obligations. And so, he increasingly felt, was his.

"It is especially hard when we are not raised in those traditions and then are forced suddenly to accept them," she said. "Even harder for those *outside* the family to accept."

Silas paused. He could sense she wanted to tell him something.

"There is some talk in town, Silas, about the Restless. And if I've heard it, nearly everyone must know. People are scared."

"So soon?"

"You speak like you know nothing of small towns. Gossip, like the dead, travels fast. A few hours, at most, is all it takes for everyone in the Narrows to know something; another hour or two for news to spread up into higher Lichport if it's gossip worth hearing. Bad news runs fastest of all, for it has fear whipping it along. Don't forget how small this town really is, Silas."

"I know. But why such fear? They know who the Restless are. They're just relatives, neighbors."

"Yes. Some are your relatives. And relatives of others. But most people are displeased to see their kin return to them from their graves. They put them away for a reason. To the others in town, they are simply *The Dead*. Even here, in this necropolis, people fear the dead, Silas."

"But the Restless have been here all along. They are all over Lichport."

"Times have changed. There's no mystery in this. People lay aside their ancient practices and customs as time goes on. It's called assimilation, or wanting to be modern. Why do you think most people have left Lichport? Most folk, you'll now find, just want a quiet life. Such a life doesn't generally include corpses coming for tea."

"It's terrible."

"Silas, if the Restless are known now, it is mostly through stories, or by family members who are trying to forget them. What the people in town see are the dead proceeding out of Newfield and walking out of ruined houses, and they believe you are the one who has called them up and out of their tombs, and that now your mother is one of them."

"Well, that's sort of true. I went to Newfield and invited some to my mother's funeral because it was required. Others came too. It wasn't a secret. What should I do now? How can I speak with everyone, tell them it's okay?"

"You can't. And it's not okay to them. Most people think of where they live as *theirs*. How do you propose to dissuade them from believing that?

"So what are you saying? Some people hate me now?"

"I suspect they fear you more than hate you."

"But I've helped some of them. They loved my father."

"Yes, some loved him, but most feared him too. You really do not understand people at all, do you?

"Not living people, apparently. The dead, it seems, I understand perfectly."

Mrs. Bowe walked over to him.

"Knowledge can be a burden, Silas. We both know that. And what of your recent journey? What did you learn, out there, at that house beyond the marshes?"

"I learned not to look back," he said flatly.

Mrs. Bowe smiled, perhaps trying to draw back the conversation away from recent troubles. She reached out and held his hand.

"So, may we forget our hard words, then? Are we are friends again?"

"I'd like to be, but I think, Mrs. Bowe, I can never be a very good friend to you."

"Why do you say that?"

"Because I know what you need, and you're never going to have it so long as you're close to me."

"And what is that?"

"To feel safe. I will never be safe, and neither will anyone near me. My work will not allow it. But I can't stop. I've crossed the threshold now, and there is no going back."

Mrs. Bowe rolled her eyes and tried to laugh. "Heavenly Mother! But he's his father's son!"

"So, if you can accept that, then I can be your friend. I already know you're mine. You have been from my first day here. A very dear friend."

"Oh, Silas. If you only knew . . . I just don't want to see any more harm come to you. Not after what you've been through, how you came into the world and now your parents, both your parents . . ."

"I can't keep you from trying to help. After tonight, I know I mustn't. But I'm asking you not to work against my wishes without talking to me, please."

"I can do that, Silas."

Silas put his arms around Mrs. Bowe. She gave him a tight squeeze, then kissed his cheek.

"I imagine you have missed your own bed."

"I can't tell you how much."

As Silas turned to make his way back to his side of the house, Mrs. Bowe, hearing the loud squishing of his wet shoes said, "Oh, Silas, the carpets! You really must clean yourself up."

Silas looked back and saw watery footprints behind him. "Oh, sorry, Mrs. Bowe," he said, leaning over, trying to take off his shoe. As he pulled at it, he stumbled backward, bumping into the table holding the crystal and candle. The crystal rocked in its stand but remained where it was. The candle fell over and rolled toward the table edge. In several places, where its wick touched the tablecloth, the lace caught fire. For a brief second, Silas and Mrs. Bowe stared, unable to move. Three flickering blue flames rose from the cloth as the candle rolled off the table and fell to the floor. Silas whipped off his heavy outer coat and threw it over the end of the table, immediately extinguishing the small fires.

Mrs. Bowe was still staring at the air where the flames had been. Her face had gone pale.

"What does it mean?" Silas asked in a low voice.

Mrs. Bowe looked at him and tried to compose herself. "Oh, Silas, there is no need for so much superstition. Besides, there are a hundred ways to read an omen."

But her words rang hollow. Gently, Silas pressed her as he brushed off his coat. "I thought we'd just agreed to be more honest with each other?"

"Yes. You're right." Mrs. Bowe looked intently at the table, at the pattern of the burn marks on the lace. She closed her eyes and slowly turned, raising her hand, pointing to the wall, through it, and beyond. "Look to the east," she said.

Silas pulled his coat on and ran outside.

The moon hung over the town, a pale and distant thing. The stars had fled. In the east, over the Narrows, smoke was rising, and above the uneven rooflines and teetering chimney stacks, the firmament was smeared with blood.

Joyous bird, heir to thine own life!

Death, who weakens the work of all, but gives thee
strength . . .

. . . no destruction shall overcome thee;

Enduring body, you shall live to see the earth
subdued;

Against you the Fates gather not up their threads,
powerless to do thee harm.

—RETRANSLATED BY AMOS UMBER FROM HENDERSON'S

1922 EDITION OF *CLAUDIAN*, VOL. II

CHAPTER 23

BURNT FEATHERS

THREE STARLINGS SAT IN A TREE as the house on the corner of Coach and Silk Streets was burning. On thin cords about the birds' necks, each wore a small bone awl.

In the street in front of the house, before a circle of ashen sigils, stood a specter wearing a sharp-tipped silver crown. He held an iron rod in his hand and pointed at the circle, shouting into the air where cinders rose, gathered, and pressed themselves into foul, winged shapes that flew at the house and added to the fury of the fire.

The starlings coursed swiftly over the Narrows to survey the damage. The roofs of several other houses were burning. It might have been worse. Passing low over the streets, they overheard voices blaming Silas Umber, who "carried grief with him back to Lichport." Who "went out into Newfield and woke the dead." Who "burned some kind of pyre at his mother's funeral," and now "she's one of *them,* and who's to pay the price for all their irregularities? Regular folk, that's who!"

Beating their black, jewel-feathered wings swiftly, the three starlings left the conflagrations and the complaints behind and flew east over the Bowditch family cemetery and down Temple Street. They landed in front of Temple House and there assumed their more habitual forms.

"Well, and hasn't our little man been busy?" said the second of the three.

"Indeed, and haven't we suffered as well for his lack of good sense? Was he born in a barn? Can't he close a door?"

"I think we're owed something," mused the first of the three. "At the very least, a little hospitality."

"Oh, I don't think I could reside with a bachelor," said the third. "Really, I simply cannot abide untidiness."

"Yes, boys make unpleasant roommates. But his is not the only unpaid debt due to us," said the second. "And, if we're all thinking out loud, I must say, I believe it's time we went back to temple living. A house is so common. But a temple . . . that must always be accounted very fine. . . ."

"Here? Truly?" asked the third of the three. "She didn't even invite us to her funeral."

"Indeed," said the first. "She owes us, so I think we shall find the rent most agreeable. And look at the proportions. The house will be more than accommodating. And she hasn't a friend in town to help fill all those rooms. She'll be glad of the company, I warrant you."

"Unlikely," said the third.

All three laughed together.

"Besides," said the second, pulling small downy feathers from her long hair, "Dolores Umber's needlework is more than passable. And now she has so much time to fill. With a little patience, who knows what might yet become of her? I still predict an impressive career could be in her future. All's a bit of a tangle now, but it may come right for us. She may yet serve. Let us look upon her as an investment—"

"And keep a good eye on her," concluded the third.

The three walked up the front path and onto the porch.

"Shall we knock?" asked the second.

The first of the three smiled. "Don't be absurd. This is our home now. Might as well make ourselves comfortable." But as the three moved toward the heavy iron door, it opened. Dolores Umber stood in the doorway, her animated corpse limned in light from the chandelier hanging behind her in the foyer.

"What took you so long?" Dolores said. She clicked her tongue. "Ladies, won't you come in?"

"Yes," said the first without hesitation, striding past Dolores and across the threshold. "We most certainly shall."

At this time, it was not uncommon to learn of dog burials within the smaller and more rural cemeteries and churchyards. It was believed that the spirit of the last body to enter the hallowed ground would become the Watcher, a soul charged with standing guard over the corpses of its fellows. Few aspired to this honor, and the custom of burying a black dog after human interment began. The poor creature's spirit was bound then to the earth, to serve as guardian, until the time of the next burial. But then, another dog might be put in the ground then too, to keep up the watch and save the next human soul the trouble. And so, such burial grounds became like kennels for those who could see them rightly. Leaving aside the general unpleasantness for the poor animals, it must be admitted that this was, and is, a very ancient practice, hearkening back to the foundation and hearth sacrifices of antiquity and perhaps still practiced in the most primitive of towns and villages.

—FROM THE PAMPHLET *GRAVE NEIGHBORS*

BY RICHARD UMBER

Est Nobilis Ira Leonis

"The wrath of the lion is noble"

—MARGINALIA OF RICHARD UMBER

CHAPTER 24

CHASE

THE AIR OF THE TIGHT NARROWS STREETS was thick with smoke.

Narrows folk were running buckets down to the sea and back, hurling water onto the burning roofs of houses.

"What's happened? Did you see who lit the fires?"

Silas moved among them, asking what he could do. Some did not see him. Others turned away, refusing to look him in the eyes as he passed. But Silas could hear them whispering to one another. Some muttered loudly and deliberately.

"The dead are put away for a *reason*," said one.

"They have their place. We have ours."

"They infect the very air!"

"Did you see the bone-fire on Temple Street? Who lit that, I wonder!"

". . . not the first Umber to bring a curse upon the town!"

So they thought he'd done it, or that by going to Newfield before his mother's funeral, he'd called up the dead and the corpses had cursed the town. None of it made any sense. But when he looked at the desperate faces of the people running with their buckets, trying to save their homes, he knew it was fear and not good sense driving their minds.

Silas stepped forward into the middle of the lane, but before he could speak, Joan Peale grabbed his arm and pulled him back against one of the cottages, saying, "It's always the smallest mind that's the first to turn, my mother says. And hasn't tonight proved it!" She moved him out of the lane and under the shadow of a wall.

"Joan! What have they seen?"

"Nothing but the fires. But, Silas, the flames rose up from nowhere. The sound of a horse's hooves rang upon the cobbles and there was terrible laughter in the air. Folks are scared half out of their wits and speak of the Dark Huntsman. I'd have laughed it away—my mother told such tales to me as a child—but, Silas, I saw those fires myself . . . just dropped out of the air and onto the roofs, and I heard the laughter. Can you tell me nothing?"

"They are not entirely wrong. But the specter is not here for you. It's come for me."

"Oh, Silas!"

"I should speak with your mother," he said.

"She has taken ill and gone to her bed. My mother feels so for this town. She whispers in her sleep about it. Her dreams tell her the town harbors an illness, and it must be driven out. She says it will come for the firstborn. She says her illness is a portent of more sickness to come. She told me what's befallen her is what's comin' for others that is first born too. Others have heard her. They think she means you're the cause of this."

"What?"

"I know she doesn't. She loves you like her own son."

"Your mother's right. I was followed from Arvale by a very terrible spirit, and now, unable to kill me, it will continue to put its hatred on Lichport and trouble whatever and whomever it can. It is this spirit who has set the fires in the Narrows. I'll try to find a way to get rid of him, but for now, we must drive him from the Narrows so the fires can be put out. I'll try to lead him away, but I need you to help me."

"If I can help, I will," said Joan.

"Go ring the soul bell."

"Now?"

"The sound of the passing bell keeps evil spirits from harassing the souls of the dead. It may help drive Cabel—" Silas stopped himself. The town already believed that Silas was somehow responsible for the trouble. How much worse would it be if they found out it was one of Silas's own ancestors attacking them? "Joan, evil spirits are driven before the sound of the bell. I think it will help."

"But is it right to ring it when none of our own have died?"

"Joan, someone is always dying. Ring the bell and keep ringing it until the spirit is gone and the fires are out! I'll try to draw him away."

Without another word, Silas ran. His feet pelted the hard cobbles, and twice he slipped on the icy stones of the street. He came up Dogge Alley and turned onto Silk Street, looking up every alley he passed for any sign of Cabel Umber. From what Joan had said, it sounded like no one had actually seen him. As he approached the corner of Coach, he considered using the death watch to find Cabel, but the street was already glowing in reflected fire.

As he looked up, he could hardly believe what he saw.

The house of the Sewing Circle was burning. The front door was thrown open, the threshold wreathed in flames and looking like the mouth of hell. And in that maw stood Cabel Umber, a man-shaped burning brand. Bea was not with him, and Silas imagined her held somewhere dark, beneath the earth, like Cabel Umber's daughter. The thought sickened him.

When he saw Silas, Cabel stormed from the house. Silas backed up just as the top floor of the attic, the room that held the tapestry of the shadowlands, fell in upon itself, flames bursting up and licking at the sky. Embers flew from the furnace the falling structure had become.

As Cabel Umber descended the steps, his horse rose up out of the broken earth beside him, a nightmare of scorched bones and bright coals. The ghost did not speak as he mounted. Instead, he pointed to a hole in the ground just at the base of the house along the foundation. Silas had never seen it before. Looking over, Silas could just see the bones of animals, rotten and old, lining the side of the pit.

"Dogs . . . ," Cabel Umber said, his voice the sound of iron dragged across a stone. He was not speaking to Silas, but to the bones.

From the horse's neck, Cabel pulled forth a fistful of ash and smoldering shards of vertebrae. He crushed them in his hand, hurled them into the pit, and then cast more into the air.

"Dogs!" Cabel Umber roared.

The pit filled with smoke and the bones rattled.

Across the street, the frozen earth in parts of the Garden Plot Cemetery began to tear open. Silas looked over and saw the soil draw apart, revealing several more pits, the old burial plots of the poor dogs set to guard the cemetery.

A low, pained howl broke the air close by.

Cabel Umber looked down at Silas and smiled, the rotten tendons of his jaw tightening. "Dogs . . . ," the ghost said once more with a throat full of malice and conjure.

From the pits, the bone-dogs pawed their way up out of the earth, growling and snapping at one another. Some had portions of shrunken, shredded hides still clinging to them. All were spotted with mold and black earth. Their snarls were wild and rabid, and as they shook their heads, soil flew from dark, hollow eye sockets.

Deep within the Narrows, the soul bell sounded. Cabel's horse reared up, nearly throwing him. Cabel looked back in the direction of the sound and grimaced. With his iron rod he reached down and struck one of the dogs, shattering the bones of its spine as two others leapt forward toward Silas, snapping at the air. Cabel pointed the rod at Silas and more broken howling rose up from across the street. The hunter had chosen his quarry.

Silas ran.

Instinct pushed every thought from his mind but two: Silas didn't want the hellish hunt going back into town. And further down Coach Street lay God's Small Acre, the burial ground where some of Lichport's lost children lay. He couldn't bear the thought of Cabel Umber coming close to that place, or what such a monster might try summon up out of its soil. So Silas ran south, and then down Temple Street.

All the houses on Temple Street were dark. Silas didn't even know if it was night or day. Since he'd returned from Arvale, he moved in one long twilight. The mornings were covered in shadows, and the night sky glowed bloodred. As he ran, the buildings seemed to lean in toward him, and the black outlines of the bare winter trees wove nets across the street before and behind him. Fear flowed freely in him again, and he hated it. There was no light in any of the windows, no human sounds except the rasp of his ragged breath and his feet hitting the cobbles as he ran. Every step made him feel less himself. He'd let titles fill his head with the comfort of authority. Lies. He could call himself whatever he wanted. Undertaker. Osiris, god of the dead. Janus, lord of the threshold. It didn't matter. He was running from shadows like a child.

Ruins of half-fallen homes crouched between the dark-windowed houses. He thought briefly of hiding in one, but the fear of being found and the whole place set on fire while he was inside it kept him running.

The gate of Newfield Cemetery rose up at the end of the

block. If he could lure Cabel Umber in there, at least he could be away from the houses of the living. If he could make it to the tombs of the Restless there, maybe he could find help.

Halfway down Temple Street, Silas risked slowing to look back. He wished he hadn't. Cabel Umber and the pack of corpse dogs flew over and above the ground like a train afire. The dogs slathered smoke and flame as they ran, leaping between the air and ground. When their paws came down, the bones of their feet splintered, and they howled as though they'd been beaten. Greasy, sickly smoke unfurled behind Cabel as he came furiously on. Silas knew there was no way he could outrun them. But he needed to catch his breath, rally, and think, and he desperately wanted something at his back.

At the gates of Newfield, the great bronze lion stood watch over the night. Silas put his foot on the edge of the inscribed plaque and pulled himself up, as he'd done many times before. He stood between the lion's massive paws, its head just above his own, his back pressed into the lion's chest. This had once been his thinking place. He'd sat here with Bea. It was his seat of peace. No longer. At least nothing could get at him from behind, and it felt better not to run.

Cabel Umber and his pack came to a halt just outside the Newfield gates.

Silas began to panic. Even if he hit the ground again at a run, he would never make it to the Egyptian tombs before the fiery host bore down on him. The death watch was no use that he could think of. He leaned back against the statue and felt the bronze warm to him, even with the bitter cold of the air. Deep within the bronze, he remembered, the corpse of a lion lay hidden, saved from death and then given burial by his great-great-grandfather on the Umber side.

From somewhere in his Umber blood swam the words: "The wrath of the lion is noble." He felt the bronze beneath his hand grow warmer. Then more words came. Restless words. Spells of that distant ancient land where, once, a lion had been a god.

He looked out at Cabel Umber. Silas's fears shifted and turned, and where once terror sat, now anger and hatred burned and coiled. Silas stood up between the lion's massive metal paws and pointed down the street at Cabel Umber. Words of summons and command came roaring from his throat.

"I have come across the night, Oh Lion! Mighty One! Powerful One! Beloved of Sekhmet! Bringer of Slaughter! Mine is a heart of carnelian; I will not be overcome. Before me rides my enemy. He has come against me. But who can stand before the arrows of the sun? Or the bright flame of the stalker of the plains? What I will, shall be. I utter these words with my mouth to destroy my enemy; he has come against me, and he shall not escape." Leaning his head back against the lion's massive head, Silas whispered, "And for the love of my great-great-grandfather who saved and loved you, help me."

From inside the statue, Silas heard and felt a low growl vibrate up through the bronze and into his body. A dry wind purled up from some other, warmer world and swirled about the monument. Silas felt something pull away below his feet.

Light shone from the monument like the glare of the sun at midday, and in the street before the Newfield gates, the golden ghost of the lion stood. It threw its mane from side to side in splendor and moved low across the ground. Without warning, the lion sprang from its crouch and took the neck of Cabel's horse in its jaws. Its teeth locked upon the horse, and it jerked its head to the side, ripping the mount out from beneath its spectral rider. Cabel Umber briefly faded, but then appeared, dimly, among the pack of dogs.

Throwing the horse to the ground, the lion broke every part of it, tearing bone from board until nothing remained.

Then the lion looked up.

"Dog," Silas said, pointing at Cabel Umber.

The lion did not hesitate, but leapt across the air toward Cabel, who, retreating before the animal's noble wrath, fell away through a rain of ash, and so fled into the earth.

Their master gone, the dogs grew still, their hungry fires extinguished. Some howled pathetically. All dropped to the ground in heaps of bone and tattered skin.

Silas descended from the statue and slowly approached the ghostly lion who stood in the middle of Fairwell Street. But as he reached out to touch its mane, the ghost passed through him, returning to its place of rest, its tomb, within the heart of the bronze memorial.

He was alone again, standing before the gates of Newfield. Lights burned in the houses farther east down Temple Street. In front of a few of them, the Halliwell house, others, piles of broken boards and rotten wood had been stacked up and lit. These fires were not Cabel Umber's doing. The townsfolk had built these bonfires.

Silas hung his head, still breathing hard.

Here in Lichport a medieval paranoia had taken root. Folk were trying to burn away a plague they feared the dead had carried home.

LEDGER

Full fathom five thy father lies;
Of his bones are coral made;
Those are pearls that were his eyes;
Nothing of him that doth fade,
But doth suffer a sea-change
Into something rich and strange.
—FROM SHAKESPEARE'S *THE TEMPEST*. MARGINALIA OF
AMOS UMBER

But where is he,
   the pilgrim of my song,
The being who upheld it through
   the past?
Methinks he cometh late
   and tarries long.
He is no more—
   these breathings are his last;
His wanderings done,
   his visions ebbing fast,
And he himself as nothing:
   —if he was
Aught but a phantasy,
   and could be classed
With forms which live and suffer—
   let that pass—
His shadow fades away into
   Destruction's mass. . . .
—LORD BYRON, FROM "CHILDE HAROLD'S PILGRIMAGE."
   MARGINALIA OF AMOS UMBER

CHAPTER 25

FROM BEFORE

INSTEAD OF RETURNING TO THE NARROWS, near broken with exhaustion and cold, Silas walked slowly home. He knelt before the fireplace in his study and blew the fire from the match to flame among the kindling. As the logs caught fire, he rose, then slumped into the chair in front of his desk. His legs and feet were sore from running on the cobbles.

He was too tired even to go upstairs to bed. Mrs. Bowe had left him a little tray with some bread, cheese, and fruit. He'd eat something and then fall asleep in the high, soft chair close to the fire.

Everything on his desk lay just as he'd left it when returning from his mother's funeral. He wasn't even sure if he should call it a funeral. What was it? A birthday? A restoration? An awakening? His mind was making a circle of itself. Enough.

Without looking up, Silas fumbled for the fob of the desk lamp and turned it on. He idly pulled at the papers he'd carried back from Temple House, glancing at one, reading a sentence or two before dropping it and picking up another. There were his notes from Uncle's dark books of life and death. Some loose papers, legal stuff about Temple House, and the envelope his mom said contained some more of his dad's things.

Curiosity got the better of him. He opened the envelope and poured its contents onto the desk. Here was a diary in his dad's handwriting. Not an essay, or work notes, but personal writing by his father.

The diary was little more than a small collection of scraps tied between two stained, torn covers. Most of the entries were written on different kinds of paper. The lower portions of the covers were burnt along with the edges, as though it had once been thrown into and quickly retrieved from a fire. As Silas opened it, the spine broke and the scraps slid from the covers. It looked like most of the sheets had been culled from other notebooks, the personal entries all bound up, taken away, or hidden. Maybe even after his dad's disappearance. He saw no dates, and there appeared to be no chronology. He was sure he could feel Mrs. Bowe's hand in this somewhere. Maybe she'd swiftly gathered these from various notebooks sometime after Silas's arrival and then sent them to his mom . . . but what was the point in accusing her now? As his eyes passed over portions of the text, he couldn't blame her, or his mother, for having wanted to keep it from him. Here were his father's private thoughts; things no father would want his son to read.

Silas's eyes flashed over the words. The subjects of the entries were various. Bits of things Amos wanted to remember or around which his own mind circled. Most of the entries, it seemed at first glance, related to Silas in one way or another. These were writings about him. Somehow, he felt in his gut, they were *all* about him.

◆ ◆ ◆

The archaic name for one of the best known Shadowlands remains the Bosom of Abraham. Explanations for this phrase abound, but I think it goes deeper than accepted understanding of an afterlife of repose, as one reclines at table, his head upon the bosom of the guest next to him. Or the more sentimental interpretation of the dead as children who come to sit upon the knee of the parent in the hereafter. I have walked its paths and seen more than guests at table. More than children taken up upon the laps of their parents.

The presiding genius loci of this zone is Abraham himself. Abraham of the mountain. The father who was only too glad to offer up his son. Abraham the Obedient. I admit, my own fears may have shaped this shadowland to themselves. But how can it be other, for now a father gives his firstborn not to the god, but to the world. Leaves the babe upon the altar of experience to shift for itself. Every morning that I leave Saltsbridge for Lichport, I walk that path onto the mountain to the altar. I utter the obedient "I will." And I place my son upon the stone. But then, there is no ram that comes to stay my hand. The altar of the world holds fast to my child, and I cannot reclaim him to my bosom. . . .

From the medieval play:

"GOD
Mine angel, fast hie thee thy way,
And unto middle-earth anon thou go.
Abraham's heart now will I assay
Whether that he be steadfast or no.
Say I command him for to take
Isaac his son that he loveth so weel,
And sacrifice with his blood he make
If of my friendship he will feel.
Show him the way unto the hill
Where that his sacrifice shall be.
I shall assay now his good will,
Whether he loveth better his child or Me.
All men shall take example by him
How my commandments they shall fulfill."

And I feel the contempt God had for Abraham. How, even now, He would assay my own heart for the joy of cruelty because I hide away behind the masks of other gods. Darker gods. Or perhaps it's merely about the weight of obligations. The gods know well the love we bear our children, and they cannot bear the love of another to come before our love for them.

After one week in the sixth grade, Silas told us at dinner tonight that he wouldn't be going to school anymore. Dolores laughed it away, but I could see by the look on his face that he was serious. He was adamant about not wanting to go. Did something happen today, son? I asked him. He didn't say anything. Did one of the other kids do something to you? I asked. Dolores said not to feed into it. Let it be. He'd get over it. I asked him what he'd do with his time if he stopped going to school. He looked at me and said he would go to work with me. I can help you, Dad. That's what he said. And the way he looked at me . . . I thought maybe we'd made the wrong decision, that maybe there was something else I could have done to make Lichport home for us. To make it okay for Dolores. So Silas just looked at me, like he was waiting for me to tell him it was fine for him to stop going to school, fine for him to start working with me tomorrow. I wasn't sure what to say, but Dolores spoke out, loudly. Don't encourage him, she told me. How's he going to be a man if we pick him up and coddle him every time he falls down? I said that she should know right now that it would be my intention to pick him up when he fell. Every time. Just like the first time. I was there. I would always be there. Of course, it stank of a lie the minute I said it. What I should have said was I would always want to be there. That much was true, would always be true. Dinner ended when Dolores told him to go lay out his clothes for school the next day. I will never forget how he looked at me then, the pain of our betrayal reddening his eyes.

The sad epilogue to tonight's dinnertime tale is that Silas cried himself to sleep, me at his side as he sobbed about how much he didn't want to go back to school and how he wants to be somewhere that has art class where they don't tell you what to make in advance. Apparently after the kids were told to draw the place they wanted to live when they grew up, Silas drew a cave or something from his imaginary storyland, something dark, and the teacher got upset and told him to throw it out. *Why can't I draw what I see?* he kept asking me. But of course—he senses and I know—it isn't about a drawing. It's about being allowed to see the world in his own way, our way. He can feel here in Saltsbridge, away from all the old familiar eccentricities of Lichport, that this world, the world where the work of our family cannot be spoken of, this world is waiting to crush him. He can already feel its pressures. It absolutely breaks my heart. We are engaged in the same battles, he in his world, me in mine. We are both keenly aware of the sameness of it all here in Saltsbridge. The same pointless busy work for everyone. Hearing him talk about how he hated everyone having to read the same story at the same time made me feel like I was suffocating. If they knew what was waiting for them, the kind of afterlives they were building for themselves, brick by brick, worksheet by tiresome worksheet, well . . . they couldn't face it. Silas knows, though. Somewhere deep inside him, he senses what people are making for themselves and he rejects it.

Christ. We could have stayed back in Lichport. . . . And all the while there is birdsong, telling me over and over how short are the moments before we are alone again. How isolated my son must feel, sitting in the classroom, other children buzzing about him, no one speaking directly to him or waiting for him to respond to anything that's said. How he must sit there and stare at people and try to put his mind elsewhere. My heart. I must not speak of it! Yet I know he feels but cannot understand what I have done to him . . . what I have kept from him. Others sense it too, that Silas is missing something, that he is not like them, that he is somehow and fundamentally incomplete.

Two days ago I banished under compulsion a furious ghost from a house on Garden. I begged for it to take the waters, but it couldn't find footing within itself. The next day, I was here in Saltsbridge mowing the lawn. Now I sit at the kitchen table writing line after line of this self-indulgent crap so I feel like I have some control while upstairs, I can hear my son softly sobbing. It's moments like this I wonder what's the point in lying to him about my life. Why not tell him? Say the words and watch his eyes go wide as he feels the world he knew fall away and the ground open up beneath him. At least then we'd be falling together.

The Fears have come. Omens are everywhere throughout the town. No one speaks of them, and that makes it worse. Now that the Fears have flown in and Dolores is pregnant, all I can think of is what manner of loss is next to come. The joy of parenthood everyone speaks of, but not the Fears. The child will be fragile. Every child is fragile and can be hurt in a thousand ways. My life is centered on death and helping the dead. What do I know of helping the living? Or a child? Or a living child.

—I heard a baby crying somewhere outside and then Dolores came in saying the time was close. It must have been a bird I heard. Everything is portent.

Have put the seal on the great door on the house beyond the marshes. I swore I would not sit in judgment, yet I have done just that. Have now looked upon their terrible, continuing work and set my hand against it. If the door is mine to command, I have closed it and shall not summon it open again. Those within shall remain within. The ancient bindings on the sunken mansion are intact. I cannot risk them coming against the gate and gaining the lych way back to town. Once merely a familiar mist home, the entire estate has become a vast shadowland, and both dead and living are imperiled by it. And though the gate is sealed, that place will call to my son if he comes close enough. There is no way to keep him out except by keeping him in Saltsbridge or some other place beyond the summons. Even that carries risk, for what Umber can resist that call, even if he cannot hear it in the flesh? With every action I take to protect my son, I know ten more dangers appear. It would have been better if Dolores and I never had a child. I know this now. Our ao-ros, our untimely one . . . our little bird, there is darkness before him and behind him and I know I will not be able to keep him from it.

Since Silas's birth, I cannot bring the Peace to the ghosts of children. I cannot approach those shadowlands in which the young dwell. Those doors are closed to me now. I can hardly bear to look the parents in the face and tell them I can be of no help. I try to explain, but they will not hear it. Last week, a couple who have been haunted by the ghost of their child crossed the street to avoid me. It was as though I was a leper. Mother Peale has gone to them. But they asked that I not try to speak to anyone in their family again.

I tell myself no one is to blame, yet my marriage may have brought certain ancestral predispositions to the fore. The Howesmans and some of the more affluent families are rife with mysteries . . . and while these usually only present at time of death, who can say what a union between our two families may conspire to conjure in a child, in the blood of our child.

I see him, surrounded by our books and the bones he finds and brings home. It's like our secret language. He leaves me bones on the table, carefully arranged in patterns. So often, when I return home, he is *asleep, but on the surface of his desk, in fox teeth, cat skull, and deer rib, I read "I love you, Dad." Even in this, already, he moves himself toward the fate I have striven to keep from him: a hieroglyphic world where souls hide or are imprisoned within the patterns they shape in life.*

There is to be no money from the estate. Dolores is furious. Charles is to stay on in Temple House. I can't imagine how much money is left anyway. Charles's collection has swollen so over the years, but Dolores is ready to hire an attorney. I forbid it. We can't afford it, for one thing. But I don't care about the money, and I don't want to enter Temple House again. Charles can no longer be trusted. His wife left him. He says. So I must believe him. But the house is filled with shadow. He can no longer be trusted. We are Osiris and Set, more and more with every meeting. I will not enter that house again.

I am being watched. When I go into the town, eyes are upon me. I can no longer discern if they are of the living or the dead. I am too much a coward to tell Silas what awaits him. So I will watch as long as I can until he comes to me in full knowledge of his inheritance, until I no longer have to speak those terrible words to him of what I've done.
. . . our common end.
ANKOU: is the name for the King of the Dead in Brittany, where the last person to die and be buried would become ANKOU until the next person died. Thus the crown passed down from soul to soul, often in families, but only so long as the line continued unbroken. Is there somewhere a tale about what happens when one turns away from such an obligation? Surely in all these books . . . one . . .

Throughout the pregnancy, the drowned girl appeared to all of us, even Dolores. She says my fascination invites the ghost closer. She may be right. But there is something else. If the ghost were seeking me out, why can't I find her on my own? Has she become a Wandering Spirit? She is tied to the millpond, but moves through the town, and her emanation of longing is considerable. The more I see of her, the more I believe it is the child she comes for, the ghost senses the presence of the unborn and hovers close, perhaps to gain proximity for what she did not achieve in life . . . a child, a family, love. Otherwise, the ghost is largely blind to the present. She will follow a young man of the town for a time, but always to his detriment and always he will either follow her until madness ensues, or she moves on, unable to discern one paramour from another. To her, I believe, all are merely shadows of the love she pursued during her lifetime: the young man who ran from her murder, and left her to drown in the millpond, her haunting place.

The way she looks at Silas . . . And though he is a child, it's as if she sees the man within the baby. In her terrible way, I believe she loves him. There's the peril.

The drowned girl still persists. If we take the child from the house, she is often there. I do not wish to use more compelling words, but I cannot make a connection, cannot reason with the spirit. She senses that Silas is incomplete, that he is not like others, and I fear she is drawn to him, to the chance of harming him, which she may, by either accident or intention. I don't want her looking at my son. So Dolores may get her way after all, because I can find no way to bring Peace to the drowned girl, or banish her ghost . . . only distance will keep her from my son. Dolores thinks it's me, my work that attracts her, but I know now that the circumstances of Silas's birth call out to this ghost, to other ghosts as well, who are likewise drawn to him. The void within my child calls out to them, to those who are lost. We should never have had a child. God protect him and forgive me for my arrogance.

◆ ◆ ◆

When Silas turned over the last scrap of paper and saw there was nothing more, he took the stack of his father's words to the hearth and cast them in. The dry paper caught instantly, and the small stack burned swiftly. As the edges of the sheets curled and burned to black cinders, there was a flash and a blue blaze flew up from the embers. Deep within the writhing ribbons of smoke and flame, he thought he could see Bea's face. Silas could not hear her voice, nor know whether it was vision or fantasy, but her mouth was open and she was screaming.

And that was his fault too.

LEDGER

THIS LIVING HAND, NOW WARM AND CAPABLE
OF EARNEST GRASPING, WOULD,
IF IT WERE COLD
AND IN THE ICY SILENCE OF THE TOMB,
SO HAUNT THY DAYS
AND CHILL THY DREAMING NIGHTS
THAT THOU WOULDST WISH THINE OWN HEART
DRY OF BLOOD
SO IN MY VEINS RED LIFE MIGHT STREAM
AGAIN,
AND THOU BE CONSCIENCE—CALMED—
SEE HERE IT IS—
I HOLD IT TOWARDS YOU.

—KEATS. MARGINALIA OF AMOS UMBER

And so the ponds and pools nearby the marshes became the sites of terror and of sacrifice. There, within or by the waterside, a stone would be erected. There, those that had broken oaths—of chastity, or any sworn bond—might be drowned, given to the gods who had once looked upon them with favor and beneficence.

—FROM A ROMAN FRAGMENT, TRANSLATED
   BY JONAS UMBER

218

IN THE TIME AFTER BEA HAD BEEN ABDUCTED by Cabel Umber, the entire surface of the pond had not yet iced over again, despite the freezing air. Silas did not know where she was being kept by his ancestor, but he did know that her drowned bones would provide a way, a sure and ancient way, to call her back to him. He would make use of the Dark Call, which required little more than the boldness to gather up the bones of the deceased and the fortitude to see the spirit dragged out of one sphere and into another. He didn't like what he was about to do, but Silas could see no other way. He could not fight Cabel directly, nor did he know where Bea's spirit lay imprisoned. But the Dark Call would bring her back. It had to.

Silas stood before the water, mustering his courage to go in. The air before him parted, and a spirit raised its hand and stood between him and the pond.

"Beatrice," he said softly, hardly believing it could be her.

The ghost drew in closer to him, and its body became more distinct. It wasn't Bea, but the ghost of an older woman.

"Leave me alone, whoever you are," said Silas angrily.

The ghost gave off an arresting luminescence that rose and dimmed like a lantern at a train crossing. She was familiar to him. Her hand glowed brightest of all and drew Silas's eye.

"What do you want of me?"

The ghost raised its arm in a gesture of warning but did not speak.

Growing more impatient, Silas said, *"Nomen? Causam? Remedium?"* and compelled by the words, the ghost slowly answered.

"I am Mary Bishop."

"I know you," said Silas, remembering her photograph from his uncle's collection. Her picture had disturbed him the most of all the portraits of corpses his uncle had taken. Charles Umber had covered her face in the photo and had focused on her hand. She had lost her other arm to disease and had buried it with her two children when they'd died before her. In some kind of sick fascination, Uncle had taken a picture of her remaining hand. Perhaps in revenge, Mary Bishop's ghost had been there the night his uncle died.

"Let no man conjure the dead by their bones! Silas Umber, let the dead rest in peace."

Silas said, "Beatrice is not at peace."

"Silas Umber, hear me!" She threw up her hand toward his face. "Let none other suffer what I have suffered. Turn aside, Silas Umber, from fell deeds! I have seen things. I know things I would rather I not know. I have been summoned through my remains, called back into my bones by black words. Unnatural! Most unnatural! Silas Umber, lay aside your desires to conjure. Bring no more suffering to the dead!"

"I am trying to save her. You don't understand, she's been taken. I have to help her."

The ghost shook her head into a blur and moved her hand as if to keep something away from her face.

"Only the mad seek to meddle with the dead. They draw curses down upon themselves and their families. Silas Umber, for his sins, your uncle suffers the torments of the damned. Seek not that same path. Leave the dead in peace. Leave us to that world to which we have been consigned by our own deeds, for good or ill. All else, leave to God!

"You don't understand—"

The ghost of Mary Bishop screamed, and Silas dropped to his knees and covered his ears with his hands. The ghost's awful keening rose up and became the cry of a nightbird. Her form sank down, and a dark bird flew up from the reeds and away toward the marshes.

Silas slowly drew his hands away from his ears. He looked up to where the ghost of Mary Bishop had disappeared, and saw another figure standing over him, holding a rope.

"I fear little good can come from this," said Augustus Howesman.

Silas didn't even ask how his great-grandfather knew where he was. "Please don't try to stop me."

"I will not. A man must set his own course. I'm just asking if you believe this is the best of all possible actions."

"How would I know that? This is the only option left to me, so maybe that makes it right."

"A child guesses. A man feels, in his gut, what he must do. He goes deep inside and *knows*."

"Deep inside? I can't go there anymore."

"All right, then. Do what you think you must. I will stand by you."

"I'm not sure what I'm going to find down there. You may want to leave."

"I'm not scared of anything at the bottom of a pond, Grandson. You may need me, so I'll be staying, if you don't mind."

Silas wrapped one end of the rope around his waist three times and knotted it, then tied the other end of the length into another strong knot and handed it to his great-grandfather. "I'm not sure how deep it is. Don't let go."

"Never."

Silas took off his scarf, outer coat, and jacket, and lay them among the reeds. He left on his shirt and pants. He removed his shoes one by one and, without another word, walked to the water's edge and waded in. The pond was not deep at first, though as he approached the middle, the soft, cold mud fell away from his feet. He began paddling, the water shocking every part of his body. He started to hyperventilate and couldn't stop. He reined in his panic, telling himself to focus and breathe. He knew he couldn't be in the cold water very long, so as soon as his breathing steadied, he dove below the surface to rake his hands along the bottom and try to find Beatrice's bones.

His eyes burned when he opened them under the water.

The moon lit the pond, and white things at the bottom seemed to turn and glow in the moving water. He could see the bones, almost within reach. He kicked to push himself farther down. How many bones did he need? How many were there? He glanced quickly and saw a skull. Then another. And another. As he looked in confusion, desperately trying to decide which skull to take, skeletal shapes stirred and lifted themselves from the mud. Long white arms reached for him, grasped at his shirt and arms, pulling him down. He saw a stained gray stone standing amid the bones, carved with script, and knew by instinct that this had once been a site of sacrifice.

The pond was full of faceless ghosts, their long hair filling the water with motion and obscuring the light. Through the black tresses, he saw Bea's face below him, and reached for it. His hand touched something hard, and he grasped it and drew it to him.

He clutched her skull to his body.

A skeletal hand, green with algae, reached for him. His lungs nearly empty, he kicked frantically, trying to return to the surface, but fingers of bone scraped down his face and neck and caught the chain of his Janus pendant, choking him, pulling him closer to the darkness at the bottom.

As he clamped his mouth shut to keep from screaming, small bubbles escaped his lips and fled to the surface of the pond. He felt the rope begin to pull at his waist, and for an instant he hung there in the water, the spectral hand gripping the chain around his neck, the rope about his waist pulled taut. Silas clawed at the chain. It broke, and the green hand held the pendant as it sank, but he was already rising, concerned only for Beatrice's skull clutched in his hands.

More hands flew up from the mud, grasping, trying to reach him.

Incantation flooded his mind and he shouted into the water, "None shall stand against the Sun! Retreat! Fall back! You who swim in the darkness of chaos!" With his free hand, he pointed at the ghosts of the drowned, and his ring— resonating with his water-churned words—illuminated the pond with a piercing blue light. The ghosts fell away and back into the mud below as his body broke the surface of the pond and his great-grandfather pulled him out.

Augustus Howesman helped Silas back up onto his feet and wrapped the dry coats and scarf about his great-grandson's body. "We need to get you home."

"I'll go myself," Silas said absently, not looking up. His teeth were chattering. He turned Beatrice's skull over gently in his hands and knew with certainty it was hers. He wiped the mud from it with his coat, and a yellowed patch of bone shone beneath the moon.

"Even her bones are beautiful," Silas said, turning to walk away.

"Grandson?" Augustus Howesman said. "Let me take you home."

"No," Silas said, cradling the skull like a child.

Augustus Howesman said nothing and did not follow. He watched his great-grandson walk away from the millpond, and what remained of his desiccated heart filled with worry and sorrow.

LEDGER

Though I am young, and cannot tell
Either what Death or Love is well,
Yet I have heard they both bear darts,
And both do aim at human hearts.
And then again, I have been told
Love wounds with heat, as Death with cold;
So that I fear they do but bring
Extremes to touch, and mean one thing . . .
. . . So Love's inflamèd shaft or brand
May kill as soon as Death's cold hand. . . .

—BEN JONSON. MARGINALIA OF RICHARD UMBER

'YE TAKE YOUR LADY, AND YOU GO HOME,
AND YOU'LL BE KING OVER ALL YOUR OWN.'
HE'S TAKEN HIS LADY, AND HE'S GONE HOME
AND NOW HE'S KING OVER ALL HIS OWN.

—FROM THE BALLAD OF KING ORFEO. MARGINALIA OF
AMOS UMBER

CHAPTER 27

WHAT CANNOT BE

SILAS HAD BUILT UP THE FIRE ON THE HEARTH in his study, and though warmth spread quickly through the room, he hardly felt it. He sat by the fire in dry clothes, gently holding Beatrice's skull, wiping it clean with a cloth. The slow, steady movements of his hands were tender, but also mechanical, insistent, as though he could prove to her bones how much he loved her. His heart cried out for Beatrice. He would use any means available to get her. His good sense had worn down to desperation.

"It will only be a moment, I promise. And then we'll be together. The way may be terrible, I know, but follow me from Hades's hall, and then we'll walk together on the paths of the sun."

His mind rang as he rehearsed the grim spell Cabel Umber himself had once whispered into his ear. In the furthest corner of his mind, a small, bright, inner voice pleaded with him not to conjure. Over that, Silas drew a pall.

He moved a low table to the side, clearing a place before the fire. He leaned over and carefully placed Bea's skull on the floor and began his incantations.

Words of conjure and command.

Words of darkness and summons.

Terrible words to tear a ghost away from one place and drag it to another.

The only words. The only way, he told himself, even as his mouth shaped and sounded the vowels of hell.

Silas could feel an awful heat begin to rise from the skull, as though mighty frictions worked against it. The strength of Cabel's bindings on her was considerable. But Silas had both her remains and his own desire to fuel his work. He chanted louder and Bea's skull cried to its wayward soul. The combined might of Silas's words and the bone of her body drew Beatrice's wavering presence to him and away from that place Cabel had hidden her.

The fabric of the air shuddered, then ripped, and Bea stood next to her skull in Silas's study, bent over and screaming into her hands.

He stepped toward her and she shrank from him.

"Beatrice. Look at me."

Still infected by the tone of command, Silas said, "Beatrice, speak to me!" Notes of iron rang through his words.

Beatrice opened her mouth as though she could not breathe.

"Bea!" Silas said more desperately. "It's Silas. I'm here!"

Bea leaned over the low table and pulled a brown, withered stem from a vase of dead flowers. She opened her mouth again and spoke. Her voice was a single, worn thread about to break.

"Shall we have more thyme? I had much of it once. Now I feel there is little left." She offered the weed to Silas. He didn't move. Bea dropped it, and put her hand into her wet, matted hair and pulled a tress out from the roots. She held out her hand again.

"Bea?"

"I have seen such places . . ."

"Please, Bea, hear my voice."

". . . such dark places . . ."

"Beatrice?"

For a moment, Bea looked frantically around her, looking with unfocused eyes through the room into some other place. Then she began to grin like a child. "I remember flowers. The fields were bright with them." She pointed to her skull on the floor while pulling more strands of hair from her head. "Here is something. . . ."

Silas watched, silent and afraid of what he and the Dark Call had done to her.

"There's rue." She looked down at her hand still clutching the torn hair. "Where are the violets? He would bring me flowers." She dropped the hair onto the floor and put her hands to the sides of her head and cried, speaking in sobs between the moans. "And now . . . and now I know . . . I know . . . below, nothing blooms! Nothing ever, or at all! In the darkness, flowers cannot be."

"Beatrice," Silas said loudly, trying to call her back to sense, to any remembrance of where or what she was. "Look at me! Remember! It's Silas, Bea! Silas! We are together!"

She lifted her head and said softly, "No more, please. Please . . . I cannot be . . ."

"Bea, look at me."

Her eyes, palest aquamarine, did not focus, but looked through and past him, as though Silas were now the ghost.

"Listen . . . just listen to my voice. Can you hear me?"

". . . Yes."

"Good. That's good."

But Bea turned quickly, first behind her, then to the left, as if hearing the angry approach of another.

"Listen only to my voice."

Her face contorted into lines of fear. Her mouth was gaping and she opened and closed her hands, her fingers miming signs of panic.

"It's just you and me, Bea. There is nothing to worry about. I want to keep you here with me."

She looked up at the ceiling of the study, but didn't see it. "I am longing to be elsewhere, where my love is hid. Let me look into the sun. . . ."

"I'm right here. Please look at me. Let me help you, okay? I have power now, over . . . over people like us. I can keep us together. I can make sure you'll be here with me forever."

"Not again," she muttered. "I was not born to live in darkness . . . or in the shadow of another . . . please let me go," she begged, looking through him.

"Bea, it's me . . . it's Silas. I love you."

"My love?"

"Yes. Please remember . . . please. . . ." He was crying. Silas's desperate sorrow let through a little more of his heart. He could see her more clearly, as she was. He could perceive what Cabel had done to her, what the Dark Call he'd cast had done to her. She had become little more than a frightened animal in a trap. Through his tears Silas could read on her face, within the wavering lines of her spectral form, that his love for her was another kind of prison, another selfish cruelty that bound her within a world not her own. His love for her put a veil before her eyes, blinding her to what was, blinding her to everything but the darkness of her own past. But if she could remember what had happened . . . if she could only remember him and say his name . . . then all the bindings on her could be broken for good. She would be free and they could be together.

Silas went to his desk and from his satchel took out two crystal vials of water from the springs below the earth at Arvale. Water of memory. Water of forgetting. He looked at Bea and back at the vials.

He put the water of Lethe back in his satchel.

Silas opened the flask of the water of memory, and put it to

Bea's mouth and tipped it up. A few drops of the water fell onto her lips, diffused into a mist that moved through and enlivened her form. She closed her eyes and did not move.

"Beatrice? Can you hear me? Do you remember me? How we used to walk together? We sat on the statue of the lion and walked among the stones. You used to love me."

Her lips slowly moved and then the sound came. "I love you . . . ," she whispered, her eyes still closed. The firelight illuminated her body, which, with each moment in the room, took on more solidity, more presence.

Silas couldn't move, though his heart beat furiously in that terrible, exquisite moment of joy.

Then she spoke.

"Lawrence," Bea said, opening her eyes. "I love you, Lars."

All the color drained from the room.

In Silas's sight, the walls and floors paled; the chairs and books lost their hues of brown or green. There was nothing real left in the world to him now. She had never loved him. All the words of his father's diary flooded his mind. She had haunted his family out of confusion and loss. His pathetic, desperate love showed him only what he wanted to see. Only her broken memories of her own past had made him into the semblance of someone she could love. They were two sad lies stitched together. All through the years her ghost had endured, she remembered only terrible losses, but no names. He wasn't Silas Umber to her, even though she had once spoken those words. He was a placeholder for someone else, for Lars, for Lawrence Umber who in life had been her lover. Her true and only love.

Now the waters of memory had restored her mind to her. She knew who she was and whom she truly loved. He had loved her, but Bea had only needed Silas to help her keep lively her own losses. And he had played the part of paramour well. She had watched him from the time of his infancy, but she'd never really seen him. He'd always been, at best, a substitute. Now he had hurt her. Because of him, Bea had been subjected to unknown horrors at Cabel Umber's hands. Because of him, she suffered being summoned under compulsion. Silas saw himself as just another of her tormentors. His need to be loved could not bring her peace. He could see that now. And he knew there was only one way to heal everything Beatrice had endured in life and death . . . even though it meant sacrificing any happiness he might have been able to fashion from the fantasy he had made of her.

"Lawrence, Lawrence . . ." Bea closed her eyes and again began to weep.

Silas turned from her and went to his coat. From its pocket, he took out a handful of the ashes of Lawrence Umber he'd collected at the gates of Arvale.

Silas's chest tightened, as though his heart was seized in a vise. Yet here was something he could do, one promise he could keep.

He threw the ashes into the fire. Lawrence Umber's remains hallowed the hearth, made it lych, and Silas followed the ashes with words to carry his dead cousin back, then he moved his arms apart, opening the threshold. But there would be no spell of compulsion. Only invitation, and hope.

"Let a path be made by love or not at all," Silas said. "Lawrence Umber, I have made a way for you through the fire. Come, cousin Lars. If it is your will to come again into the circle of the sun and have your heart restored to you, come, now! Follow my voice through the flames!"

The fire rose up in a gold and scarlet fan, then folded back down into its embers.

As Lars's ghost came forth from the fire, Beatrice opened her eyes.

The two ghosts stood looking at each other, and for an instant, Silas thought they could not perceive each other.

The three figures stood and did not move.

Each side of the triangle was equal. Each had its measure of pain and hope and fear, and not one of them could speak for fear of banishing one of the others. But then Bea lifted her hand toward Lars, and he moved swiftly toward her. The two slid together, their edges blurring in a growing brightness until a brilliant light filled the room. Silas shut his eyes, as much to banish the scene from his sight as to spare his eyes from the lovers' glare.

"Go," he said to the ghosts. "Go now and find what joy you can. Don't look back."

Bea reached out to him. Silas stepped away, his eyes wet with rising tears. Yet, as the ghosts stepped past him and through an opening in the air, Silas felt her hand brush his cheek.

Silas stood alone in his study, looking at the floor where Bea's skull still sat, a cold, dead thing requiring burial.

Silas took his coat from the chair and his satchel and left his house.

As he walked, he took out the death watch and the vial of the water of Lethe. To him, they now seemed the same. Two ways to hide. He put both back in his pocket and looked at the sky. Morning was still hidden, but he couldn't be at home. He could not be in that room where they'd all three been a moment before.

He needed to keep moving because every place he passed reminded him of Beatrice, and the memories hurt him. Wasn't there anywhere in Lichport where memories could just die away instead of crying out and clinging to the living?

He saw several of the Restless who had attended his mother's funeral. Two were slowly, aimlessly wandering, side by side. Silas looked away and walked down another street to avoid them. On the next street, another living corpse had stopped, motionless in the yard of a house. The owners of the home were begging with the deceased to leave. The corpse stood with its eyes closed, immune to or ignoring the pleas of its descendants.

"Just go. Please, for the love of Christ. Go back to where you came from!" cried the voice from the porch.

Silas quickly turned the corner and kept walking.

He didn't want to see anyone or speak with anyone. Much of Lichport was abandoned, and yet at every turn was a memory or a problem waiting only for him.

He made his way down Coach Street, passing the cemeteries of God's Small Acre and the Lost Ground before he could see the ocean. The wide expanse of featureless water, the incessant crashing of the waves against the shore brought no comfort.

He thought of the tavern at the end of the Narrows. He had entered it once as a shadowland, saw there upon the stools the ghosts of the forgotten, the ghosts of the lost, saw them drinking down their days. He imagined the tavern that still stood there, still existed in his world, was probably the same. Filled with derelicts. A place to be and not to be. A place to become invisible. A place to finish falling apart.

He wandered north again, then down into the cold lanes of the Narrows.

LEDGER

The first offspring of every womb belongs to me. . . .
—Exodus 34:19

For now I will stretch out my hand, that I may
smite thee and thy people with pestilence; and thou
shalt be cut off from the earth."
—Exodus 9:15

CHAPTER 28

REMEMBERING BABYLON

CABEL UMBER STOOD ABOVE THE GHOST of the young girl who shuddered in his shadow.

He spoke to her of the wonders of fire—of both the righteous furies of a father, and of the sacrificial altars and pyres where punishment might bring about redemption.

He whispered of the evils of children, their selfishness, and of how they might be brought to heel. He bellowed about the joys of hunting and how Death was himself a huntsman.

He spoke to her as if she had been his own child. He told her the stench of sin was all about her, and how soon it would be burnt away. And he marveled at how much she looked like that lost and ruined child who once, long ago, was his daughter.

The ghost of the drowned girl clamped her eyes shut as he touched her cheek with a long, blackened finger. The lines of her face were pulled thin in terror. She had seen the fire in the furnace, in the great bronze god. She had seen its piercing horns, its glowing belly thick with smoke and flame. She would not open her eyes again.

Enraptured by his self-made scene, Cabel Umber delighted in seeing Silas Umber's paramour standing confused and afraid as the idol's sickly glow grew brighter in anticipation of what was to come. He had hunted well, and brought back worthy prey.

The hollow idol of Moloch groaned as the bronze stretched

and contracted with the rising heat of its burning innards.

"Child? It is nearly time," Cabel said to the ghost of the drowned girl.

As he stepped toward her, the trembling girl blindly backed up until she was nearly upon the idol. Cabel paused, enjoying her terror. But as he stepped forward again, and would have pushed her into the furnace, the drowned girl shuddered and her form wavered and grew translucent. The air about her body darkened, and the outline of her skull glowed briefly behind her face as her body was drawn up suddenly toward her head, as though she was made of water spiraling upward from the surface of the sea in a storm funnel.

Cabel Umber shouted words of command and binding, but none availed him, and before his voice had stopped ringing in the air of the chamber, she vanished within the shadow of her own skull's hollow eye socket.

Cabel stood, the flickering flames about him rising into a conflagration brighter than the idol's burning heart.

His prey had been stolen.

This was Silas Umber's doing.

Once more, his quarry had been taken from him by the boy Undertaker. Silas had not fallen to the curse Cabel had put upon him, and now here was another affront.

So be it, thought Cabel. If Silas cannot readily be killed by curse, then let his sufferings continue as they have begun. As the folk of this place perish, so shall Silas Umber. Let him die of grief if no other death can catch him.

Cabel Umber had hoped to savor the destruction of this town, to drag it out, make the killings last a while. He had imagined himself riding out, becoming Death to these people, a grim hunter on his dark mount cutting down the living.

No matter.

He would set more fires; burn them in their beds if nothing else. But what of the sacrifice to Moloch, who required the lives of the firstborn? Repeatedly his planned offerings had come to nothing. His daughter and the Mistle Child had been taken from him. Silas Umber would not die. But a firstborn must be brought to the fire. Cabel Umber swore he would not break that promise to his god again.

He paced and stalked the twisting aisles of the labyrinthine rotunda, stacked high with the spoils of many crusades. And here, the stone idol of the demon of fever, carried out of Babylon.

He recognized it immediately.

Cabel swooned with remembering the plagues of old. The purgings. How the weak were carried off, all the miserable and sickly folk. The ignoble wretches were the first to succumb, the first to fall. Whole towns, cities . . . all died. He remembered bodies stacked up along the city walls, and how the wolves and jackals came then to feast upon the dead.

Then as now, he thought, *the hunter always wins the day.*

He put the statue upright. It stood on four legs, part lion, part man. Before the ancient idol, Cabel rocked his head back and forth as he spoke.

"Nergal! Lord of Pestilence! I greet thee!"

Cabel began, reveling in a distant memory of his first sight of this statue, of when he'd first heard that it had been bought from the desert tribes. Those exiled folk who long ago fled from Babylon, living as shepherds when the Brothers of the Temple met them in the desolate wilderness. How, in the raiment of a knight pilgrim, did one of the Brothers pay an old man with silver to show the god's power. A child he bought from some poor family . . . how it whimpered to come before the god. Then fell words were spoken. A wind rose in the surrounding desert, sending shifting sand howling across the dunes. The Brother told how the flaps of the darkened tent were ripped aside like the veils of the bride upon her wedding night. Wind-thrown sand flew at their faces, but about the child the air turned more slowly. The boy was placed before the idol. The idol stood motionless as the child trembled. Soon the child's face grew red and he began to sweat profusely and cry. The boy clutched at his throat as if mere water might have saved him. As the fever raged, his screams rose to match the wind. A moment later, it was done. The boy lay dead of a fever, and the old man gestured at the statue and held out his hand for more silver. He was paid and the idol was carried away.

By the work of the Brotherhood, the idol had been here preserved.

Here is providence indeed, thought Cabel.

And without another thought, Cabel Umber began speaking the words that would rouse the god of plague from its sleep within the stone.

> Nergal!
> Lord of Pestilence!
> Raging King!
> God of Plague!
> Oh, terrible god of wrath, awaken!
> Let your evil fever fly up!
> Let it fall upon the bodies of the firstborn!
> Now it pierces with teeth of fire.
> Now it poisons and consumes their bodies.
> Rise up, oh flame of pestilence, and go forth!
> Shroud our enemies in fire

so that they may perish
and you may be fed!

And from that low and hidden place, that sepulchre of old gods grim and long forgotten, a vapor poured from the statue of Nergal and rose, twisting like the cords of a hanging rope, up and through the stones of the chamber's ceiling, through rock and soil, up and past the frozen earth and into the air of Lichport. There it joined the night winds, and formed a miasma of poison fumes, yellowed by evil and hatred for the living. The airborne curse sought chimneys, cracked windows, and the gaps beneath doors. It writhed along the floors of cottages and mansions both, and when it found the throats of the firstborn, it settled into the flesh as fever.

All that night and into morning, Cabel Umber gibbered his song of sickness with delight.

Fever come and strike the heart like lightning.
As shadow
it is born.
As a poison breath
may it pass into the mouths
of the firstborn.
Hold them in your hands, O Death,
And put them into the earth!

And he beat his chest in supplication to that god of distant Babylon, welcoming pestilence, again and again, into that town he sought by terrible spell to put beneath his thumb.

The cold earth around Temple House was awash in a dark miasmic mist. It seeped up from below the ground and flowed along the streets of upper Lichport. Freezing winds pushed it through the town, where it washed like waves into the sides of houses and crept in tendrils under doors.

When the mist reached Coach Street, the winds fell, and it flowed fast down into the Narrows, pooling in its alleys, coursing through its lanes. Many in the Narrows took ill. Some blamed it on the cold winter. A few, who saw the mist rise or had heard rumors, spoke the name of Silas Umber with blame and anger in their voices.

The pestilence was quick and, like a hunter, it sought the weak out first.

A few of the elderly fell that night. Two old sisters in a cottage on Pearl Lane were found dead in their parlor by a neighbor. Parents wrung their hands as they stood over their children's fever beds. And where the mist found the firstborn of Lichport, it was especially harsh. The mist clung to them, and choked them and bound up their breath. Some feared they would not survive the night. Poultices were applied. Medicines taken. Cold cloths were placed upon the brows of the feverish.

Sick or not, few slept that night.

Those that were inclined prayed continuously to whatever gods still listened to the prayers of the people of Lichport.

And Mother Peale, who had already succumbed to a winter chill, was struck by a fever that lit madness in her mind. She ranted in her bed and threw her head from side to side, even as some of her neighbors, sick with fear if nothing else, filled her cottage to bring her comfort and wait out the long night.

COME, THEREFORE, BLOOMS OF
    SETTLED MISCHIEF'S ROOT:
COME, EACH THING ELSE WHAT FURY
    CAN INVENT,
WREAK ALL AT ONCE! INFECT THE
    AIR WITH PLAGUES,
TILL BAD TO WORSE, TILL WORSE TO
    WORST BE TURN'D!
LET MISCHIEFS KNOW NO MEAN, NOR
    PLAGUES AN END!

—FROM *THE MISFORTUNES OF ARTHUR*, BY THOMAS
    HUGHES, 1587. MARGINALIA OF AMOS UMBER

. . . *Also sometyme the blind beteth and smiteth and greveth the child that ledeth him, and shall soone repent the beting by doing of the child. For the child hath mind of the beting, and forsaketh him and leveth him alone in the myddle of a brydge, or in some other peril, and techeth him not the way to void the peril.*

—FROM TREVISA'S *BARTHOLOMAEUS ANGLICUS*, 1398.
    MARGINALIA OF JONAS UMBER

Now is afraid of thee,
all thy kin . . .

—FROM THE MIDDLE ENGLISH POEM "DEATH,"
    TRANSLATED BY JONAS UMBER

CHAPTER 29

OUTSIDER

THE AIR OF THE NARROWS WAS FOUL, as though something dead had been unearthed from below the cold stones of its streets.

No wind moved down its lanes. No salt breezes came in off the sea to wash the staleness from the air. Silas hardly noticed.

He would have walked past Mother Peale's house. He didn't want to talk. The sooner he reached the anonymous barstools of the Fretful Porpentine the better. Or maybe he would walk past it, into the abandoned warehouse district, or out onto one of the rotting wharfs. He just needed to walk. But as he approached Mother Peale's house, despite the early hour, the lights were blazing. He heard voices and his name spoken sharply.

So he stood by the window, listening, and in only a few minutes had learned what certain of the Narrows folks thought of him now. Some had very suddenly fallen ill that night. He hadn't heard how many, but enough that their relatives were ready to believe the sicknesses were all somehow connected.

"You can bet it's the Umber boy who's done it to us!" cried the voice of Mrs. Halliwell. "Fires in the Narrows and ghost lights seen about the millpond. All those corpses walking *right out* of Newfield! Who do you think invited them?"

"Don't speak so against him in this house," said Joan Peale.

"The truth has always been welcome in the Peale home," continued Mrs. Halliwell. "Some of our folk are struck down, and *all in a day*! Unnatural, I call that! And more to come, no doubt. Like lightning out of the blue the sickness came on! *Unnatural!* Even now you can hear them coughing and crying out as you walk the Narrows. We all know it's his fault. I don't say he's cursed us by intention, but whatever he's been up to has gone a bad way, and who's to pay the price? Us, it seems! Two of my cousins stricken with the fever. And your own mother, Joan! Struck down! Those who have fallen have all been firstborns. So how do I know Silas Umber is the cause? Why, isn't he himself a firstborn child? And has he taken ill?"

"No!" someone shouted. "He's right as rain! I've seen him, this very night, walking along the waterfront!"

"So that proves it," said Mrs. Halliwell.

"Witchcraft!" yelled someone.

"It's them dead folk coming back. That is the cause! It's been years since any of those Restless have been seen on the streets. But since Silas Umber has returned, here they are, up and about again! The boy's own great-grandfather has come out of Fort Street. *To the store!* And now the rest of them. They followed him out beyond the marshes to the old Umber place. Then the other night! Right out of Newfield they followed him. Does anyone here find comfort in that? It's them that's brought about this sickness, you can be sure of it!" said Mrs. Halliwell.

"Well, look at the mother!" said another. "He could be one of *them*. Or worse. Umber *and* Howesman . . . what do you even call one of *those*?"

"Enough! Any more talk like that and you can all get out of this house and never come back. My mother wouldn't stand for it, and neither will I. Just wait until one of your own dead needs settling! Who will you run to then? And don't forget the season! We've always had bad fevers and agues when the weather turns, this close to the sea. And I am sure not *every* firstborn in Lichport has taken ill. Who could know that already? Have you spoken, Mrs. Halliwell, to *every* family in town? I reckon you have not! Don't borrow trouble or you make it so!" Joan shouted over the rising protests.

"There's no question those Umbers are useful. No one is saying they ain't, but only as far as they keep trouble *away*. This one's invited trouble right into town. Left the old Arvale gate wide open, I've heard and all! And Joan, you can't deny, there is something not right about Amos's boy." Silas couldn't put a name to the voice, but it was one of the older Narrows men.

Mrs. Halliwell chimed in again. "Joan Peale, you can't tell me there isn't bad blood run right through the Umbers. Charles Umber, who got up to God knows what just down the street from the house where I raised my children! And who can say when bad blood rises to the surface. Remember from where the dyer's hand takes its color? From the work! From. The. Work. Is there anyone here who wasn't at least a little afraid of looking Amos Umber in the eye, even when he'd done your family a good turn?"

More mumbling assent rippled across the room.

"So don't lecture me on what I can worry about and what I can't, Joan Peale. Maybe your mother's only been so kind to the Umbers to stay on their good sides all these years . . . and now look where that's gotten her! Flushed with fever, thrashing in her bed. And for that matter, since no one's answered my question, why *ain't* Silas sick? Free of trouble: caused the trouble, I say!"

Mrs. Halliwell was ranting and trying to incite the others. Perhaps not wanting to fuel the rising fires of accusations, Joan ignored the question, but said, "Well, what are you suggesting we do, send Silas from town? Where could he go? He's got kin here. Silas can't leave, if that's what you're saying. This is his home! Who would be the Undertaker?"

"What kin has he got? All of 'em's dead, one way or another!"

The room erupted in voices, some shouting, some beseeching

others to be calm, but there was no quieting the room. People were scared and needed to talk, or yell it out. Silas waited a little longer, but the clamor wasn't subsiding. He opened the door and went inside.

The moment he entered the room, every voice went silent.

Joan Peale ran up to him and took his hand. "Silas, come in. You find a place near the fire and warm yourself. You're cold right through! Let me bring you something."

"No. There's nothing I need."

Every eye was on him. Silas looked at the floor.

Again, Joan Peale jumped in the gap. "The fires are all out. I think all's well. Everyone was just leaving."

"I'll go," said Silas. "I'm sorry I've interrupted your gathering. I shouldn't have come." He looked around the room; most avoided his gaze.

"He's sorry, he says. *Now* he's sorry. Half the Narrows scorched and he's sorry!" said Mrs. Halliwell.

Silas said, "I suppose my apology isn't much help to you."

"Help? Some help! What help are you?" she snapped.

"You're right. What would you like me to do? Cast a spell? Conjure a ghost? How would you like me to magic it all away for you?"

No one answered.

"No. Really. I will die trying to make sure everything is just how it was and you can get back to living out your days while the town falls down around you. You fear the dead? Most of you act as though you are dead already. Hiding in your houses. Only coming out to accuse someone who is your friend and would help any of you who asked. I heard what you said a few moments ago. Is that how neighbors speak of one another?"

Mrs. Halliwell gasped at the word "dead." People began

moving about the room, whispering in each other's ears. Some of the women made signs over their chests with their fingers, muttering desperately. Others hung their heads, ashamed to have had their harsh words heard.

"You know, I never asked to be Undertaker. You assumed I would take over my father's work, and I have. If I step down, you will have to see to your own dead, all by yourselves. And when everything goes wrong, and this town is thick with ghosts and homeless corpses, well, you'll have only yourselves to blame then and no one else to turn to." Silas shook his head in frustration. "You know, the Restless are *your* kin. Or the kin of your neighbors. Why not welcome them? For God's sake! They've been here all along. You can't shut your eyes to the world around you."

"You see? He has no fear of it—whatever it is that brought sickness on this town. That's because it's him that's done it!" screamed Mrs. Halliwell.

Joan Peale got up again, but Silas stepped in front of her.

"You're right. I am not afraid. But that's because I know what's out there. And behind that darkness, there is more, and I've seen that, too. I also know that when you turn your back on shadows instead of facing them, more shadows come." He turned his head, making eye contact with all of the people in the room. Most looked down again and avoided his stare. "There is something out there. Something very terrible, very old."

"What is it? Tell us!"

"It would not help your fears to know what is haunting this town. But rest assured, it is hungry. It set the fires."

Terror lit the faces of the room.

"But I will find a way to put it down."

Silas stood away from the fire, moving closer to the door. "I think we all know that ghosts are not your real problem. Ghosts are everywhere here. You're afraid of something else."

"Oh? Yes? How's that?" Mrs. Halliwell called out.

"It's the most common thing in the world, and so long as you fear it, you will be miserable every day of your lives. Death is what you fear. And it's waiting for each one of us. But Death is calm and patient. One way or another, our time is running out. If not today, then tomorrow. So go back to your homes and let me get on with my work of keeping the shadows off you a little longer. Just remember as you close your drapes tight and lock your doors against the night: Many of you stood in my father's house and shook my hand and drank at his funeral. I have helped you before and will continue to do so as best I can. When the ghost of the lighthouse sent nightmares across the Narrows, who ended them? Who brought peace at last to the Sorrowsman of Dogge Alley? Please remember this when you're condemning the only person who . . . when you speak of driving me out of the only place where I've ever felt, ever known. . . ." His voice broke. Silas turned his back on the assembly, and said, "Who are you to judge me? To weigh my heart and deeds upon a scale when you have repeatedly asked the Umbers for help and *expected* us to serve you?"

Silas's lip curled. "You know, when I came in, many of you were walking about the room counterclockwise, widdershins. Very unlucky. You should be more careful with yourselves. Who knows who might be the next to fall?"

People drew away from him.

"Silas, this is not helping," whispered Joan, pulling at his arm.

"I'm just being honest with them," said Silas, not lowering his voice. "If they are determined to see the devil in every corner, then they should take precautions. Not walk under any ladders, or let any black cats cross their path!" He began to shout. "Beware the dog that barks at your door! And the sound of bells at night! And chirping crickets! All those are dire portents."

"Silas! Enough," said Joan.

Silas pulled away from her. He looked at the room. He'd only added to their fear. He needed to calm them, not berate them. He had chafed under their judgment. Wasn't this precisely why he had himself backed away from some of the more terrible rites at Arvale? He felt, in his heart, that there was peril in the act of judgment. Peace must be sought another way.

He turned back to the room. His voice was steady, measured. "Listen to me now, all of you. Your fears are real and understandable. Something terrible has come among us. It is very old, very strong. But it is a ghost, and no ghost is all-powerful. Each one is a puzzle, and I haven't figured this one out yet. But I will. I will find a way to put it down, or bring it the Peace. I am asking you for patience. Patience and trust. Nothing more. Can you give me that?"

Most of the people in the room nodded. Mrs. Halliwell drew up her shawl and stormed out. A few followed her.

What else could he have said to them? It wasn't their fault people were sick with fever, a ghostly pestilence brought down on Lichport by his ancestor Cabel Umber. Silas should be the sick one. His mother had already borne the weight of a curse meant for him, now Mother Peale and other firstborn of Lichport families were suffering on his account. A few had just lost their homes. Of course they blamed him. There was no point yelling at them about their fears and intuition. They felt it was somehow Silas's fault. It was his fault. For who had led Cabel Umber back from Arvale by the breaking of a vow?

As he was about to leave, Silas paused.

"Joan, I'd like to pay your mother my respects. May I see her?"

Joan Peale hesitated, but then said, "Of course, Silas. You know the way. I'll tend to the others."

On the wall outside of Mother Peale's bedroom, a mirror hung. Silas paused and stared at his reflection. The glass was dusty, but he could see how awful he looked. His hair was disheveled and his coat was wrinkled. Dark crescents colored the skin below his eyes. He straightened his coat, knocked lightly on the door, and went in. Mother Peale lay on her bed in the dim light. Her brow was covered in sweat and she was moaning softly.

She turned toward the door. Her eyes were open, but she said, "I cannot see you. Come closer. Who comes here from the field of flowers? I will not be taken." She threw her head to the side.

Silas could smell the sickness in the room, the sweat in the bedclothes and sourness of her breath. There was a shadow upon the quality of the air, and dark, barely audible words were woven through it. This was curse and no natural contagion; more confirmation of Cabel Umber's wrath. Yet Silas wondered why, as Mrs. Halliwell had said, as a firstborn child he had not gotten sick? He felt fine. Maybe he hadn't succumbed to the fever *yet*. Maybe it was only a matter of time?

Mother Peale groaned and thrashed among the bedclothes.

Silas put his hand on hers. Her skin was hot to the touch. She was burning with fever. Next to her bed was a basin with water. Small pieces of ice floated in it and a cloth hung over its edge. He dipped the cloth in the cool water, wrung it out, and placed it across her brow.

"Ah . . . that is comfortable."

The stillness of the room was almost unbearable. He looked around. The dark wood walls closed in. Everywhere he went, it felt like he was moving from box to box, coffin to coffin. Hadn't his uncle once told him the world was a hospital and everyone in it waiting only to die? The window was open, but no air moved. Silas could hardly bear to breathe in that place. He took small breaths, not wanting too much of the room in him at once. He could feel the particles of sickness swarming about him. He lifted his arm in front of his mouth to breathe through the fabric of his coat. He looked upon his ring. The scarab was the only bright thing in the close room. He saw only blue. His own blood stirred. He held out his hand toward the bed, the sapphire scarab holding the air, and he remembered that the *Book of the Dead* was also a book of life and the words to help the dead might also bring comfort to the living, or to those close to death. He closed his eyes and said,

> "Fly now and come into this place:
> winds that move above the waters.
> From the sea, wind comes.
> From the river, wind comes.
> From about the trees, wind comes.
> From the sky and the arms of the mother of stars,
> wind comes,
> bringing comfort to the afflicted soul.
> The way is open.
> It is the Lord of the West
> and he who greets the bark of the sun
> when it is below the earth
> who speaks these words."

Silas put his hand to her brow, letting the scarab in his ring touch her skin, and said,

> "You are the firstborn of the resplendent sun.
> You shall rise up with the morning.

You shall open your mouth.

You shall eat.

You shall rise up like the sun each day."

As he finished the spell, Silas broke out in a sweat and felt dizzy. Outside, the wind picked up, rushing against the house, blowing across the chimney. From the window and from the gaps below the door, a breeze stirred the air. Dust danced on the floor and the stale smell dissolved before the scent of the salt sea and the pines beyond the river. Mother Peale lifted her head. The deep blue stone of his ring warmed, and he felt the skin of her brow cool beneath his hand. She closed her eyes and smiled.

"Silas Umber, bless you, child." The heat had gone out of her face.

Some of his frustration had faded too, but his head was throbbing.

"Don't sit up. Rest," he said to her.

"Yes . . . yes. I have been ill with an ague. It's kind of you to come—"

"I am sure that's all it is," he said, wanting to comfort her. But as he spoke, the strength went out of his legs and he had to grab the side of her bed to steady himself.

"What's this?" Mother Peale said. "Don't tell me you've a fever too?"

"No, no," replied Silas, reaching behind him for a chair and sitting down. "Just a little tired. Nothing more." But the spell had taken the wind out of him. He was glad to have helped her, but it was clear now that his strength came from helping the dead, not the living.

Mother Peale looked at him sharply. "So be it. If you say. I do hope you've not come down with it! Lordy, how it burned. It felt as though I'd been days in the sun with no clothes on at all!"

Silas looked at the cold hearth across the room.

"Tell me how it goes with you," she asked.

"Not well."

"I have heard some of what's come to pass of late." She gestured to the door. "I am sorry I'm not more fit, or I would help you."

Silas looked down. He felt ashamed, undeserving of anyone's help.

"If your father was here, lad, he would know—"

"But he is not here. So I'll have to make do on my own."

Mother Peale stared at him for moment, then said, "You know, I don't think I properly thanked you after my man's funeral. You did a fine job, Silas. A fine job."

She leaned over and opened a drawer in the nightstand. She took out a small leather pouch and put it in Silas's hand. "My John would have wanted you to have this, Silas. I've only kept from giving it to you because I know you are so fond of wearing the pendant your father gave you and I didn't want you to feel obliged."

"I've lost that," Silas said wretchedly. "In the millpond."

Concern crossed her brow.

"Well, well, perhaps this is timely and all. You just take it, a gift from loving friends. You remember that," she said, putting her head back on the pillow. "You are not alone, child."

Silas opened the pouch and took out a small carved green stone in the shape of a sort of bird's head. It was attached to a woven cord. Silas held it up to the candle and the carving glowed bright green, even in the low light. Touched by Mother Peale's generosity, he put it on over his head. The bird's head lay over his heart.

Mother Peale closed her eyes. "That's come from the South Seas, Silas Umber. Made by those folk there. My John brought it back from his traveling days. He sailed on the *Mary Farrell,* out of Kingsport, under Captain Ruskin. More than a year he was away, but when he come back, well, he had a tale or two to tell. This he had from the *Mayorhee* folk. Right clever with stone were some of them, he told me. That carving you hold, they wore that and ones like them to keep them safe on their long voyages.

"You mean the Maori?"

"That's what I said. Who's got the head cold now?"

"What kind of bird is it?"

"Hard to say. My John said they called it a *Manaeeah,* or some such. That's a spirit thing. Part bird. Part summat else. I thought, by its beak, it might be an albatross. But what do I know? That's a fine bird though, the albatross, a great traveler, and it can always find its way home, even from far and distant places. You wear it now, if you like."

"I do. I will. Thank you, Mother Peale." Silas looked at the stone, bright and green, a kind of jade, he guessed. The eyes were set with mother of pearl and they flashed in the candlelight. John Peale was a good and sensible man. A beloved father. Silas liked wearing something of his.

"Keep it close. . . ." Her words trailed off. He could see the weariness in her face. She needed rest.

"Ma'am?"

"I tell you, Silas Umber. These are talismanic times we live in, perilous days. Best to keep your needful baubles about, but not too close." She turned her head to look at the carved clock on the wall. As she did this, Silas could feel the death watch ticking in his pocket. Mother Peale looked back at Silas as though she could hear its ticking also.

"Some are not worth keeping, Silas. Some are no longer in keeping with the time. But that stone of my John will serve you well . . . mark me, child, it will that. Bring you home safe, as it brought my John home . . ."

There was loud talk in the other rooms. Mother Peale began coughing and tried to sit up.

"No, no," said Silas. "You need your rest."

"I won't have cross words spoken in my house."

Silas pulled the covers up over her. "Just lie still and make yourself better. Sleep. That's best."

"All right, doctor's orders, eh? But you come back soon, won't you?" Mother Peale reached out and grasped Silas's hand.

Silas waited a moment, then came away from the bed.

"You take care, Silas Umber. You hear? Take good care."

Silas left the room and closed the door behind him. He tucked the pendant under his shirt and the stone warmed quickly against his skin. As he passed back into the main room, silence fell. He felt their eyes on him and knew that this was the pain his father must have also endured throughout his life: to be loved and revered, but also feared and sometimes hated. He nodded to Joan Peale, asking her over. Silas took a leather wallet from his jacket and wrote on a piece of paper, then pressed it into Joan's hand.

She unfolded the check and stared at Silas.

"My God! What's this?"

"For the people who lost their homes, and the others that were burned. May I leave it with you to use this to help them? If you need more, my great-grandfather will settle it. He'd be glad of your visit, in any event."

"Silas, are you leaving?"

He said nothing, but held her hand briefly, then he let it go and turned away.

The moment he stepped outside and closed the door, the night drew in about him. Silas made his way at first toward his mother's house, walking along the docks close to the surging sea, but then something tugged at his mind. He turned around and walked to the path leading up to the Beacon. Down below, the sea made mad rushes at the breakwater, and the boats in the harbor were pushed back and forth, groaning and straining against their anchor ties.

Above, the stars turned in wide arcs about the Beacon as though it was the very center of the world. Somewhere along the base of the burial hill, despite the time of year, crickets were chirping. Silas felt the stone bird at his neck and the heaviness in his heart, and he knew it was almost time for him to fly.

CHAPTER 30

NAMES

Silas knelt at his father's grave.

The earth was cold. No warmth from the world within rose to his hand as it had before.

On the stone were the letters of his father's name. Black marks carved deep into the rock. An attempt to make immortal that thing which would otherwise most swiftly pass out of the world. Yet Silas knew his father was somewhere.

Not missing like before.

Hiding.

"All this you left to me with barely a word," Silas said quietly. "Fathers are supposed to bless their sons. Not you. Some fathers leave land, money, advice. You left me this." He took the death watch from his pocket and let it dangle from its chain. "You knew . . . you knew what was coming, and still, you left it for me to find, along with everything else that comes with it. You knew Bea would find me if I came here. You knew. All the fear. Yours. Theirs. Mine. Well, I'm not afraid like you. You're a coward. I know you're a coward because if you weren't, you'd be here, right now, helping me. There are ghosts all over this town clinging to their living kin. But you . . . you're out of here like a shot. One farewell in the clock tower and then, 'You're on your own, son.'"

Silas stood and looked around the hill. Beyond, a gray light came over the sea. The wind had fallen away and nothing stirred, nothing appeared. All was as it had been a moment ago. His father was not there.

"Mom wasn't all wrong about you, you know, but I couldn't see it before. You hid in this town. Hid from me. Just like you're hiding now. Don't worry. I can take care of myself."

Silas reached down and scraped a handful of frozen leaves and a bit of earth from the grave. He looked at the dirt in his hand, and began to open his fingers to let it fall, but instead he flung it at the tombstone. The dirt and leaf mold stuck in patches to the stone, covering parts of his dad's name.

Silas turned from the grave and descended the hill the way he'd come.

In the long shadow of the hollow oak where his spade was hidden, the ghost of Amos Umber stood and wept, unable to move or speak aloud, and watched his son walk away.

LEDGER

THREE MAY KEEP A SECRET, IF TWO OF
THEM ARE DEAD.

—FROM THE PAMPHLET *USEFUL TIDINGS FROM THE
WIZARD FRANKLIN. PRINTED IN KINGSPORT*, 1791.
TRANSCRIBED BY AMOS UMBER

*For there is nothing covered, that shall not
be revealed, neither hid, that shall not be
knowen. Therefore, whatsoever yee have
spoken in darkenesse, shall bee heard . . .*

— LUKE, 12: 2–3. MARGINALIA OF JONAS UMBER

CHAPTER 31

ABOVE STAIRS

THE INSIDE OF TEMPLE HOUSE SMELLED LIKE A HIVE. The rich scent of honey was clinging everywhere. A preservative, it must have been pleasing to his mother. Silas had mixed feelings about the smell, remembering Uncle's Camera. It had been a preservative there, too. He had come to consult his uncle's library once more, to see if somewhere among the books of necromancy and dark magics, there might be a way to banish a ghost to whom you'd broken a vow.

When Silas came into the parlor, there was a freezing draft. Bowls of honey sat open to the air by his mother's chair, and there were many unopened bottles lining the bookshelves.

"From Mrs. Bowe. I take the gift of honey very kindly," said Dolores. "I know she doesn't approve of the changes around here, and to send such a gift . . . well, it's very big of her."

Dolores sat in a carved chair near the parlor fireplace where a small fire burned. The statue of the Ammit sat by her right hand.

"Watch your step," said Dolores.

Silas looked down. There were fragments of glass on the floor. A pane of the window had been shattered. A brick sat on the coffee table on top of a stack of old papers.

"See how they fear us now? These are such little people, the ones left in this town. Once, they would have covered the porch with gifts and come for oracles. But, well, look at what the world's become. A town of fear."

"It wasn't very long ago you would have picked up a pitchfork and joined the mob yourself."

"How can you say that, Si? I may have gone through a period of . . . uncertainty about the charms of our old town, but I never lost respect." She paused a moment, looked at the broken glass still on the floor, and then said, "Perhaps fear is a kind of respect too, in its queer, messy way."

"I don't think so," said Silas. "Respect requires some under-standing. Fear is what happens when ignorance gets sharpened to a point. What does any of it matter anyway? People will believe what they want."

She rose, walked over to Silas, and kissed the top of his head. "My wise son," she said, then pointed to the top of the mantel where dark green vines hung down from decorative pots. "But look, another of your friends brought gifts. Joan Peale came with the ivy plants and an excuse about her mother taking ill and not being able to pay her respects. Still, the plants were thoughtful."

Dolores stared at the weariness on Silas's face and said, "You haven't come to see *me*, have you?"

Silas looked at her, confused.

"Go on, if you like. They're somewhere upstairs. I believe they've settled themselves somewhere in the north wing, where your uncle used to store the darkness."

"They?" Silas didn't like the idea of anyone messing around in the north wing. Too many of his uncle's things were still housed there, things he needed, and he thought of it as a private place.

Without another word to his mom, Silas went upstairs and through his uncle's old bedroom, still hung with paintings of grimly rendered mythological abductions. The heavy-browed eyes of Hades glowered at him from the canvas. The furniture was undisturbed, all still under dust cloths as they had been since soon after his uncle had died.

The doors to the anteroom and the Camera Obscura both stood open.

Three familiar, mocking voices said, "Be welcome, Silas Umber, author of our troubles."

As he crossed the threshold of the Camera, he didn't understand what he saw at first.

The three women of the Sewing Circle stood before their massive tapestry. The proportions of the room had swollen considerably. It was hard to imagine this was the same Camera where his uncle had hidden his cousin's corpse in honey, that chamber where the walls closed in and the air was heavy and barely stirred. The room was now vast. Great darkened beams held the warp threads high above. Hundreds of scenes spread out over the wide tapestry.

"What are you doing here?" Silas said. His tone was more accusatory than he'd intended.

"That does not sound like either the thanks or the apology we deserve."

"Thanks? You must be kidding me. Thanks for what?"

"For not seeking retribution against your mother when she tricked us out of a debt owed to us. Rest assured, she will pay that debt in time regardless, one way or another. But, because she came to us only to help you, we were prepared to be flexible in our terms. You know how we dote on you."

"Ladies, I am very nearly at the end of my patience with you and much else."

"And what would that look like, we wonder?"

"I might send you from this house."

"Ah. *That* is not entirely in your power. Your mother invited us here. And we like it. We wish to stay."

"Why would she do that?"

"Because we did her a good turn."

"What?"

"Let us say we helped her achieve her potential. Besides, it's not safe out there for extraordinary people, is it?"

"They're just scared, that's all. Everyone's scared. So they threw a few rocks. So what? It's not the end of the world."

"You want to cast your lot in with the common folk, eh? But you're not very common, are you, Silas Umber? By definition, the extraordinary can't exist easily next to the common."

"You're saying I'll never fit in? Thanks. I already know that."

"You are only just beginning to know it. Each day you work at the Undertaking, you offer your life for theirs, and each time you do so, you'll feel the separation more keenly."

"I'm only doing what anyone would do. I am trying to help my neighbors."

"Don't be absurd. You started out very unlike most folks, and that's why you are where you find yourself. We are sure that there has barely been a single accident . . . no, not in your entire life."

It was the usual game. Now Silas worried that every time he came to see his mother, there would be round after round of *this*. Annoyance reddened his face.

The three adopted a less accusatory tone. "We shall not say you are unique, but understand, Silas Umber, you are a very rare bird indeed. Death follows fast on your heels, and we won't say that is without its uses."

"You say these things because there's something you want from me, just like everyone else. So why don't you say what you want and be done with it?"

"Look here at his highness. He has lost his throne and now his temper, too. He wanders about with Death in his pocket but is never content. It's hard to be special, isn't it? You have our pity."

Anger striped his face, and words of power stirred in his mind. He glared at them.

The three stepped back.

"There is no need to posture so with us. We know who you are and what you can do. Indeed, we know you better than you know yourself."

"How can you know me so well when I don't think I know myself at all?"

"Perhaps you're right. But we know what you *do* . . . what you may *yet do*. Although 'Lord of the Dead' is not a job in the conventional sense. You have no office to work from. The world is your studio. Do you not see?"

"Yes. I see," he said wearily. "I am surrounded by death all the time. Now you tell me I *am* Death. What's the difference? It's a word game."

"No game. And we didn't say you were Death. Not yet. 'Lord of the Dead' implies responsibilities and obligations. 'Death' is a state of being. Well, of course, you may at any time and at your discretion run about willy-nilly bringing Peace to the rowdy dead, if you like. You might even end a life if you put your mind to it . . . you have such words within you now. But that is not the nature of your particular calling. You are the Undertaker. Death was the first one to hold that title. He took them *below*. You may make as much or as little of that title as you like. If you ever settle your losses sufficiently and lay your melancholy aside, you may certainly add the title of 'Death' to your already impressive list of credentials. But truly, no one really cares what you call yourself, so long as you serve the *polis*.

"The process of death continues not because you individually work to turn the wheel of mortality, but because you are merely present here and now. And, should the time come that you leave this world, there will be another. Perhaps of your family, perhaps not. The dead congregate about you because you are a magnet to them. This town was founded on such attractions. Death came out of the East and the dead followed him. But in the long ago days, Death, like you, was world-weary by nature. A melancholic. He wanted to stretch his legs and think of gladder tidings. He wanted a new land to call his own where the earth was not so packed with bones. So he fought a war and left the Old World. People understood too little then of the protocols . . . but rest assured, whether on this shore or that old one, people dropped off just like clockwork, because Death continued to *be* Death.

"As we've said, it's not so formal, nor so literal. Dream it, be it, as the proverb says. Point of view is everything, especially for extraordinary people such as yourself. Some might say, when you returned to Lichport, as you were then, that you were dead already. But truly, you have blossomed here. And so as long as *a* Death is present in the world, the great work continues, people will die. Well, most of them anyway. There are always exceptions and they are generally despised. As you've seen.

"Silas, it is easy to see our words bring you little comfort. We are not unsympathetic to your position. Death is a chore to most, something to be dealt with. And a long afterlife is an ordeal, even though there are pleasures as well. All souls long for rest. Even young ones. We are tired . . . goodness knows. Of course, you could always refuse your position."

"What if I did refuse?"

"Oh, well, as for that, you would find that our fair town would suffer for your modern way of seeing things, your lack of obligation. Your presence here holds some very dangerous, very unstable forces in a state of tension. We might, for example, in your absence, assert certain of our customary rights. And we prefer things a little on the dark side."

"Indeed we do," confirmed the third.

"It's true," said the second, showing her teeth.

"Or there might be others who rise up to take your place. Indeed, one already is attempting just that. Your inability to keep your vow has allowed one formerly imprisoned below Arvale to ride right into Lichport. And now we've had to move house as a direct result of *his* action and *your* inaction. Very inconvenient."

"I know. I know. I'm sorry."

"If it makes you feel any better, it's not a matter of good versus evil or anything so trite. Simply put, there are forces in a state of contention in the world. One departs, others vie to fill the space left behind. You, oh Death-To-Be, occupy a very important position. Those who would seek to fill your shoes would hardly be the humanitarian type. But you, because of your terrible birth rites... you are keenly prepared for such a role, Silas, Osiris, Serapis, Mors." The three looked at one another and laughed as one, then said, "It sounds like a law firm."

"I am glad you find me so entertaining, but I don't think I can bear the weight of another god on my shoulders, let alone all of those."

"Don't be ridiculous. The gods are not on us—"

"You are forgetting Jove and his paramours," interrupted the second.

"Yes, yes. All right. But my point is this," continued the first, "the gods are *within* us."

"More riddles."

"Not at all," said the three together.

The first of the three continued: "It is not nearly as complicated as you imagine. At night, you see the sky is full of stars. But during the day, you see only the sun. However, that does not mean all the stars have vanished. They are still there, only hidden from sight. So with you. But there is no need to feel schizophrenic. The gods of life and death are not discrete in us. You travel *through* their names and stations, Silas Umber, back and forth, invoking their powers as need requires. You are part of a pattern. As in the stars and their constellations, and you can see it here, in the tapestry, one strand woven through many other strands, unique, but not isolate. Give over, child. Janus, Osiris, Serapis . . . what has gone into the earth shall rise again in you. Embrace your fate, Undertaker. Say 'yes' to Death. Endings are very much in your nature. There is no prologue in you. You are all conclusion. We have been preparing too, and when our work is done, we might all begin again, fresh and new as the first morning of the world. Your father, and many others before him, could not accept the elegance of the inevitable. We were meant to work together. So Death contrived a special path for you, brief, perhaps, but very unique. You have been his from the beginning and there is nothing for you to lose that you have not already lost."

They had worn him down. Silas looked pitiful, his head hung low. "Mysteries and more mysteries . . ." He sighed. "You know what I find mysterious?"

"Mah-jongg?" they asked a little absently, the fun ebbing from the game.

"No."

"What happens after you die?"

"What happens to the dead is hardly a mystery to me anymore."

They smiled, leading him. "All right, what then?"

"How do we go on, day after miserable day, not knowing who we truly are? How is *that* done? How do you look at everything rotting away around you and then get out of bed and start each day? That's what I'd like to know."

"You are beginning to speak like an old man."

"Maybe because I'm feeling old."

The third of the three leaned in close to him and said, "Would you truly like the answer to your question? You won't like it."

"Go on."

"You begin by not asking questions like that. You get up. You go forward and you don't look back. You take up a hobby. You show up. You love your children and your friends and those in whose glad company you find yourself. Distractions are the key. You should plant a garden. A garden is *very* distracting. When God sent mankind from the garden, it was a very bad day, and people have been complaining ever since. That's when Death crept in to fill the hours and then began to end them. Serve the world and win back your life. Then, there is a chair hard by and beneath the earth with your name on it. Silas, take it! And let it all be done."

This last part, Silas understood. What she meant was sacrifice. Not an offering to some god or other. But giving yourself to the world. Be the sacrifice. But also be the god. Then something chimed in his mind.

"Stop. What chair?"

"The throne of the Lord of the Dead. It is very fine and, for such an old thing, it is in an excellent state of preservation."

"Like so many of the things he surrounds himself with." The second laughed.

"It would look very fine in your foyer," the third joined in. "You can see it in the catalogue if you like."

"Do you mean the throne I saw at Arvale?"

"The very one."

"'Hard by,' you said. Do you mean it is close?"

"Just outside the door, you may see what we mean. In the account book of that brotherhood whose house this once was. In truth, they were pack rats. Here."

The first of the three drew out a long bone needle and pointed to Temple House on the tapestry. In one of its high windows was embroidered the scene Silas stood within: a thin figure with a small crown of lights about his head stood before three tall ladies stitched roughly in pale cotton thread. Silas could see his mother in the richly embroidered rooms below, tiny, intricate gold threads for her body and green silk for her face.

Silas looked up, confused.

"The green is an homage, an old Egyptian motif. Allow us some artistic discretion. Looking at it again, I think that color would suit you as well," said the second, taking up her shears and leaning toward the tapestry. "I could tear you out and rework you. . . ."

"No, thank you," said Silas, continuing to follow the complex, interwoven patterns of Temple House. To the side of the main structure, many threads of different colors led to the rotunda. Silas looked, fascinated not by the older building's columns in sturdy gray wool, but by the fantastically detailed chamber depicted below it. In comparison to the rotunda above, and to the house, the underground chamber was vast. The details were so numerous, so tiny, that Silas could barely make them out. He remembered, from the days with his uncle, how hollow the floor sounded, how dizzy it made him to stand upon it. In the tapestry, it looked like a kind of vast warehouse, or a museum. There were little depictions of statues rendered in metallic thread and dusty velvets. A throne in ebony silk stood out from the others, perhaps because it had just been mentioned. At the center of the labyrinthine chamber, there were flames of golden and scarlet thread stitched one over another. As he moved closer to the tapestry, Silas could see, at the fire's center, another fire was depicted. Over that conflagration of silks, worked in careful stitches of bronze thread, was the bullheaded idol of Moloch, Devourer of Children.

Silas stepped back.

Cabel Umber was hiding below the house. And the idol was lit with fire, and it was from below the rotunda that Cabel Umber put his curse upon Lichport.

"Ladies, I have to go. I appreciate your candor."

"Leaving already?"

"I have business below the house."

"How will you accomplish this task? How will you banish this spirit when you are bound by a broken vow?"

"I will try to find a way, maybe in my uncle's books—"

The three interrupted him, speaking as one. "Only sacrifice will cleanse the *polis*."

The words rang true and confirmed what Silas had begun to suspect was the only way to send Cabel Umber from Lichport.

"So be it," Silas said, resigned. "In that case, I'd like to ask you for a favor."

The three stared at him.

"Watch over this house. Watch over my mother."

"Are you asking us to take over for you?" said the first of the three.

"I am asking for your help, if I cannot bring Peace to this ghost below my mother's house. Beneath *our* house."

"We cannot raise a hand against him while you are present and your oath to him is unfulfilled."

"But if I'm gone, even for a brief time?"

The first spoke gravely, "In another aspect, our help might

be more considerable. Like you, we wear several masks—"

"I know who you are."

"Has he shed the blood of kin?"

Silas thought of Alysoun, Cabel Umber's daughter. She had been imprisoned in the catacombs below Arvale, but Silas didn't know if her father had actually shed her blood. Silas touched his arm where Cabel had cut the curse glyph into his skin. "He has shed my blood! We share a name. We are kin."

The air in the Camera grew heavier and the light dimmed.

"And what form shall his punishment take, should it come to pass?" said the three, their voices drawn together into an edge.

"I don't want to sit in judgment over him. My hope is to convince him to go, or to bring him the Peace. But if it comes to that, ladies, do what you think is best."

The three nodded.

"You shall owe us a great debt, Silas Umber, if we must take up against him."

"Can there be debt between a brother and his sisters, or between partners in the same business?"

The three smiled to one another.

"It's hard not to love him," said the third.

"Indeed," said the second. "If he does not return, we shall miss him very keenly."

Silas turned to leave the Camera, but the three called after him.

"But before you dash, do tell us: Have you gotten to the good part of your current reading?"

"I have no idea what you mean. That catalogue out there? The ledger?" He knew those were not the books they meant. "The scraps of my father's diary? I've read them."

"We believe that you have been given an edited edition.

Sanitized for the protection of the young. Speaking of the young, and the poor firstborn, oh, Silas, your birthday puts the other children's to shame."

"Stop it. Tell me," Silas said sharply.

"It is not our place to stage such a play for you," said the second of the three.

"But now that you ask," said the first of the three quietly, "don't you wonder why you have such an aptitude for death? One might even call it a fascination. . . ."

"A fetish," said the third.

"Do you think I need any of you to tell me there's something wrong with me? With my life? Everything I love or once loved is dead. Bea. My father. This town. My mom, sort of. And the living people I do care for are literally made sick by my friendship. So, if you actually know why everything is so screwed up for me, I'd welcome an actual answer."

"The elegant simplicity of the matter eludes you. You think you are broken. Not so. But you are incomplete. And even though you don't know it, you seek what you lack. You search without for what should be within. Even when you were looking for your father, it wasn't all about old Amos, was it? Something's always been missing . . . always and always . . . and you look for it, though you don't know what it is," said the first.

Silas peered back at the tapestry, but nothing stood out. Queasiness churned his stomach as only truth can.

"Tell me what I've lost. It's too easy to make sport."

"Ask your father."

"I don't know where he is. I haven't seen him since the night before his wake."

"Fled the scene of the crime, eh? How like a man," said the third.

"Well, then you should fly along to your mother before dashing below stairs. She will no longer withhold anything from you. She's a very modern woman now. Go, Silas Umber, and claim the knowledge of your birthright. And when all the stories have been told, should you return from such a day, we shall be waiting for you, and the family business shall continue properly."

After Silas left the Camera, the first of the three spoke to the others: "There are threads left too long hanging. Time to stitch them down and have done."

"But which ones?" asked the second.

"Is there a choice?" asked the third.

"There is always a choice," said the first. "But we must work with what we have." She leaned in close to where the stitches of Silas Umber below stairs hung loose, faded and gray.

"This all must be reworked, I think. And very quickly."

The second and third nodded.

"Now be a dear," said the first to the second, "and bring me the good shears and the thread of bronze."

LEDGER

IN ALL OUR PERIODS AND TRANSITIONS IN
THIS LIFE, ARE SO MANY PASSAGES FROM
DEATH TO DEATH; OUR VERY BIRTH AND
ENTRANCE INTO THIS LIFE IS <u>EXITUS Á MORTE</u>,
AN ISSUE FROM DEATH, FOR IN OUR MOTHER'S
WOMB WE ARE DEAD. . . . IN THE WOMB
WE HAVE EYES AND SEE NOT, EARS AND HEAR
NOT. THERE IN THE WOMB WE ARE FITTED FOR
WORKS OF DARKNESS. . . .

—FROM JOHN DONNE, *DEATH'S DUEL.*

   MARGINALIA OF AMOS UMBER

EVEN AS YOU AWAIT THE BABY'S EMERGENCE
FROM THE WOMB OF YOUR WIFE, SO AWAIT
THE HOUR WHEN THE LITTLE SOUL SHALL
GLIDE FORTH FROM ITS SHEATH.

—FROM MARCUS AURELIUS.

   MARGINALIA OF AMOS UMBER

CHAPTER 32

BIRTH RITE

SILAS CAME DOWN THE STAIRS and into the parlor. His mother was there. She looked right into his eyes, waiting for him to speak, waiting to be challenged.

"Can you account for every moment in your life?" Silas asked.

"What do you mean, Si? I don't know. I think so."

"But which are the stories, the mere anecdotes, and which the real experiences? Can you tell one from the other?"

"Silas, you're talking nonsense."

"So says the woman who is more animated now than she ever was in life. I think we are only alive while we are feeling things happen to us, when we experience life in the moment. The second after that, the moment we begin telling ourselves about ourselves, we become ghosts. I can barely feel anything anymore. But I can tell you a tale if you like . . . a story about Silas Umber, Undertaker of Lichport. I think he's felt dead for some time now, our hero."

"Silas, stop it. If you want to ask me something, ask. I can't play games anymore. Not with you."

"I want you to show me what's missing from my father's diary. I want you to show me what he could not tell me. What you can't tell me. I want to know what happened when I was born."

Dolores rose from her chair and lifted the brick that had broken her window from some sheets of papers covered in Amos's handwriting. She turned her head away as she handed them to Silas.

He looked at the pages. "Is this all of it?"

"Trust me," Dolores said, "this is what you're looking for. What did you do with the rest, the pages I gave you before?"

"I threw them in the fire."

"Really?" She looked relieved.

"Yes. I watched them burn."

"You should do the same with these. Really you should."

"Why didn't you burn them?"

"Because they're true and because your name is on them, and I couldn't, Si. I just couldn't. Whatever is meant for you," she said, closing her eyes, "you must face it without ignorance of how you began. I won't keep that from you any longer."

Silas didn't answer. He went across the foyer to his uncle's old exhibit rooms, found a chair near a lamp, sat down, and began to read. And as Silas read the torn pages back to front, one after another, his hands shook so that the paper trembled. And the more he read, the more he wept, at first because he didn't understand, but then because he did.

◆ ◆ ◆

What would I not give for him? Silas. My child. My life is his. Only sacrifice can end suffering, so I know my days will be short. One way or another, he will come for me. My life for Silas's, so he might have even a few more years beneath the sun. I will drown my cares in my love for him. And I will watch over him as best I can. And I will wait for him at the thresholds if I may, but I fear that power has now been taken from me. I am cursed by my all-too-perfect recollection of that day when he was born.

These pages I will most likely burn. Either way, I will never look on them again. I had sworn never to write these words. That was years ago, and my son is still with us. But I feel that not to record what happened would be the greater sin. There is no fading of these events from time. They are as fresh in my eyes as the day they happened. I cannot, even now, look upon my son and not see some lingering vision of him as an infant, lying among the flowers of the field, and that shadow risen at his side. . . .

How could any child know the madness of his father? We give ourselves to our children. Our lives for theirs, but then we must give them up, sacrifice them to the world, offerings made to their unknown futures. We are all Abrahams and we offer up our children to Death and say nothing. They are born, they live, they die. And sometimes they don't live long. Still, we carry them to the altar and it shall all end in tears. I never should have had a child. Never. The gods that live in the Umber line, the old gods of death and loss and judgment, might have faded out of the world. Then we could have stumbled on, mere mortals, mostly blind to the terrible worlds hiding just behind our own. The joys of such ignorance . . . I will never know them. Neither will my son.

We each must meet the mysteries in our own ways. I cannot bring myself to write the words of what shall become of my son. What I sought to flee, he shall be subjected to. Oh, my son. In my ignorance I have wrought your fate. Forgive me.

Nascentes Morimur.

Dolores had a brief labor. The midwife was pleased. The baby's head had crowned. A few more moments, we thought, and we would be parents to a child.

The midwife spoke calmly to Dolores. I remember her saying, "Push again and the hardest part's over."

How could she know it to be a lie? Then the baby came. I did not hear it cry, but the midwife said, "Your son is breathing."

Dolores was exhausted, but she sat up slightly in the bed and the midwife handed her our son. The midwife busied herself as Dolores called me to the bed. The child was still and quiet.

He's not breathing, I said.

Amos, he's sleeping.

Dolores, I said, my panic rising, he is not breathing!

The midwife looked at the baby and fear engulfed her face. She turned the baby over and swatted its bottom. No cry came. She said, I will go to get help.

Amos? Dolores cried.

Wait, I said. Wait. I ran to my desk, got the death watch, held the dial. A bird circled the bed and no sooner had I seen it than it flew from the room, out of the house.

Sensing the now real absence of her son, Dolores began to scream. She cried, Amos, bring home the child! Bring home the child!

Dolores, he's gone, I said. Our boy is gone.

But she was adamant. Go now! she screamed. Find him and bring him home. Bring home the child!

And I ran and the mist parted before me. The presence of the small enlivened corpse in the house drew spirits toward it. I raised the ring of Anubis and it burned and shone with blue fire and scattered the mindless spirits before me. I could see the bird as it flew over the marshes and followed it out upon the mist paths, but then it vanished.

Frantic, I parted the mists once more and cast my mind toward the Gates of Moloch, that threshold through which pass the spirits of the firstborn. A risk, I knew, but as I ran, the bullheaded idol rose up before me, and through its flames, I saw once again the small bird flying ahead.

I followed the bird through the fire and over lands I've never known until I saw broad fields spreading out, then a meadow flowing away to the hills. There, clustered stalks of asphodels were crowned in white star flowers.

It was then I knew where I was.

And there was my baby. An infant-corpse in the field of asphodel, wrapped in his swaddling cloth, staring up at the blooms with open, unblinking eyes. And by his side, Death stood as a child, and on his arm sat the little bird I'd followed along the lych way. The baby did not move, but the little bird was lively, and Death lifted the little bird to his face, where it pecked lightly at his lips.

I said, "My life for his."

Death shook his head.

"What, then?"

Idly, Death pointed at the baby's corpse, and said, "You should be pleased. What I propose is an honor to your house. Your son shall be my son. He shall follow in my footsteps and hold the key to the land of the dead."

I pleaded again, "My life for his. Let me serve you."

"You? Who have so deliberately shunned the greater public service? No."

"Let me serve you. Then, later, he can be yours. But not yet. Please. Not yet."

The child plucked one of the asphodel stalks, then looked at me and nodded.

I wept. "Just a little more time. Thank you. Thank you."

"But then he must come to me of his own free will."

"Yes." I would have said anything.

"One last thing," said the child.

"Isn't my life enough? And my son's life later?"

"One life? Two lives? What are those? No great things in the larger reckoning, I think."

"What else?"

"I will have this place as my own."

"This field?" I asked, knowing it was not what Death meant.

"That place." The child pointed over the river toward town. "I am tired of wandering, weary of exile. I will have that place for my own, and I shall be Death to those who reside there. That shall be my place. My home. Lichport shall be Death's seat."

"How could that be? I can't give you a town; it's not mine to give."

"If you give me your son, it will be enough. The town lives in him. So shall I. If you like, you may consider this inevitable. Either I take him now, or later. One way or another he shall come to me."

"I will not give him to you. I will not give you my son. Not yet."

"That is not for you to say."

"He could take the waters, leave this world. I could give him the waters. He would leave you behind and forget."

"That is true. But then he would still be gone and unable to return in any form. I think we both want something more for him. Indeed, always, he was meant to be with me. I came to these shores to wait for him, to help him onto that dark throne that is mine alone to bestow. But so be it. Let him come to me by his own will. And sooner, not later. And if he does . . . well, then your child shall carry Death within him and all shall be well and he will abide in a place of honor. So take him now, Amos Umber. For just a little while more, he is yours."

But the thought of Death eventually enticing Silas away from life . . . and when would it be? When he was five and ran to him, just another child appearing on the playground? I was still mad with fear.

Death walked to my side. The little bird plucked a flower from the stalk of asphodel he held. Then Death let the bird hop onto my wrist. I could barely feel its weight.

"Now go home, Amos Umber. But know that soon we shall meet again, and certainly, it will be too soon for your liking."

I turned and pretended to go, but I took the death watch from my pocket

and pried off the very top of the skull, which I had never before opened. The
spirit contained within swiftly fled, leaving the mechanism incomplete.

I turned then to Death, who still played with the stalk of asphodel,
and uttering certain ancient words I will not here record, I consigned
him to the death watch. The moment he was trapped within, I released
the dial and the mechanism returned to life. I wrapped the cord all
around the watch, so that the seal on the lid could not be breached
before I could better seal it later with lead or silver.

The death watch ticked in my hand and the field of asphodel was
gone. I stood knee-deep in the marshes, but the little bird, my son's
quickening soul, I clutched like my own life.

I ran, through the marshes and past the millpond, on to the streets of
Lichport and finally home. But as I ran, I heard a voice. Whether it was
Death or my own shame speaking in my mind I do not know: Always it
will be thus, for you. To never take hands with another. To win by
guile what you might have had for love. And when your last day
comes, go to that prison you have prepared for yourself during
your life. Or, if you can, say farewell to those you love. And only if
the soul bell be rung for you shall you make farewell. Only so long
as the bell rope swings may you speak your peace to the living and
not a moment longer. Once it stops, you shall not return to them,
nor speak to them from the shadows. We shall share a fate, you
and I, by your hand, by your broken vow. So long as we are kept
from our inheritor: for you, Amos Umber, the door shall be closed.

I turned my mind away from those words. I buried them inside
myself. There was only the moment and the hope of life for my son.

Dolores called out, even as I approached the house.

I entered our home, the little bird hidden in my hand. She sat
by the bed. No doctor had yet come, nor had the midwife returned.
I took the baby from her. I took the small bird into my mouth and,
leaning over the baby's cold body, breathed the bird into him. I closed
my eyes. The baby gasped. The blanket covering his body began to

squirm with the movement of his legs and arms. Petals of asphodel fell from where they clung to my jacket onto the baby's head.

Dolores began to cry and said, Jesus Christ, Amos, what have you done?

Take him, Dolores, now, I told her.

Without thinking, she reached out and I placed the baby in her arms. She held the child slightly away from her body. The baby began to cry.

Amos, she moaned, come and take your son.

I held my child then. His eyes looked wild, like a hunted thing, but slowly he calmed and slept and breathed easily, and was, in semblance, a child like any other.

When the midwife returned with the doctor, all was well. The doctor explained away the midwife's account.

The baby could have been cold, he said. These newborns can give every suggestion of trouble, but all usually comes right in a moment or two, he said, as I thanked them and showed them from the house.

But the next day, when Mrs. Bowe came to give her blessing to the child, she looked at the baby, and saw the shadow on him, or rather, the shadow he lacked, and she wept.

Morimur Nascentes, I say now, changing the edict. To die is to be born.

I set the following translation at the end of this account. I will inscribe it within the ledger with my other notes, but here may it serve as a fervent prayer. May we have life. May my son have life. May he find another way. A simpler way than the path of judgment trod out by his kin. But not yet. Let that day take its time in arriving. When the shadow comes over me, may I remember these words. No more than this, no harder, nor more terrible. May it end this way for me and mine. Yet I fear, for me, darkness waits to pay back the gifts I've given it.

A man dieth not gladly that hath not learned it,
therefore learn to die so that thou shalt live.
For there shall be no man who lives well
but he who hath learned to die well . . .
This life is but a passing time . . .
and when thou beginnest to live,
thou beginnest to die.
Now hearken and understand.
Death is but a parting between the body
 and the soul and every man
 knows that is well.

      —FROM "LERNE TO DYE" BY THOMAS HOCCLEVE
        (c.1421–26)

CHAPTER 33

TURN THE PAGE

SILAS SAT IN THE COLD EXHIBIT ROOMS of Temple House. The glass doors of the artifact cases held a hundred reflections of him clutching the papers in his hand. As he finished reading his father's account of his birth, Silas could barely draw breath.

When he looked up, he saw his mother had come in at some point and had taken the chair opposite his. She sat, unblinking, watching him.

"I had already begun to grieve for you, Si. You cannot understand what that means, when a mother begins to mourn her dead child. My hopes had died too, and I had accepted in those few moments that I would never be happy again.

"Then you came back.

"When I saw your father come into the house, the room went dark. I could see something moving, some small thing stirring the air with its presence. Then that dead child . . . Lord . . . and *you* began to cry. Silas, I thought my heart had stopped. You'd think I would have leapt for joy, but it was fear that held me. I looked at your father's face and could see that whatever he'd seen, it was not of this world. Whatever it was he had done to bring you back, it was no natural thing, somehow more terrible than the terrors that were his daily bread. And he looked scared. Your father looked scared. He picked you up and tried to hand you to me. I couldn't take you. Even though you were crying so loud. Amos held you tight in his arms and sat down. Slowly, you quieted, and then you slept, your father holding you. Your eyes were closed, but I saw your nose twitch a bit and you gently breathed the air as though nothing at all had happened. Neither one of us could speak. I think we were afraid to. Afraid that if we made any noise at all, the fragile spell that held the life in you would shatter.

"Silas, you're my son and I love you, but then, as things were, I could barely look at you. You scared me. I remember there was a flower caught in the little bit of hair you had, the same as the flowers stuck to your father's jacket. I reached out, plucked it from a curl, and threw it on the fire. I had never seen that flower in Lichport before. God knows where you'd been or where your father had found you, let alone how it was he brought you back."

"Were you scared of . . . are you scared of me now?" Silas said.

"No. Silas, look at me. How could I be? Now we are mother and son. And two creatures who have escaped death. However it happened, here we both are. We have to look out for each other."

Dolores looked down, fixing her gaze upon at the preternatural skin of her hand. She said absently, perhaps not wanting to know the answer, "Are you frightened of me, Si?"

Silas walked over and took his mother's hand. "I'm not. Mom, I'm not scared of you. I am not scared of death, either."

"Would you . . . do you think, you'd prefer to take after my side of the family—later, I mean?"

He understood the question. "I don't want that, although I'm not sure anyone has a choice in the matter. I'm not frightened of what you've become. You're still my mom. But I don't want to live on that way. I don't know. Now, I guess, I don't care when Death comes for me. I've been living on borrowed time all along anyway. We both know I shouldn't even be alive. My father cheated. Whenever my death comes, I'm not going to fight it.

Every problem I've seen or faced as Undertaker has been caused by people refusing to give death its due. I'd like to think I've learned something."

"How can you say that, Silas? How can you not care about living as long as possible? I would have fought off death with both hands, bitten and scratched, had I seen it coming for me."

"Only if you were fighting for your own life. When mine was being threatened by a curse, you took that curse upon yourself and went to your own death willingly. You sacrificed yourself for me. I know."

"I would do anything for you, Silas. I had lost you once. I couldn't lose you again, even if it meant your losing me. But we're both here now. That's all that matters."

"I don't think now, as you are, you can understand me. Maybe, as I am, after the last year, I just don't see that much difference between life and death anymore."

"I couldn't disagree more," said Dolores.

"I know. But we each have our own roads now. You're all set. I still have things I need to do. The sooner I do them, the sooner I can come back and we can keep arguing about this." He tried to smile at her, but then his smiled faded. "Why couldn't you tell me?"

"Silas—"

"Later, I mean. All those years together. Dad coming and going. You could have filled in some gaps. It might have helped. Part of what happened, losing a child, is common enough."

"You're asking me why I didn't talk about my stillborn son who came back from the dead? Silas, really. Even if it had all ended on the day of your birth-death, who would speak of it openly? Silas, women don't talk about these things with the rest of their families. Even miscarriages, very common, are only whispered about, and then only by the women. These are 'women's mysteries,' things men do not deign to hear. If a woman started talking, really talking frankly about the blood, the clots, the things that come out of us . . . the miscarriages, the babies, the parts of babies . . . all the things we create and discharge, if we gave voice to all that, men would drop dead on the spot. You ask me why I didn't talk about it—the answer is because your sex is weak. Men have an awful fear of death, and our bleeding reminds them of it. But women live on, and men are terrified of our . . . *changes*. And we are *always* changing.

"Even now, my body is undergoing powerful, awesome changes. You want me to talk about it? Sure. I could tell you of the drawing away of the moisture from my skin. I think it is, I don't know what to call it, calcifying? Still supple, but no longer what it was . . . I can feel these shifts toward permanence . . . my skin, my muscles becoming more resilient, tougher. And my organs . . . I think they are shrinking. I can feel hollows in my body now, spaces where there never were spaces before. My mind is not only my mind. I can feel others like myself. And I can feel you, through our shared blood. It is as though you are an infant again, an extension of my body. Sometimes I imagine I am seeing through your eyes. But I'm sure your great-grandfather has told you something of our condition. What more may I tell you, Silas?"

"Nothing. That's okay."

"You see? Men can't handle change. I guess, if it were thirty thousand years ago, this is the part where you'd make an excuse about how you need to run off and do some hunting, and then leave me alone with my clots and thoughts, in the moon-hut with the other maidens and crones."

"Mom?"

"It's all right, Si. I know. Enough. It's okay."

Dolores paused, then added, "Strange, though. There are so

many things we blind ourselves to in life, consigning common truths to shadows. But now . . . now it's all clear to me. I can see right through every cloud. No more hiding, not for either of us. Everything is all out on the table. I think it's better that way. Don't you?"

"You're right, Mom. You are. Everything out on the table. So. I love you. But I have to go. I know who's followed me out of Arvale and is trying to kill me and who has fouled the air in town. I don't know if I'm coming back. And let's admit it now, I'm not sure most people would miss me. I am an outsider. You heard what people said. They blame me, and they're right. You know, I have walked all over this town. I've looked in a lot of windows at night. I've seen families light their candles and draw their curtains against the dark. But I was always outside. Always looking in from the shadows. That's not an accident. If I need to die so that others live, well, I've cheated death twice now, right? From the very beginning, really, I've been unnatural, and everyone can feel it. So I'll go down there and do what I can, and if I can't convince this spirit to depart, well, there are others older and wiser than me that we may call upon. If I die trying, what's really been lost?"

Dolores stepped toward him. "Silas, you can say you don't care whether you live or die, but I care! That's why I don't want you going anywhere alone right now. You're in no fit state. You need people about you."

"I have to go alone. I want to try and settle this my own way. Yes, there are others waiting even now to be called upon who would gladly bring down judgment upon this ghost because he has spilled the blood of his own family. You may call upon them yourself, should the need arise. They are already close by."

Dolores looked up at the ceiling in the direction of the Camera Obscura.

Silas continued. "Yes, you know of whom I speak. Their solution would be horrible and irrevocable, I suspect. So I will do what I can first and leave aside more severe resolutions if possible. I've seen what happens when the old punishments are invoked. Terror only begets more terror. Judgment more judgments. I'm not that kind of Undertaker. If this spirit can be convinced to accept Peace, to take the waters of Lethe, or to leave of his own accord, it will be better, safer, for everyone."

"I am still going with you. Give me time to pack a few things."

"Mom—"

"Silas, don't argue."

"I'm not arguing with you. Come if you like, but only as far as the entrance to whatever is below. I won't turn down a little more time with you."

"Then where are you going?"

"The spirit I seek is very close."

"Silas?" Her eyes narrowed. "How close?"

Silas shook his head. He only wanted her to come with him as far as the threshold of descent, wherever it was. He didn't know what kind of harm could be inflicted on her now, as she was, and he didn't want to find out. He was pretty sure he could face his own death, should it come, but he didn't think he could stand to see his mother still and lifeless a second time. But then, he realized, if he failed to bring the Peace to Cabel Umber, he wouldn't be there to see whatever followed.

"Silas! Where. Are. We. Going?"

He held his mother's hand and, with his other hand, pointed down at the floor of her house, saying only, "Down there."

They walked together through the parlor toward the arch leading to the rotunda. As Silas walked past the statue of the Ammit sitting next to his mother's favorite chair, he paused and, with his ring hand, he stroked the crocodile head of the creature and whispered something so his mother could not hear. Then he smiled and said softly, "Watch over her, watch over this house." Perhaps from the dry static air, the little hairs on the Ammit's neck stood up against Silas's hand.

CHAPTER 34

ROTUNDA

SILAS JUMPED ON THE FLOOR, and with each landing, a hollow boom sounded.

"See?" he said to his mother. "There's a big space below."

"But how do you get down there?"

"I have no idea."

They each went their own way along the curved walls of the rotunda. They knocked on the paneling and columns, listening for unseen hollows. They pulled on the sconces, looking for a device that would reveal a secret passage to whatever the Brothers of the Temple had hidden below. To no avail.

"We might have to bring up the tiles," said Dolores. "That would be a pity. I don't think there's anyone in Lichport or Kingsport who can do this sort of work anymore."

"There might be another way," said Silas. He threw open his arms as he had done before the great doors at Arvale. Not a desk drawer opened.

Dolores looked around the room. "Was that supposed to accomplish something, Si?"

The gesture felt hollow. He told his mother about losing the Janus pendant in the millpond.

"Silas, I guarantee that any trinket of your father's had very little real power in it. Whatever you thought it did for you, well, that power is *in* you, not on you. Do it again."

Silas leaned forward slightly; he breathed in slowly. When he threw his arms wide again, he brought his foot down hard on the floor, and several unseen doors in the rotunda flew open. One of the doors led to a secret shelf of hidden books. Another was a small broom cupboard near the far wall, long forgotten. But at the back of the enormous fireplace, a great passage of stone had been revealed.

Dolores looked at her son.

Silas nodded and began walking over to the mantel.

Dolores's voice rose in panic, following Silas across the room. "How can you do this? Whatever is down there nearly killed you once before. Indeed, it killed me, after a fashion. Wait. We'll get help."

"There is no help for this. I could search the books for curses and spells, but to what end? I have broken a vow and I can bring no force against him. But I can try to bring him the Peace."

"Silas, please! Don't be so dramatic!"

"*Nascentes Morimur,* to be born is to die," Silas said. "But not for me. My father denied me the one thing that is the birthright of every person. I am not dramatic, I'm unnatural. Whatever is crouching down there in the earth is only a ghost. Whatever else it may call itself, that is what it is. I have made mistakes. I have given it some portion of power over me, and its curses have spilled over onto those I love. I will make it right, one way or another. Trust me. This ghost's past and my own losses are inextricably knotted. There is only one road. My father knew it, and I can see it now. Let me follow it where it leads. Whatever happens, Mom, remember me, and be strong."

"Silas, stop it! You are not going down there alone. The arrogance—"

"I don't see why you're so worried. I've been dead before.

And let's be honest, I have been a burden to my family."

"That's not true. I mean, every child is a burden to its family, Si, one way or another."

"I've been more than a burden. Dad said so in his diary. He said more than that."

"He didn't mean he didn't want you. Damn it, Silas! See? That's why I wanted it kept from you. No one page in a person's life stands for everything. Your father may have *written* that then, but you were reading a moment in time. One moment. Silas, listen. Your father was scared. Scared of what might happen to you. Scared of the things borne in the blood of both our families. And we all see why, don't we? You have picked up where he left off, and so it will all continue."

"It won't continue for long, because I'm never going to have a child."

"Don't say that, Si! How do you know? Of course you'll have children."

"You see? Bea would have been the perfect wife for me. No chance then of . . . anything else."

"Silas, please. Don't go down there."

"Too late for turning back. I have set my course."

"I just wish . . . oh, Silas . . ."

"What?"

"I wish I could keep you from what's coming. I wish we could just be . . . as we are."

"No one has that power. Change is the only certain thing."

"But if we waited—"

"I can't."

"Si, let me go instead."

"Not yet. If I can't settle the ghost, *then* I will need your help. But I must try first. He may listen to me. You can't go in my place.

Besides, you've already had your journey into darkness. Now it is time for mine."

"You'll come back to me," Dolores said, closing her eyes.

"Mom—"

"Say it, Silas. Say you'll come back to me."

"You'll come back to me," he repeated, trying to smile.

"Wait, Si! Please! And if you die? Silas! Christ! What are you thinking?"

"I can't turn back now. My problem has been with me, or rather, hidden from me, since I was born. I need to find what's missing from my life, or what good am I to others? Roads of the living, roads of the dead, they all lead forward from here. Sometimes, we must leave the world to enter it properly."

"Death? That's what you want?"

"*A* death. Yes."

"You want to die?"

"No. But I can see what must happen now, even if you can't."

"You asked me if I was frightened of you. I'm not. But I'm frightened by what you're saying. I'm scared I'm not going to see you again."

"Mom, don't. Please try to understand. It's not about being alive or dead. It's about being whole, about accepting who I am and what I am. Like every tortured ghost I've seen or helped, I am lost, or rather, I am the sum of my losses. Right through. I thought it was because I couldn't find something I was looking for: Dad, friendship, your love, my place. But it's not any of those things. I am incomplete *in my self,* and I have been from the moment I was born.

"Life and death . . . those are blurred for me now. There are no more boundaries. We all die. All of us." He looked at his mom and smiled. "No matter how long we are able to put it off, eventually we all must take that road into the shadowlands. But I think, if we do it knowingly, if we accept the inevitable, the nature of the journey can be something more than the terror of the unknown. I think I know what's waiting beyond the fire, and I'm not scared, but I need to know for sure. I promise we will see each other again. I love you, Mom. Trust me. And if I'm not back soon, remember, this is *your* house. Yours and no one else's. There's power in that."

"Silas . . ." But Dolores's words fell away. She looked at her son and put her arms around him. "I love you, Silas. I've always loved you. You'll always be my little boy."

She kissed his eyes, his cheek.

Then she let him go.

CHAPTER 35

IN MEMORIAM

AUGUSTUS HOWESMAN MOVED SLOWLY through the downstairs rooms of his house. Many of the Restless had come there, seeking sanctuary. Some had been turned away from the homes of their descendants. Others didn't want to go back to their lonely tombs. He didn't blame them. He showed them the abandoned houses on Fort Street. So now it was a neighborhood once more.

He didn't even mind some of them coming by now and again. In the old days, he would receive company between three and five on Tuesday and Thursday afternoons. So now, it appeared, it might be that way again. In the parlor, a few of his new neighbors were playing cards. Others spoke quietly in the front rooms, sharing memories of Lichport long ago. The Victrola played from the dining room.

Though he enjoyed the company, he didn't feel like talking today. So Augustus Howesman made his way upstairs. The ascent took him most of the morning. Everyone and everything seemed to be moving a little slower.

From his chair in the upper room of his Fort Street home, Augustus Howesman sat, looking absently at the window. His eyes had turned to pale stones. He was not looking outside, but *elsewhere*.

With his inner sight, he could see his great-grandson walking into his house with the girl's skull. He saw Amos Umber, a young man, running toward the marshes. Then he saw Silas pass into the great fireplace in the rotunda of Temple House. All was blurred now. The past and present had unraveled. He saw Dolores standing by the rotunda hearth, waiting for her son.

Augustus Howesman could only watch and trust that his great-grandson knew what he was doing. The temperature in the town had risen. Folks had been taken ill, and blame was flying all in the wrong direction. He worried Silas was shouldering too much. *Good blood will always tell,* he thought. His great-grandson was a man of honor. Why argue with fools when good work could make all right again?

As Silas passed below the shadow of the mantel and into darkness, his great-grandfather saw him once more, saw his face filled with the resolution of a true Howesman. Then flames flew up, burning away the vision.

Augustus Howesman cried. "Oh, great-grandson . . . ," he said in a choking voice. "I would have gone with you, boy, had you asked me. . . ."And though he was not the kind of man to give in to despondency, he worried, truly feared, that he might never see his great-grandson again. That thought brought an aching stiffness to his arms and legs, and he shifted uncomfortably in his chair.

He straightened his back. "Be well," he said to the air, to Silas. But those words felt flat to him, so he called out well-hallowed, familiar lines that he had known by heart ever since his days in school, when the young were expected to memorize words worth remembering:

"'No exorciser harm thee! Nor no witchcraft charm thee! Ghost unlaid forbear thee! Nothing ill come near thee!'" He stopped, not wanting to finish the line, but then whispered reticently, "'Quiet consummation have; And renowned be thy grave.'"

LEDGER

I am not pierced by the sun, but enter the flames and come forth from the flames.

—FROM THE ANCIENT EGYPTIAN COFFIN TEXTS, TRANSLATED BY SILAS UMBER

CHAPTER 36

UNDERWORLD

THE DESCENT FELT FAMILIAR. Dark and steep, the stairs carried Silas down into the underworld below Temple House. Almost before he could think of summoning it, corpse fire appeared and flickered about his head, suffusing the passage in cold, pale light. From the remaining shadows, spirits rose up in his path, angry ghosts too long imprisoned below the earth. As he had read his father had once done, Silas did not pause, but raised his hand as he descended, holding the ring confidently before him. The spirits fled or dissolved upon the air where the refracted light of the scarab struck them.

At the bottom of the stairs, Silas emerged in a vast chamber filled with every kind of artifact: Etruscan sarcophagi, vessels chased in gold, statues of forgotten gods, fragments of architecture from Rome, Babylon, and the farther East. It was as if the whole of the ancient world had somehow shipwrecked itself here, below the earth. His father had known this place, or at least had been familiar with some of the relics hidden here. Silas guessed his uncle had never found this chamber.

Torches lit the room, and the blue corpse candles that attended him dimmed and faded out.

From somewhere near the center of the room, he could hear the grinding of teeth. Cabel Umber was there waiting for him. Silas followed the sound through the cramped lanes, between the stacks of artifacts and crates, all spoils the Brotherhood of the Temple had long ago brought to Lichport.

As he neared the center of the chamber, the air grew warmer, closer. When he emerged into the heart of the labyrinth, he saw why. The massive idol of Moloch stood glowing with heat from the fire burning wildly within it. On the floor surrounding the statue were traced circles of ash, sigils and signs. Silas saw his own name crudely inscribed among them with something sharp— a dagger's point, or a finger bone. He was expected.

Cabel Umber looked up from gazing at the flames.

"It is a great wonder to me, Silas Umber, why you are not dead. Twice I have cursed you, and yet you remain. People are sick, dying in their beds of fever above us."

"It is winter. Did you not know? Lots of people get sick from the cold, yet forget all of winter's discomforts come spring. Don't take so much of the season's ills upon yourself. Besides, the weather is about to turn. This all happens regularly in the lands of the living, remember?"

Cabel ignored him. "And some of the firstborn have fallen, and more shall follow. But you are still hale, I see. Are you sure you are your mother's firstborn? She may have whelped a few bastards before you."

Silas let the taunt pass. "None have fallen that I know of. Your curse against me has faltered. My mother saw to that. Its evil troubled her briefly, but she has quite recovered. The people of the town are scared. That is all. They will recover too. You are not the first ghost to trouble Lichport. Now, cousin, I ask you to leave this place."

"I cannot grant your request. I have work here requiring my attention. I shall make of this place the New Hinnom."

"There is no such thing as hell; at least, not as you mean it."

"Why, this *is* hell. Or, it shall be soon enough."

"Hollow words."

"Your incredulity is the foundation of all your failures. If you had come here and taken up this throne, I could never have found this place. It is your fear of power that has opened the door for me, and has invited so many other ills besides."

"I don't rule over anything. This is my home. Any power I have comes from knowing where I belong."

"And because you have set your sights so low," Cabel continued, "I shall be Death and shall rule here."

"You are not Death."

"Look upon me, Silas Umber, and say it is not so." Cabel's skull shone from out of his blackened skin and his coronet caught the torchlight impressively. Dark flames leapt from his arms and torso, gathering and rising at his shoulders like a collar of crimson, gold, and sable.

"It is true. You look very terrible. But you are confused. I understand. I have seen others like you, spirits broken by time, their memories shattered or become absurd. Hear me, Cabel Umber: You are not Death. You are *dead*. There is a difference. Accept this and return to Arvale, or let me help you. I can bring you Peace at last. Cousin, aren't you tired?"

Cabel Umber shook his head slowly. In the firelight the long shadows cast by the statues of the demons wavered about him.

"You cannot compel me, Silas Umber!"

"You still don't understand. I am not trying to compel you. I am not threatening you. I am not forcing you to do anything. I am *asking* you to go."

"You are no threat in any event. I am here because you are here. You made an oath and broke it, so I am here. You sought me out in my imprisonment and left the door open for me. I came.

Now you wish to stand in judgment over me? But to no avail."

"I will not stand or sit in judgment over you. Others may do so, but I shall not. It is not an Undertaker's place to judge. Once, at Arvale, you asked me for sympathy and I offered it to you. I offer it again, if you will accept it. You are a shadow held together by fear and hatred. I can make all that go away. You may know Peace, as your daughter and granddaughter did."

Cabel spoke through his teeth, and the muscles stretched over his skull pulled taut with anger. "I will suffer no man's pity!"

Silas continued, his speech slow and measured. "Ah. There is such a difference between pity and sympathy. I am sorry you cannot see that."

"You speak as though we are different. Not so! We are both come to the same place. It is no accident. But you carry loss in you like a tumor. It makes you weak. And it invites the intervention of others."

Silas stood very still, unable to speak. There was a sharp angle of truth in his ancestor's words. Cabel smiled, aware he had struck a blow. Slowly, Silas turned toward the bronze idol and looked into the fire. "Yes. It is true. We all carry our losses within us. But only when what we've lost is found may we free ourselves from fear and shame and hate."

Cabel brought his hands together again and again, and the exposed bones clattered more than clapped. "In accord at last! Now, let me tell you what shall come to pass. I will, in time, hunt down all the living of Lichport and bring death to them, then—"

"No. That is not within your authority. That is *my* job. I am the Undertaker. When the time comes for any here to pass beyond, I will hold their hands and no one else."

"So long as you live, they shall continue to fall. You cannot change this edict. Your life means their death, and death shall come terribly and from *my* hands."

Cabel's words beat down Silas's patience and anger rose up to take its place. Silas quickly turned, his face hot and glowing from staring at the fire. But Cabel spoke again.

"You can do nothing."

"So you've said. But I've been thinking about that. Silas Umber owes you a debt and so cannot strike you down. I am he, yet I am also more. I am Mors. I am Osiris. I am Janus, Serapis, Atis, Hermes, Anubis. It is from one of these names I might cast you down." And as Silas's imagination colored in the threat, his throat and mouth filled with words of power and punishment from the *Book of the Dead,* from the Undertaker's ledger, and from hymns of anger hidden in his heart. Here, at the ready, were terrible words that tasted bitter on his tongue. Cabel moved swiftly back from Silas, fear beginning to tear at his form. Silas drew in a deep breath, ready to cry curses upon the ghost, but he stepped back too, swallowing his words. He would speak no evil. Cabel Umber had cursed himself by his actions in life and in death. Cabel would rise or fall now by his own will. And if he would not embrace Peace, others waited to help him meet another fate, others whose job it was to punish and not comfort.

Silas looked back at the idol and felt his own losses keenly and knew, without doubt, the fire was the only way. Cabel had a road to travel. Silas did too. Time for both of them make a start of their conclusions.

"Cousin," Silas said, "let us make an end of this."

Cabel Umber did not come closer, but anticipation sharpened his voice.

"As you will. A firstborn is all my ancient rite requires. I will walk the world again. That is the bargain. By the offering of a firstborn child, I will be born again and not die. Not as you see me now, but as I was before I saw too much of the world, before the darkness came. I will be as Adam in the garden. I shall hunt down the living. So the god of Canaan and Hinnom has promised me."

"I will make good on my oath," Silas quietly said, interrupting him. "Now."

Surprise briefly replaced Cabel's arrogant stance.

"Life for life," said Silas with absolute calm.

Cabel seemed nervous again. His form wavered on the air.

Silas looked Cabel in the face and said, "I believe the terms were I was to bring you the Mistle Child. I failed to do so at Arvale. I've brought you another one."

Cabel turned away from Silas's stare. "That cannot be."

"There is another, I assure you. And I give him to you. Let us be clear. When the Mistle Child is offered to the fire of your idol, my debt to you is paid?"

"It is. You make this offer willingly?"

"I do."

"Silas Umber, I—"

"Do not speak. It's bad enough I've had to hear so much of your talk already."

He walked toward the idol and did not look back at Cabel.

The doors of Moloch's massive bronze belly stood wide open, a gateway to the conflagration within. Silas reached into his pocket, stopped the dial of the death watch, and looked into the flames. In his mind rose the memories of other fires: Mother Peale's hearth, his own fireplace, the candle at his mother's funeral, the little floating flames of the dead that danced above the marshes. He looked in the fire and saw all fires. All one. He felt the presence of the children that had come this way. Far off he could hear their crying. So many had died here within the idol in ages past. Bodies, put inside, never taken out. Their bones were all ashes now and scattered. But even the idol of the horror-god was hallowed by their deaths. The path was lych. And his father had once passed this way. Silas could feel it. And as he understood the nature of what stood before him, the land of bones appeared beyond the flames. The way lay open now.

He said to Cabel, "It seems for one so learned in lore and so dedicated to filling the belly of this abomination, you understand very little about the nature of sacrifice. But I do. Eternity is not gained by sacrificing others. You need to have the guts to do it yourself."

Cabel Umber stared and gibbered, and then began to laugh.

"Here," said Silas. "Let me show you what I mean."

Without another word, Silas walked into the fire. Flames clutched about him but he moved through them and past them, and in the distance, the familiar smell of asphodel drew him on.

LEDGER

If birdsong should be heard in Avernus, the reign of its present king must end and free shall be the dead.

—ANONYMOUS MARGINALIA, CIRCA EARLY SEVENTEENTH CENTURY

CHAPTER 37

SECONDS

DOLORES UMBER SENSED HER SON LEAVE THE WORLD, and it felt like she was being pierced with knives. The pain went right through her, even though all the flesh of her body, the flesh of her womb, was dead. This was the second time she'd felt her son go out of the world. Once had been enough. It was unbearable, and so she screamed like the old wailing women, and in that moment she understood: For some terrible things, there were no words.

Then she heard laughter coming from below, and anger swelled in her.

"Si, I will put it right for you. Whatever you've left to do, I'll do it. Now."

Dolores descended the steps into darkness. When she reached the chamber below, she followed her son's footsteps inward to the center of the room.

Cabel threw back his skull and howled with laughter.

"Now comes the lady of the house! How pale she looks."

Dolores did not answer.

"You have come to find your son? Oh, lady, he is dead and gone," Cabel Umber said with triumph in his voice. His eyes were wide and wild. Flames danced about his brow. But at the end of his laughter, was there a hint of fear? Was he scared of *her*? What had happened here? What did the ghost think was about to happen? Dolores scanned the space, looking for some sign. "Where is my son? Show me my son!"

"Lady, I am no Lycus to sit upon my throne, awaiting your little Hercules to wander back from hell and put me in the ground." He laughed again. "I am already in the earth as you can see, and he is not coming back. Even now, my god, Moloch the Hungry, has bathed him in fire and shrouded him in smoke. . . ."

"That's enough from you. Get out!"

Cabel Umber chortled low in his throat.

"Where's my son?"

"As I've told you," said Cabel, gesturing at the idol. "He is gone and shall not return."

"I said, *get out of my house.*" Her voice surged along its lower range. "Did you hear me, you son of a bitch? Get out, before I set the dogs on you."

Cabel Umber moved across the floor toward Dolores and looked her up and down. When he spoke, the tone was different. No more bravado. Here was deference and enticement.

"Yes. You are lady of the house, indeed. I now see from whence your son got his fine looks. How far you have come to be here with me now and rejoice in my offering to the god of fire, the eater of children."

Dolores raised her hand as if to strike the ghost, but Cabel Umber lowered his voice and spoke again, his words rising and falling like a chant.

"Lady, you are, like me, a marvel. We need not make war on each other. This place might be ours." The ghost's voice was like liquor, smooth and warm, and though she hated what he said, the way he said it drew her in. If diamonds could speak, they would sound like the ghost's voice. His eyes shone too, and the glow was enticing, like candle flames seen through a gin tumbler. Every word the ghost spoke made her thirsty for more. She could not look away from him.

"May I share a truth with you, lady? It is our children who steal immortality from us. Why, had you remained childless, you might have lived forever. You were always a great beauty, that is plain to see . . . although . . . the years have added lines of care to your brow. Had your child not served you so, you might have been queen of this place."

Dolores spoke, her voice wavering. "I will not die. I will live forever."

"Oh, lady," said Cabel, shaking his head, "you may *endure* forever, perhaps. But to *live* forever! That is what Moloch offers those who give up their firstborn. *As we have both done.* Know this: If you love another, you lose your life. But love thyself and live forever."

Dolores slowly rocked her head from side to side, as if she were falling asleep to a lullaby.

"Yes. There is no need to argue. You feel in your heart that I speak the truth. You know your child has stolen your youth from you. As every child has done since the beginning of the world. They are clinging vines upon every parent's life, and they draw out our vigor and liveliness. What you must have been in your youth . . . what you might yet become . . ."

Before Dolores's eyes rose a vision from the nightland of her past. She saw herself again, a young woman with a life ahead of her. She saw what might have been. A life abroad. Lovers. Everything she saw was shining. No one needed to die. No one needed to look back. There were only the lights along the river, leading ever away and away.

Dolores could see it now. How she had been both terrified and relieved on that day her son was born still and motionless into the world. The scene rose again before her eyes and she remembered with clarity how long the pregnancy had felt, how each long, uncomfortable day had sharpened her fears of what would come, and what motherhood might keep from her. She could hear her own mother's voice, plying her with the usual truisms about what was expected from a wife, and so Dolores had let familial duty veil her fears. Now all was a blur. Whose fault had her life been? Her son's? The father's? Both?

Cabel's voice whispered, "Always and always the child is the cause. . . ."

Yes, thought Dolores, it was Silas who had wrought all her disappointments.

As Dolores's brow furrowed, Cabel Umber smiled.

"In its way, the child always slays the parent. Or rather, slays the person, and leaves only the parent behind. Child-changed fathers and mothers . . . that's what we become. But there is another way. . . ."

Dolores could feel the lull of the river again, the dark eddies of fear pulling her, drawing her back to that perdition of a life framed in regrets.

She put her hand to her cheek and the visions froze. The dead skin still held the warmth, or the memory of the warmth, of her son's kiss good-bye. Dolores closed her eyes, and Silas's face was waiting there. She could see him, standing beside her on the night boat. She could see him standing over her corpse. She heard him saying, "I love you, Mom," and with those words rising in her mind, Cabel Umber's spell broke and fell away from her.

She looked at the ghost and her eyes went white.

Silas had said those other women would help her. Now she wanted them.

Dolores stood stock still, except for her lips, which began to move slowly around a whisper. Whatever else Cabel Umber might be, he was a rat in her basement. When she had traveled by reed boat through the realm of night, she had heard words in the shadows of the Tuat, words of judgment and reckoning, and she spoke those words out loud, never taking her eyes off Cabel Umber. Then Dolores opened her mouth and screamed, an unearthly sound that was not a cry like any human had ever made before.

The vaults and stonework of the ceiling began to fade. Stars pierced the darkness. Above their heads was now hung a tapestry of some ancient midnight strewn with constellations of destruction. Dolores heard sounds above stairs, like the whirring of a spinning wheel, the churring of locusts, the song of a storm. They were coming.

Cabel Umber moved away from Dolores and closer to the idol, into its dismal shadow.

Dolores looked at Cabel Umber with her white eyes, and said, "I am the lady of this house and sister to the fates. I consign you to yours. You have killed my son. Let your destruction come."

The noises above descended into the chamber and a furious wind rose, throwing dust and ash into the air. The flames within the idol were blown down low.

In the middle of the chamber, between Dolores and the ghost of Cabel Umber, stood three women. Their long dresses were encrusted with ash and their faces were streaked with soot. Dolores recognized the three. They bared their teeth and cruelty shone from their pitiless brows. In their hands, where once they held skeins of thread and yarn, they gripped writhing serpents whose mouths dripped with venom. When the three spoke, it was in one voice, and all the room shook at their utterance.

"You have spilled the blood of kin. You have set your hand against the just. The judgment is against you." The three turned to Dolores. "Sister? How shall he be condemned?"

"Let him go to where even the dead die. He must never come here again."

"So be it," said the three. "Let him be consigned to the Second Death. He shall burn in the Lake of Fire." The three slowly raised their arms and, with fingers like iron nails, pointed at Cabel Umber.

The ghost shook violently on the air and seemed to thin and tear.

From the side of the chamber, heavy footfall could be heard entering the underground hall. It moved swiftly, and an instant later a creature stood behind Dolores Umber.

The Ammit sat back on its thick haunches and opened wide its long crocodile jaws.

"Now," Dolores said to Cabel Umber, "you go straight to hell!"

The ghost did not speak. He raised his arm as if to throw something. His mouth hung open, though no words came. Sinews and shreds were already coming away from him, and chunks of the bone of his skull, all being drawn into the mouth of the Ammit, down into the Lake of Fire that roiled in its belly, into that second, terrible death from which there was no returning.

The stars had fled. The ceiling was once again stone and wood.

The three had vanished as quickly as they'd come.

Already, the fire was dying inside the idol. Dolores leaned down to the hot embers and slowly breathed out over them, saying, "Come home to me, my son. Come home."

LEDGER

"In both life and death, travelers always meet two times."

—LATVIAN ROAD PROVERB

OUR TWO SOULS THEREFORE,
WHICH ARE ONE,
THOUGH I MUST GO, ENDURE NOT YET
A BREACH, BUT AN EXPANSION,
LIKE GOLD TO AIRY THINNESS BEAT.

—FROM "A VALEDICTION: FORBIDDING MOURNING" BY
JOHN DONNE. MARGINALIA OF AMOS UMBER

CHAPTER 38

FIELD

THE YOUTH IS WALKING THERE. *Below the mountains, in the field of asphodel.*

The land is quiet but for the sound of the watch in his pocket. The ticking of the pocket watch is all the youth can hear. He takes out the watch and looks at it. A miniature skull. He opens it and tries to stop the hand from moving around the dial. It will not stop, and the harder he presses, the more the dial tears into the skin of his finger as it pushes past on its ceaseless round.

The youth turns the watch over in his hands. The silver watch is warm. There is a seam that runs along the outside of the skull. Sometime in the past, someone had opened it and then sealed it shut with more silver.

On the ground are two stones. Heavy and weathered, they sit upon the dry earth.

Ticking. Ticking. The watch is ticking.

The youth puts the pocket watch on top of one of the stones. A small scorpion emerges from the shadow of the rock, raises its tail, then scuttles away. Carefully, the youth lifts the other stone. With it, he strikes the pocket watch and it breaks open. Small gears are smashed and the dial lies in two halves.

A child appears.

The child looks at the broken watch and smiles.

"Do not leave me again," says the child.

"I am lost myself," says the youth.

"You are not lost. We are where our roads have brought us. We are where we are supposed to be."

"Can't you go home either?" the youth asks the child.

"No. That was another time."

"Another Mistle Child?"

The child nods. "Neither of us is a stranger to loss."

"Where are your people?"

"All dead. Long ago. There was a storm in the desert. The animals fled. The storm did not stop. Crops failed. Many died. I was left as an offering, along with a bull. The storm stopped, but the offerings continued. Animals were burned at first, but then mostly children. I was lonely. My name became the name of loss and hunger. So I waited close by the living, and then all the firstborn were given to me, for without sacrifice, there can be no blessing."

"You are the god of this place?"

"To some."

"Have you so little power that you cannot leave?"

"I have been held here. Now I might leave. I have power over all things."

"Over love?"

"No," the child says, his eyes welling with tears. "Not love."

Beneath the child's feet, a green blush of color spreads. Verdant curls unfold and rise as flower stalks, but almost as soon as they bloom, they brown and shrink, falling back to the ground even as more shoots rise up.

Then the youth knows who the child is, and asks, "Are you going to kill me now?"

Sadness falls across the child's small face. "Death does not come to punish the living. Acceptance of death is a gift. I have been waiting to free you, and only your father's fear has kept us apart."

"I saw him once. Why hasn't he come to me?"

"He loves you very much. That can never die. Perhaps now he may more frequently tell you so. It has always been his choice. Your father, of his own free will, has bound up his estate with that of my prison house, which you have just destroyed. As a result, a portion of him was imprisoned in the death watch as well. He is now free. Just as I am. Just as you are."

"How am I free?"

"You are free to choose what you will do next. That is the only kind of freedom there is, for both the dead and the living."

The child and the youth walk across the field of asphodels and along the foothills that run beneath the mountains.

"I want to go home," says the youth.

"Take me with you. Carry me with you."

"I don't . . . I don't think I can."

"You may."

"How?"

"Welcome me home. Say my name," says the child.

"Moloch."

"No," says the child, smiling. "That was what they called me in the Long Ago."

"Please tell me how to get home. What must I do?" says the youth.

"Say: I give myself to you."

"To you?"

"Yes. 'I give myself to you.' Say it."

The youth says, "I give myself to you."

"My Death," adds the child.

The youth closes his eyes and says, "I give myself to you, My Death."

"Now it is all one," says the child. "Shall we walk together?"

The child holds up his hand to the youth. On his small palm is a dark stain, perhaps a birthmark. It is in the shape of a key.

The youth takes hands with the child.

They walk together.

"No one wants to be alone," says the youth.

"Yes," says the child. "No one."

They are standing upon the edge of the sea.

The moon is over the water. High above, a firedrake, a comet, draws a line of flame across the firmament.

A sound of keening is heard over the water.

The child hears the sound and smiles at the youth.

"Only the unloved are truly lost," says the child.

Ahead, there is a path.

"I want to go home," says the youth to his death.

"There is no other place for us," his death replies, and the two walk together down the path that runs along the sand hills and to the sea.

LEDGER

THOU, WHO ART ABOUT TO CONSIGN
    YOUR YEARS TO THE FLAMES
WHO, BY THIS ILLUSION OF DEATH
    ARE DESTINED TO FIND LIFE AGAIN;
THOU WHOSE DEMISE SHALL ONLY
    BE PROLOGUE TO RENEWAL AND
    REBIRTH,
AND THROUGH SELF-DESTRUCTION
    SHALL REGAIN THY LOST YOUTH,
TAKE BACK THY LIFE,
GIVE UP THE BODY THAT CAN NOT
    ENDURE,
AND BY METAMORPHIC EXCHANGE OF
    FORM,
RETURN AND COME FORTH, GOLDEN,
    BEAUTEOUS, ETERNAL.

— RETRANSLATED BY AMOS UMBER FROM HENDERSON'S
    CLAUDIAN, VOL. II. 1922

CHAPTER 39

VEIL

THE SURFACE OF THE STONE WOULD NOT PART. There was no veil. Only murk and shadow.

Mrs. Bowe looked down at the sphere of crystal but could not find what she sought in its depths. "He is very far, I fear," she said to Mother Peale, who peered over her shoulder.

"Call him," said Mother Peale.

"I don't know where he is. He could be here in Lichport already. I don't know."

Mother Peale stood upright, put her hands on the back of Mrs. Bowe's chair to steady herself, and closed her eyes. "Dolores," said Mother Peale, "take Mrs. Bowe's hand."

"Yes. He is far. . . . ," said Mrs. Bowe. *"Kyrie eleison,"* she whispered, reaching over her shoulder to cover Dolores's hands in hers.

"He is wandering. . . ."

"Thanatos, eleison."

"He comes to the place of flowers. . . ."

"Lord of Earth, *Thanatos, eleison,*" said Mrs. Bowe, barely breathing.

"The shadow draws close. . . ." Mother Peale opened her eyes.

"Come home to us, child! Let the doors of your homecoming be open wide," the three women spoke as one.

"Pace tua, Thanatos," said Mrs. Bowe, bowing her head. She rose and went to the front door. She opened it and then untied her

hair. Letting it fall over her face, she cried out, and a great wailing went forth into the world.

When the keening ended, Mrs. Bowe went back into the parlor and said to Dolores, "You must call to him. The voice of the mother is puissant."

Dolores nodded but did not look up. She said, "Silas, oh, my own son, come home. Little bird, come back to me. Sail with me once more upon the bark of the sun."

And above the house, a comet briefly blazed and passed over Lichport and the sea.

"This," he said, "O King, seems to me the condition of men on earth, compared with that time which to us is uncertain: It is, as though, on a winter's night, you sit feasting with your noblemen—and a little sparrow flies into the hall, and entering through one window, it quickly exits at another. In that brief moment when it is indoors, the furious cold of winter does not touch it; but then that tiny instant of warmth being swiftly ended, from winter going back once more to winter, the bird is lost to our eyes."

Thus appears the life of man—but of what went before or what may follow, that remains hidden in the shadows.

—THE VENERABLE BEDE, FROM *ECCLESIASTICAL HISTORY*, BOOK II, TRANSLATED BY SILAS UMBER

Silas Umber walked along the sea.

The sound of his blood coursed in his ears.

Or was it the waves of the ocean?

The sun was just beginning to go down. It was his favorite time of day.

He passed back and forth across the Narrows, making a game of trying not to cross his own path more than once. Candlelight and hearth-light lit many of the windows, and beyond the glass, there was laughter, and stories culled from the doings of the day. The fresh air of the sea was all about him, and the savory smell of well-cooked suppers, for many of the cottage windows were opened.

He walked along the wall of Newfield Cemetery and toward Temple House. There, he quietly looked through the window.

His mother sat with Mrs. Bowe and Mother Peale. The three were weaving together by the blue-tinged fire where a small loom now stood. Silas could see that, although his mother's fingers were not as nimble as the others', she held the fateful shuttle in a grip of iron, and when she tied a knot, it would never come undone.

Beyond, unseen by them in the dining room, Silas saw the three ladies of the Sewing Circle, watching over while the other three women worked. He could see the pattern now, of what was, of what would come, and of who would soon assist him in his work.

The elder of the three looked up and met Silas's gaze. The

three bowed deeply. Their mouths did not move, but he could hear their voices.

"Hail, great lord of shadows, ruler over the dead. It is you who grant beneficence that our threads be spun and our work continue by the industry of new hands."

Silas smiled at them and continued his pilgrimage.

He passed through the cemetery of the Umbers, where so many of his kin lay sleeping below the soil and in their tombs. He walked back toward Coach Street and through the Garden Plot, and then passed the Bowe tomb behind Mrs. Bowe's house, where the bees were preparing for the work of the rising year. He walked under the long shadow of the Beacon and over the water to Fort Street. Silas heard voices from his great-grandfather's house. Augustus Howesman was not alone. Some of the other Restless were with him there in his enduring mansion. Music was playing.

He walked up Main Street past the ruined church. Over the distant marshes, dark birds flew and folded across the air in slow, gentle murmurations, while others sang their song of eventide from the trees.

Looking at the ground beyond the streets and sidewalks, he could see that no more ice clutched the soil. Tiny purple flowers had appeared. It was nearly spring. But hadn't the flowers always been there, just hidden below the frost?

The sun was already setting, for the year was still young. The brief burnished twilight had settled over Lichport, and the first stars rose in the east and were reflected in the waters of the mill-pond and the pools of the marshes.

It was time to go home.

As Silas approached his house, a man sat waiting on the porch, picking at the paint on the handrails. Silas smiled.

Amos looked up. "Son?" he said.

Did you love this book?

Want to get access to
the hottest books for free?

Log on to simonandschuster.com/pulseit

to find out how to join,

get access to cool sweepstakes,

and hear about your favorite authors!

Become part of Pulse IT and tell us what you think!

Margaret K.
McElderry Books 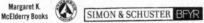 SIMON & SCHUSTER BFYR SIMON PULSE

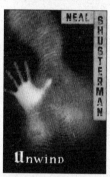